I0551647

THE ASSEMBLED

By Ben Devine

A Book of the Therion Engine Series

INTRODUCTION

The Assembled is set in a time and place which draws
from the context of our modern world but examines the
imagery in the Book of Revelation. When the Book of
Revelation was written, an ancient person having a prophetic
vision would be at a loss to describe the technologies they saw
which were beyond their comprehension. The resulting
fantastic imagery is open for broad interpretation. More
importantly, if viewing the Book of Revelation as a warning,
the social and political climate that will lead to the battle of
Armageddon could unfold in both mundane and spectacular
ways. The Assembled explores a world where many paths to
Armageddon are possible, but where the most probable is that
human nature will be in contest with basic morality. Good
versus evil in surprising forms.

This is a work of fiction. Names, characters, places, and incidents either are the product of the author's imagination or are used fictitiously. Any resemblance to actual persons, living or dead, events, or locales is entirely coincidental.

1st Edition

©2021 Benjamin C. Devine

All rights reserved. No part of this work may be reproduced or used in any manner without written permission of the copyright owner except for the use of quotations in a review.

ISBN 978-0-578-92538-7

For questions and permissions please email
DMDLLC2020@gmail.com

To Z.C., who taught me about the Antichrist.

CHAPTER 1

SMALL PARTS

When I lay awake at night—between the time I stop thinking about the day and when I begin to dip in and out of consciousness—Sometimes I wonder how my life would have been had I not met some of the people who have passed in and out of it. I have a story of all the places I have been and all the things I have done. But I often find that when I tell my story, the most interesting parts are always about other people. My life is just a collection of other peoples' lives and pieces of their stories. Through this realization I have come to understand the world in a way that ties all men together. It is the people we meet throughout our lives that shape us into who we are. But as we are shaped, we also impart some small piece of ourselves on others as we go along. Sometimes word by word. At other times it is deed by deed. With each life we touch, we mold it just a little. The overall effect being that the little things we do for one another grow into something greater than ourselves.

The world, and its history, are molded in much the same way. Each person who passes through this life, no matter how low their station or short their existence, shapes the clay of history. This is true even if they do so only by small things like building a home, planting a field, making some object, or having a child. These things happen every day, without monumental planning or grandiose intention, and shape the world little by little. Then of course, there are the greater examples. Things that people—ordinary people—did at one time or another, and by doing so turned their ordinary personage into immortal legend. It is the little things that seem so ordinary at the time which can become—for all we know—turning points in history.

I cannot claim to be of great importance. I am a simple soldier. I am Daniel Marconas, formerly of the 3001st Imperial Rifle Regiment, serial number A000710714. That is a number I will never forget, but that I am sure history will bury, as it has so many others. However, I have one claim—one story—that may save for me some small recognition in the annals of the human race. A story where the people who came into my life are the people who shaped history and whose names became everlasting. Although my part was small in the scheme of things, it was my actions which paved the way for a truly remarkable man to fulfill his destiny.

To begin, I must say that no story beginning in that time is complete without mention of the man who ushered in that dark age: The Architect. Trained humbly as a designer, he inevitably was so much more. He was a renaissance man. A man of art, science, language, and philosophy. To the world's chagrin, he was also well suited to the arts of war. The Architect was the one man whom all the world came to know. Some saw him as a visionary, while others saw him as a demon. It was by his hand the world was nearly perfected, and then nearly destroyed.

The Architect quickly became almost unimaginably wealthy when he designed a machine that could create energy from basically nothing. It burned only the chemicals it took in from the air and was primarily powered by a magnetic mechanism. It was simple, not costly to make, and highly efficient. Suddenly not even the sun and wind were needed anymore. Solar farms and wind fields were left to rust. Hydroelectric dams were breached and abandoned. Coal mines and nuclear plants were boarded up and abandoned. The oil barons and sheiks paid him great ransoms to limit the sale of the machine, but in the end, he alone controlled the ebb and flow of energy. No one turned on a light or traveled an inch without money flowing into his accounts from the sale of his engine—which he branded *The Therion*.

While most people would be content to hoard their wealth, his fortunes burned a hole in his pocket, so he spent it as fast as it came to him. At first, he bought mundane things to complete his trappings of wealth. He bought houses, yachts, cars, and other trinkets to help him find meaning and beauty in a world where nothing was denied him. Despite these diversions, he became restless and graduated from a penchant for the excessive to a deep and consuming desire for control. Then, he bought companies. He bought politicians. He bought land, cities, and whole regions of the Earth. When he ran out of things he could buy, he bought armies.

His money aside, he had many other talents. His brilliant negotiations unified many nations of the world into one great confederation. For those who would not join peaceably, he deployed his mercenary armies to beat them into submission one by one. In the course of ten years several quick and definitive wars made the world one nation. In his path of destruction, he soon sent another army; an army of architects, engineers, and construction workers to shape the world to suit his vision.

Soon, there was no one left to fight. Under his direction, for seven years, the world saw peace and prosperity on an unprecedented scale. There was no war, as he could intimidate any aggressor. There was little terrorism, as his armies ensured subjugation. There was no famine, as he could buy enough food to feed everyone. He built hospitals for the sick, created jobs for the poor, and financed art, music, and science; all the while taking in vast sums for the sale of his machine.

The time of peace and plenty came to a violent and abrupt end when he raised one building that changed everything: a pantheon. It was a great temple to the gods of all people. In this world of thousands of gods, he built one home for them all. He had the best of intentions to overcome that last, most ancient divider and wash away the final traces of animosity which had been festering for thousands of years. Unfortunately, The Architect misunderstood the nature of religion. When people build a temple to their own gods, they build it to bring their gods closer to them. The Architect sought to bring all gods closer—not to the people, but to each other. The endeavor was flawed from conception.

Men need their gods. The promise of relief in this life and the next that religion inspires helps to lift the everyday weight of existence. But gods are made by men, and their character cannot help but be tainted by man's desires. Selfish and proud as men are, so too must their gods be.

What The Architect did not understand was the sense of pride that religion breeds in the human mind. The Architect took all the gods and made them equal in one house, and this was an offense that the faithful could not abide. The Temple was an offence to the righteous and devout of all creeds as it diminished the gods to the devout and mixed them all together in one great dilution of all sanctities. The effect of this ultimately destroyed the world The Architect had created.

In every corner of the Earth, great uprisings tore the fabric of society apart. Ancient hatreds and evils were fed by modern weaponry and unlimited energy. The engines The Architect had used to unite the world fueled a war of unprecedented scope, destruction, and ruthlessness. Those who held to their gods revolted against The Architect's empire and divided the world again into a thousand factions all vying for power over one another, and at the same time all working towards one goal: To destroy The Temple and punish The Architect.

Angered and offended at the threat to his temple and his empire, The Architect's hand of creation turned to a hand of iron. He crushed pocket after pocket of rebellion with no mercy. His loyalists and his appointed bodyguards, the Praetorians, slaughtered their way around the world. But it was all in vain. For every rebel killed, a thousand flocked to the banners of their priests, imams, and other holy men. Soon, there was nothing but war. The only trade was war. The only skill a man needed was making war. The only commerce was the business of war. The fighting raged for years, and then decades. Men turned to monsters. Those outside of The Architect's law resorted to atrocities lost since ancient times. The Architect made his policies for dealing with the outlaws just as harsh.

The Architect's cruelty did not go unpunished. Several years after the completion of The Temple, his palace in the redesigned Holy City was rocked by a massive explosion.

Although The Architect was severely wounded, he survived. His heart, lungs, liver, and kidneys were replaced, and several feet of intestine were removed. The doctors expected his body would reject the newly implanted organs, but he recovered quite miraculously. During The Architect's resurrection, his empire surely would have crumbled if not for the dutiful maintenance of his seven ministers. Most prominently, the herculean efforts of the Praetorian Prefect Mikhail Chernob, who breathed new life into The Architect's public image during his absence.

Known originally only as 'Chernob'. Through his execution of his duties, he accumulated a variety of monikers befitting his ruthlessness. Among these were Chernob the Black, and General of Death. He burned prisoners alive by the thousands, or remove all of their limbs and left them lying helpless on the ground. To suppress rebellions before they happened, he separated families from their children as a way of subjecting certain jurisdictions. He formed eugenics programs to breed more docile populations in some troublesome areas. Ultimately, his final moniker was a direct result of his one and only public appearance beside The Architect.

At the celebration of his victory over the last elected government in the world, The Architect honored Chernob by appointing him sole command of all the armed forces as a sign of faith. Chernob's acceptance speech warned that what The Architect had created could only be destroyed by clinging too tightly to tradition. He espoused the dangers of religion, cultural identity, and other barriers that still stood in the way of a true single, global nation. Although it took seven years to come to pass, his predictions became true after the completion of The Temple. Religious zealots and nationalists chipped away at the edges of the empire. His predictions coming to pass so accurately, thereafter he was known as The Prophet.

After his recovery, The Architect doubled his effort to end the war—not just by conflict, but by constricting the sinews of war itself: Money. He collected all the precious metals he could gather and established his own currency system. Without his cartouche, nothing could be obtained.

Inevitably, wars cannot last forever. There must be men to fight wars. There are men who start wars and men who end them. I cannot say who started the war. Whether blame lies with The Architect or with the gods who incited men to war against him, only history can decide. What I can say is that I knew the man who ended the war. This is his story. This is my story.

CHAPTER 2

THE FIRST KINDNESS

He was born into war. There, right in the middle of the street, as jets dropped ordinance in neighborhoods we had yet to clear. Enemy artillery rained around us, coming in from across the river. It didn't matter what was destroyed; everything was going to get blown up anyways. If not today or tomorrow, then some other day when our commanders decided we needed to take this city, or the enemy decided they needed to assault that city. He was born right in the middle of that destruction, in that time of utter senselessness and cruel desperation.

I was running for the next scrap of cover with the remnants of my unit, doing the same thing we had done in a hundred towns and villages up and down the front. We watched with apathy as civilians tried to flee. They tried to get away from us, or the artillery, or bombs. They tried to get away from the hell of it all mostly. Some fell and stumbled along, while some were wiped out by the shrapnel that picked its victims without prejudice. On this occasion, I noticed that one woman ran slower than the rest. As I crouched behind my little shield of rubble, I saw her drag her feet and hold her stomach as she cried. Then she collapsed. I watched her squirm in the street for a while as I waited for the captain to signal us on.

Eventually, the artillery died down. Most likely, they were bringing up more boxes of ammunition. Perhaps they were just waiting to find more targets and pinpoint our position. Finally, curiosity overcame me. I gave in and walked over to the woman writhing in the road. In a complete loss for real words of care, I asked, "Are you okay?" There were dead bodies all over the place. The thick of war was happening all around us. The landscape, the dwellings, and all their contents were thoroughly destroyed. Who knows how many of her friends and family were dead, and I asked, if she was okay.

I knew right after the words left my lips that my question to her was a vestige of a world that was extinct. By all rights, I should have been devoid of any last fragment of human kindness after what I had seen in eight years of war. Men killing wantonly, looting, raping, and pillaging. There was, of course, torturing prisoner in retort for the countless brothers killed or maimed. The torture was only occasional, because most of the time all combatants fought to the death. We knew that living defeated in the hands of the enemy was not an option. In this war, there were only victors and dead men.

She looked at me with eyes full of fear and hopelessness, saying nothing. She turned over on her back and screamed. It took a second to sink in that she was going to give birth right there. I tried to talk to her, telling her to hold on until we could get her out of the street, to try and relax, and all the other soothing things that typically come to mind when one has absolutely no idea how to help someone. Two of my comrades saw what was going on and rushed over to us. I grabbed the nightgown she had on and tried to get it out of the way, and in my nervous hurry only managed to get tangled in it myself. She gave one last blood curdling scream, sighed, and went completely limp.

Checking her pulse, my comrade said, "She's dead."

As I sat there with my hands on the ground between her legs, I felt something hit my arm. I pulled back the cloth, and there lying in the street was her baby. Not crying, not hurt or dirty, just lying there looking at me.

"Is it dead, Maconas?" asked the sergeant.

"No, it's very much alive," I said.

As we three soldiers knelt there in the street—in complete disbelief of what had just happened—the artillery started back up again, and they were right on top of us.

"Leave it!" yelled the sergeant. "It's going to die anyway. That baby was born to die. We have to get out of here."

They ran off, following close behind the rest of our unit. They left me sitting in the street with the child. It still wasn't crying. Completely innocent and unaware of the

11

circumstances of its birth, it just looked at me. I don't know why he was brought into the world in such a time and place, but the cruelty of it was disheartening. How could I help it at all? One idea came suddenly. I couldn't just leave it there to suffer. I pulled out my knife to end its pointless, wasted life, and was about to stab it right in the head when its foot touched my other hand. More so, it laid its foot on my hand.

Call it decency, or sympathy, or even stupidity; but I just stopped and stared back as the child stared at me. I've seen babies. I have seen them be born. I have watched them die. They always cry. This one did not. He had every right in the world to cry, as I saw it. Mother dead, no family, no home— he didn't have anything to live for. I guess the ignorance afforded to him by just being born was a blessing. Well, if he was going to accept the tragic state of his existence in quiet forbearance, then the least I could do is give him a chance. Why I did it, I'll never really know. I didn't owe it to him. I didn't even really care if he lived a day longer. I took that knife previously intended to end his life, and instead cut the umbilical cord, severing him from his dead mother and setting him free into the world—cruel and ruined as it was. I cut the mother's nightgown off and wrapped him in the pieces. She didn't need it anymore. It could be her last parting gift to her child. Besides life, that's all she could give.

***

It wasn't long until the utter stupidity of what I had done hit me. I was still a soldier. I was still at war. In fact, I was still on a battlefield. We worked from street to street dodging artillery and the occasional potshot from snipers as we crossed the intersection of some shattered street. My unit looked back at me, shaking their heads and cussing. They called me every demeaning word in the book to let me know that they thought I was weak for what I was doing. I thought a thousand times about just throwing the baby down to get rid of him. I've seen half my comrades do worse. This was the age of heartless men. I fought alongside them every day and killed them too. The enemy were no more noble than us. However inspiring their propaganda was.

As I absorbed the harassment from my comrades, I finally became resolved that it was too late for me to just throw this child aside. His life was already unfortunate enough, and I couldn't find it in my heart to save him from sure death only to place him right back into it. I had taken responsibility for him, and it was ingrained in me to finish what I had started. Perhaps that was the only reason I continued to fight in that bloody war; simply because it wasn't finished yet. Perhaps it even kept me alive. I couldn't die until it was done. With all the evil things I had done and witnessed,

I never thought I would still feel the influence of my upbringing. A sense of duty was instilled in me so long ago, that still had its hold on me. My parents were long gone for all I knew, but some things never leave you. Carrying through what I had taken responsibility for is a thing I don't think I will ever shake.

Nonetheless, I wished I could be rid of the child. I wished for it to die from exposure, or for some fragment of shrapnel to hit it and not me. Anything to make it go away and release me from my responsibility. It wasn't mine. I didn't own it. I had no part in its creation, only in its still being alive—as foolish as that part seemed. I carried it as we pushed through the city. Occasionally, we had to stop and return fire. I held the baby in one arm and propped my gun up on some piece of rubble or railing so I could at least look and feel like I was helping my unit. We all had our duty to do to uphold The Architect's law.

CHAPTER 3

DIANA

After the day's fighting died down, I resolved to take the child to a friend. I describe her as a friend only because I lacked a real word to explain our relationship other than friendship. On my part, it was love; but on hers it was not so strong. It was through her that I learned the difference between love and lust. When I was younger, like most other young men, or men of any age, I suppose I held a somewhat utilitarian view of women. The goal was to have sex with all that could be had, with any notions of love reserved for someone only after potentially. Many young men have the same approach, I suppose; being unromantic and impetuous in their early years.

I remember the first girl I ever fell in love with. It was the middle of my junior year in college, and I thought I was in love. I would have done anything for that girl. I thought we would be together forever. I bought a ring and was working up the nerve to propose when I heard through a friend that she had other ideas. Apparently, love didn't mean much to her, because she gave hers freely. Heartbroken, I joined The Architect's service to get away from women for a while, and to help the Architect's Central Command put down what everyone thought was going to be a short rebellion. Ironically, it was the service that brought me to my next love.

I first met Diana about two years after joining the war. Our unit—separated from the main army with wounded men, myself among them—had been lost in the woods. The first dwelling we came to was Diana's family's house. They took care of our injured as best they could. I was significantly worse off than the rest, having taken a bullet to the neck and half a dozen to the left side of my body. Once my unit located the main army, they left me for dead.

I didn't hold it against them. The unit could not be held up for one man. The dying were left to die. It was the way of our war. If it hadn't been for Diana's diligent care, I would have perished there in that remote corner of the woods.

Fortunately, since I was the only one left after the unit moved on, she devoted her every waking moment to being my nurse. I think it was more of a diversion from her provincial life than out of real care, but nonetheless, she kept me alive. Once I gained my strength back and could focus less on surviving and more on who was taking care of me, we talked. We talked for hours. She had so many questions: What was happening in the war, where had I been, who was winning? I was glad to have someone to talk to. Not only did she enjoy my stories, but she shared so many stories from her happy youth. It almost made me forget the rest of the world was on fire. For a time, in that corner of the world, there was only me and her. How could I help but love her? We got along so well. Conversation came naturally, and after months of talking, it was easy to see we had so much in common. I could have stayed there the rest of my life. I thought about it. It would have been so easy, and so perfect. However, I was a soldier, and soldiers must fight. I couldn't stay there knowing there was unfinished business.

Once I gained my strength, I spent a few weeks helping out on her family's farm in my vain effort to repay them for their kindness. I left her with a promise to come and see her whenever I could. I had been fighting all over Europe for years and been with many women, but of all the women I had been with, none stirred me more than Diana. I had never touched Diana, and I loved her more than I loved myself. I don't know how many times I had made romantic advances and whispered sweet nothings in her ear trying to earn just one night with her, but she still followed an old religion and wouldn't have me. I asked her to marry me once. I don't know what kind of life I could have given her, but my profession as a soldier wasn't the reason she had said no. Religion was the reason. She didn't say as much, but I assumed she saw me as a godless heathen or saw herself as too pure to marrying me. Somehow, I didn't care. I still came to see her whenever I had the chance, even if only for the pleasure of her conversation and not her bed.

After acquiring my infant passenger, our unit received orders sending us to a city to the north, and we would pass within a days' travel of Diana. I asked Captain Ajax for a week of leave under the guise of a solo scouting mission. This was permitted every now and then when one man traveling alone might look a lot less suspicious to the enemy, and for the most part they would not take notice. Ajax and I had served together long enough, he knew exactly what I wanted when I asked for such a mission—especially since I asked to leave every time we passed through this region. He would always tell me the same thing.

"If you find anything, Maconas, you get your ass back here ASAP."

Captain Ajax was one of the toughest men I've known, rebel or loyalist. He wasn't a tall man, but he always *seemed* taller than everyone around him. Perhaps that was because we were always stooped over trying to avoid incoming rounds while he stood there and barked orders, his bright red mustache dripping spit and his hands pointing to each man as he urged them forward. I've seen him take shots to both arms and both legs and fight through. He was always the last to report to the medic and made sure that all his men were treated first.

Still, he was also one of the most heartless men I have known, and I have seen some of the worst. He would use his elbow to crush the skulls of the enemy prisoners. He once removed the jaw a wounded rebel for fun. He never took part in the looting that soldier did, but I never saw him cringe or blink an eye at anything the rest of us did. There was no smell, no sight, no atrocity that could move him. At that time, I believed that he was the only kind of man that could be a leader in this terrible war. Men don't follow weakness, and to the men of my unit, he had none. I had served with him since I joined, and there was at that time no man I would rather serve under.

I left with the baby in the morning before my unit crossed the bridge into Monthermé. I followed the river east. It was a bleak morning and it drizzled on me the entire day. The river rolled black beside me. A little after noon, I left the river road and started off on the forest trail that led to Diana's homestead. It was common for the more clever civilians to build their houses far from the commonly traveled roads. Rather this than having their house and goods on display for every roving army and vagabond to see and envy, like when the war started. Those old houses lay ruined, burnt, and covered with nature's vines and weeds; all pulling down man's vanquished past to envelop it back to the earth.

Diana's homestead was only half a day's walk from the river, but it took me longer than usual because of my passenger. He didn't cry the entire time we traveled; only fussed a little every now and then when I got him wet or had to roughly climb down a hill. I made a little sling out of my blanket to carry him. When he got too fussy, I would stop and give him concoctions of mashed up things from my rations. It was hardly mother's milk, but it was the best I could do. Other than the long time it took to get to the homestead, it was a smooth trip. We arrived at dusk. Diana's father was sleeping on the porch with his old service rifle. Diana was in the garden, picking vegetables for dinner. I could see her head bobbing up and down in the tall rows of plants.

I walked up to the porch and put my finger on her father's forehead. "Bang."

He started and reached for his rifle, but I grabbed the barrel as he swung it towards me and stood there smiling.

"Some watchman you are," I said.

"I've done my share of watching," he gruffed. "You're the only person that ever comes around here anyways. What do you have there?" He pulled back the blanket from the baby's face. "Well damn, that's a baby. I haven't seen one of those in a while."

I took the baby out of the sling and handed it to him. "Well, he's for you. I've been looking at him all day."

"He ought to be worth a bag of salt or two."

We both chuckled at the joke. By this time, Diana saw me and walked back up to the house. Her thin figure was illuminated in the fading light as she approached.

"I haven't seen you in a while, Daniel," she said as she swung her arms around my neck.

Her breasts pressed against my chest, and sadly I knew that was probably the farthest I was ever going to get with her. She looked at her father holding the baby.

"Aw, who is this precious thing?" she asked as she kneeled to get a closer look. "What is his name?"

The question struck me as odd. I felt foolish and cold for not giving a thought to naming him. I guess some sentimental faculties had been long lost to me in the war. I thought for a moment. He wasn't mine; I had no right to give him my name. I didn't know his mother's or father's names. I looked at the corn. It was tall corn. I thought of what month it must be to have such tall corn.

"His name is August," I said.

As Diana cooked dinner, I told her and her father about how I came to have August. Diana agreed to keep him. It was the best I could offer him in this world, and it was probably better that he would have had with his real mother. After dinner and after Diana's father went to bed, she and I and August sat on the porch.

21

"Do you think he will live?" she asked.

"He should," I said. "He's already survived his first battle."

She smiled and chuckled a bit. "Does this mean you will come back and visit more often? It's been over a year since you've been here."

"I come back when the war permits. I can't abandon my unit. I sometimes wish I had never left here after I got shot up. No one would have missed me."

"Well, why don't you just stay now? Don't scouts disappear all the time?"

"I wouldn't feel right about it. Plus if they found me, they would execute me for desertion. Someday, this will all be over. Then I can come back for good."

"That would be nice. I miss you when you are gone."

"I miss you too," I said.

August was fast asleep in her arms as she rocked gently beside me. I took in the scene. The child and Diana. The dew-speckled cornfield in the moonlight. It may have been the happiest night of my life. It was—to this day—the only time and place I felt at home. I stayed with Diana and her father for four days before my leave was over and I was scheduled to return to my unit. I gave them all the ration cards I had with me to help them get supplies for August and promised to come back soon to see them all.

CHAPTER 4

BAD TIMING

It was nine years before I made it back to the homestead. A nuclear attack in the north wiped out Central Command's Baltic Army. After the rebels cleaned up the survivors and smaller units which had not been with the main army, they shifted most of their units into our sector on the old Belgian border. The fighting dragged on as we played cat and mouse with them. Who constituted as the cat and who was the mouse changed every month. We tried to keep ourselves spread out to avoid the same fate as our northern brothers, but it was a hard game to win. Our forces held out, but dwindled. We had no way of knowing how our enemy was holding up.

One day we received intelligence that a large concentration of rebels—mostly mechanized light infantry and artillery—was just outside Monthermé. It wasn't far from Diana. Ajax must have already known I would ask for leave again. As soon as we got just outside the town, I approached him. Before I said anything, he handed over my pass, already all filled out. "Get back here ASAP."

I took the side of the river across from the road to avoid detection. I crossed the river when I was near the path I would usually take. I knew something was wrong even before I got to the homestead. The smell of smoke filled the air as I jogged through the forest. As I got closer, I could see flames and smoke through the underbrush at the edge of the clearing. I ran out of the woods and to the smoldering house. Diana's father was lying on the porch. I rushed up, drug him off, and away from the house. He was barely alive; beaten beyond recognition and hardly breathing.

He struggled to say, "They took Diana and August."

I stayed with him until he was gone. He lasted only minutes.

I had no way of telling how long ago the raiders had left, but since the house was still burning, I assumed it had been mere hours. I picked up their trail at the edge of the clearing and tracked them for about an hour until their trail split. The path I took was littered with bare footprints—likely Diana's. There were gouges in the ground where she had fallen and been dragged before regaining her feet. The more signs of mistreatment I saw, the angrier I got and the faster I worked. Where the trail was clearest, I was almost at a sprint. It was nearly dusk before I stopped. I fell in the forest leaves and panted for what must have been an hour. My muscles burned and my lungs seemed to hold only a handful of air. I wondered how far I would run to find her and decided I would run as long as my body would allow and my breath would hold.

The sky grew orange as the sun began to set above the forest. I probably had less than an hour of workable light left and decided to use it as best I could. I stood up to walk but my muscles were tight and could barely support my body. Walking was a conscious effort—and running only a dream. The light faded and faded until I could no longer see the ground. There was no moon that night, and my night vision goggles were broken. The best I could do was creep along until I could see no more at all.

My eyes began to play tricks on me. I saw faces in the branches and leaves. Slight twitches of twigs made me draw a sight and look for something to shoot at. Unable to track anymore, and nowhere near able to sleep, I stood and peered out through the forest until I thought I saw a glow to the south. I walked towards it, and the glow of a fire against a distant tree line materialized out of the blackness.

I moved slower as I approached, watching for the turn of a head or swing of a rifle in the shadows. The fire was bright enough I could see there was a clearing. I dropped down to my stomach and crawled below the briars until I reached the edge of an outcropping. I peered out from behind a bush into the clearing below. Four men sat around a rock to the left of the fire, eating. Two others stood talking closer to the fire. By their insignia I presumed they must be scouts or rangers from the main rebel army in the vicinity. Perhaps even deserters. I looked for a long time for Diana and August. If they had been discarded along the trail, I would have found them. They must be here, I thought.

Then a mass by the fire caught my eye. I put my scope on it, and the horror of what I saw drained the blood from my face. There, by the fire, was Diana's limbless torso. Paralysis took my body and made the rage building in me all the more unbearable. All I could do was roll onto my back and stare into the black sky through the orange-lit trees and fight back the urge to scream.

I stood up with a start and drew a bead on one of the four despicable creatures feasting on Diana. I held for a moment while I waited for my arms to stop shaking. Plans formed in my mind for every shot as I tracked the movement of all six men. I wanted to kill them all. I wanted them dead already. The shock began to slip away, replaced by a deep, seething hatred. If I shot them outright, I could only get two or three before they scattered into the darkness. If I waited until they were asleep, I could cut them all down one by one. I withdrew from the clearing to a creek I had crossed before and found a smooth stone on the bank. I sat on it and sharpened my knife as I stared into the pool, checking from time to time to see if the glow on the trees had faded away yet.

After about two hours, the fire faded. I put my knife away and took my pistol out, dropped the magazine, and worked the slide a few times. Part of me hoped I didn't have to use it. I hadn't shot at anything at less than two hundred yards in years. My knife would do just fine tonight. I reloaded my pistol and put it back in its holster. I left my rifle and kit by the stone and crept back to my perch on the outcropping. Five of the soldiers lay around the dying fire. It took me a while, but I finally found the sixth behind a tree at the edge of the clearing. He was walking around the clearing just inside the tree line. I waited patiently for him to pass me.

I stood with my back against a tree, my heart pounding as I listened for the footfalls or the snap of twigs. The wind picked up, obscuring the sound of the footsteps. I could not tell where he was. Suddenly, I saw the barrel of his rifle nose past the edge of the tree. My heart jumped to my throat and in a reflex I drove my knife through the underside of his chin and out the back of his head. He slumped to his knees and fell to the side, eyes locked on the handle of my knife. It took me several minutes to wrestle the blade from his head.

With the knife freed, I crept down to the fire. One by one, I grabbed the cannibal bastards by the chin and cut their throats. The whole process took less than a minute. When I was done, I sat down with the fire to my back and surveyed the gushing corpses. Each little stream of blood ran down the sloping campsite and joined into one, which flowed towards me and pooled beneath my lap. I waited until the fire burned down to embers and the clearing darkened. I laid down right there and slept until morning.

I woke long after the sun had risen and it had dried the blood I laid in. Gathering what was left of Diana, I buried her by the stone in the river where I had left my gear. I did not otherwise mark the grave. I had come to resent the sanctity of graves. It pained me to think of proud and beautiful men and women turned to broken and bloody shadows of themselves, and the memory of their entire lives reduced to a single stone—or worse, a hastily crafted wooden plaque. After years of war burying my good friends, I decided that remembering the small things they left me with was the best memorial I could craft for them. A joke or a piece of advice. Things that cannot be walked away from. A grave is just a hole, and a headstone is just a rock. A memorial is nothing without a memory.

Then again, some men deserve no memory or memorial at all. The bodies of the cannibals, I left to rot in the sun and be devoured by whatever animals that would see fit to eat them.

I searched for signs of the boy and found neither body nor grave, so I decided to go back to the fork in the trail to pick up the other path. Even if August was dead, at least I could get my revenge on a few more of those detestable cannibals. I tracked them for three days before encountering a wide river. I found the prow imprints of fast boats on the bank and one pair of small, bare footprints in the mud.

There was no hope of tracking them on the river, so I turned around and set off to return to my unit. I could only assume that August suffered the same fate as his surrogate mother. I thought at the time it would have been better if I had left him in the street in his real mother's arms.

CHAPTER 5

DISBANDMENT

I walked slowly back to Diana's homestead to sift through the ashes. The animals had already started on Diana's father by the time I got back, so I put his remains with the charred timbers of the burnt-out house. As I stood there tending the fire, I went through his wallet. I found a few expired ration cards, a veteran's card, and a faded picture of Diana and her mother on vacation. I put the picture in my helmet and set off to find my unit with the smell of woodsmoke and burnt flesh assaulting my senses.

As I crossed the river, I found it tinted red and littered with floating bodies of rebels and Central Command regulars. There were more and more as I traveled to where I left the army. I got to Monthermé just before morning. Dying wisps of smoke rose into the sky. The rising sun revealed the town as I crested the hill above it. Deep furrows from gun carriages and mounds of spent artillery cases told the story of what happened. The rebels had beaten the regulars back to the town as they tried to hold it and get across the river. The rebels had massed their artillery and pounded the town to dust, along with all its inhabitants. The bridge that would have allowed

Central Command to escape was piled with bodies all the way up to where the center of it was demolished. On the far shore, there were a few scattered corpses of those that almost made it. Looters were beginning their daily work picking the city clean.

"Did anyone survive?" I asked a looter.

"A few stragglers swam across the river, but the rebels cut the bridge the day before the Archys got pinned down. They planned this one out good," he said with a slimy, nearly toothless smile.

I bartered my way across the river on a looter's skiff. I followed the road for a few miles until I came to a group of Central Command regulars huddled around a shoddily constructed tent. I made my way through the crowd to the makeshift structure. Inside was Captain Ajax, handing out slips of paper.

"We could have used you," he said as I walked in. "Did you find what you were looking for?"

"They were long gone, sir," I said, consciously trying to keep my voice from wavering.

"We're done for, Daniel," he said as he passed me a slip of paper. "Good luck to you."

I looked at the paper. In large black letters at the top it said, "Discharged." After the battle, the captain received a dispatch from headquarters. Central Command had ordered that all units consisting of less than twenty men were to be disbanded. I guess they figured that we weren't important enough in small numbers to be of any use.

A few of us newly discharged and now unemployed soldiers made camp close by that night. I was not looking for any comradery, so I made my camp away from everyone else. As I sat alone staring into my fire Captain Ajax approached.

"You're pretty fixated on that fire. Did it do something that made you mad?" he said.

"I'm just thinking. Trying to decide what to do next," I responded.

Ajax sat down near me and helped himself to my coffee.

"I'll tell you what we need to do. We need to find ourselves another unit. There are still rebels out there that need killing, and we're just the men for the job.

"I don't know," I said.

"I'm joining the Praetorians," he laughed.

"They only take orphans now."

"That's a myth."

"Is it also a myth that they never show their faces?" I asked.

"If I had done any of the fucked up depraved shit that they've been accused of I'd hide my face too. They're supposed to be the top notch, elite, special forces, but they're also cold hearted murdering bastards. Anyways, if I can't join

32

a Praetorian main unit I've heard they have auxiliaries. They take all the misfits and send them riding around burning shit down.

"Well, I'm sure you would be perfect for that sir."

"You're kind to say that," Ajax said.

He drank most of the coffee he had in his cup and then poured the rest out. I watched at the wet cold grounds steamed where he poured the last of my rations.

***

Not having any prospects for proper employment and not having any place to call home, I wandered with my only aim to find something to fill my belly. Aside from employment with Central Command, there were opportunities with even less scrupulous units. Much of the worst work was undertaken by intermediaries; better known as mercenaries. While this work did not appeal to me, there were typically no minimum durations of service, so I could quit whenever I chose. This was especially appealing when considering that execution or death was the only way to get out of a Central Command conscription. Being given this rare chance at freedom through my unit's disbandment, I was keen to carry on the cause without volunteering for more regular army service.

I signed on with a group contracted to capture and screen refugees trying to enter the Paris Control Zone. It was one of the few places where The Architect's forces still held control in the north. Reflecting back, it was misguided to get involved with such a job. But being desensitized, having no guiding authority to dissuade us, or fear of ever being held accountable made it seem completely normal. This was furthermore enforced by the fact that we were contracted to the Central Command, giving our actions the legitimacy needed to make us feel like loyalists instead of criminals.

At first, the refugees were mostly from the surrounding towns looking for better opportunities and some modicum of security. However, entrance into the control zone was extremely regulated. We found refugees all over the perimeter, waiting for their chance to enter extrajudicially. It was hard to tell the difference between the genuinely downtrodden and those that were bent on nefarious purposes. The process for determining the difference and dealing with our captives was less than scientific and not at all humanitarian.

Those refugees which had no discernible loyalties were allowed to enter under probation to work the factories. Those who were tried and true loyalists were conscripted either to the factory rolls or into the army. Those we determined likely to be rebels were interred. The fate of authentic rebels, those who possessed religious symbols, were caught praying, or who refused an oath to The Architect were summarily executed. The refugees of Europe being much more thoroughly disarmed than their counterparts in the Americas, we were able to do with these wretches whatever we willed. I'd like to say I had the same disdain for the work then that I do now, but at the time—given my experiences elsewhere in the war—no amount of savagery seemed out of place.

For twenty-four years, I stayed in the Paris Control Zone and plied my gristly trade. The war raged all around us, but we stayed relatively safe. The rigors of factory work and conscription slowly took a toll on the workforce. Then a plague dramatically reduced the available labor in the city almost overnight. The local overlords relaxed the regulations on refugees. At first, those who had been previously within the city without permission were given amnesty. Partly to encourage their enlistment into the factory force, but also to make the prospects of gaining entry less daunting to those on the outside who might consider it. This newfound citizenship swelled the ranks of the workers, but also released a sense of entitlement among the newly elevated.

Before these changes, refugees were only capable of lodging in whatever hellhole would have them. After, they competed for apartments and houses in more secure parts of the city. This caused tensions with longtime citizens who found their bids for upward mobility coming at a premium. To compound the housing crisis, the factory bosses made no distinction between the new and old citizens. Jobs which had previously been reserved for the most skilled and experienced were handed out to the lowest bidder. Myself, having been substantially rewarded for my role securing the perimeter, found my job outsourced to a newly formed unit of immigrants.

Not content to work in a factory job and finding it increasingly hard to find work otherwise, I joined the City Security Force. Not long after I joined the force, a wave of refugees descended upon the city. Weakened defenses without and a great magnitude of sympathizers within meant there was no stopping the tide. The Architect's engines powered the factories endlessly and made the outflow of weapons seemingly effortless, but the unlimited power was useless to assist the simple biological process of growing plants. An effort was made to subsidize the meager harvests with chemically produced supplements, but some of the raw ingredients still required time and of course sun. Although the overlords took over the distribution and production of food, they could not supply to everyone's satisfaction. Eventually, riots gripped the city. The surrounding countryside was stripped bare even to the last blade of grass to fulfill the growing population, but once there was no food to be had work at the factories stopped and the citizens descended on each other with animalistic disregard for life.

Although the movement of people across the Earth was not without precedent, the violence that followed was inevitable. With factory rolls filled, new housing non-existent, and food itself in finite supply; competition turned into insurgency.

One night, as I stood with my fellow officers behind my riot shield watching as waves of club-wielding rioters closed the distance, I decided there was nothing left there for me. I dropped my shield and ran towards the city gate. Behind me, I could hear the thuds of shields and the footsteps of my fellow officers as they surrendered themselves to the fact that all was lost. I ran briefly to my tiny boarding room and gathered my old gear. From there I ran straight to the city gate, which lay wide open, and ran out into the black night. I ran and ran until my lungs gave out.

CHAPTER 6

REUNION

After the fall of Paris, I decided to rejoin The Architect's service. In the north, as well as in other places where The Architect's power was weakest, local commanders were given commissions to muster bands of loyalists. It was a desperate strategy to carry out that which the Central Command and the Praetorians could not. The only problem for me was that it was extremely difficult to join a loyalist unit. Decades of insider attacks, betrayal, and double agents had made loyalist units wary, and the only way to get in was with recommendations. I decided the only way I would be able to reenter the fold would be to find an old comrade to vouch for me, or find a previous commander to whom I could appeal for my enlistment.

I heard of a successful unit operating on the old Belgian border—my former sector. It was the only unit left in the north with any kind of operational ability. I didn't know much about this unit other than it was locally raised loyalists, but since this area was the old haunt of my previous unit, I assumed it was the best chance for me to find someone to give me a reference. On foot and with no idea where to find the unit I was looking for, I could only attempt to locate them from local intelligence. I was able to determine their last engagement by enquiring with several locals I found along the way. Once I picked up the unit's trail, I followed their sign day and night until I finally found them moving warily along a forest road.

As their column moved through the valley, I crept along the back side of the ridge; popping up to the top every now and then to look for the commander. I made sure to stay within sight of, but well behind their last scout to avoid detection. He was a fat little man with tattoos of naked women all over him. After about five miles of shadowing their flank scout, I decided if I was going to see the commander I needed to get to the head of the column. I got my chance when the scout sat down to catch his breath.

I watched him for a few minutes as he took off his kit and cleared a place to lie down. I should have assumed this meant that he knew their destination was close and that the column would be stopping soon. Unfortunately, I assumed that he was a common lazy scout and was taking a break at the risk of endangering his fellow soldiers. I passed his position, keeping a good distance from him but maintaining an eye on him. Once I was sure I was out of earshot, I picked up my pace to get ahead of the column.

The unit was moving through a valley which gradually opened into a wide meadow. The soldiers began to disperse and set up their camps. I knew it was only a matter of time until they would search for firewood, so my position in the tree line would eventually be compromised. I laid down behind a rocky outcrop and used my binoculars to look for the commander or anyone I knew. It was incredibly difficult to pinpoint anyone in the mass of soldiers, and it was taking all my focus to single anyone out. Small groups who had finished making camp worked their way to the tree line. I had been lying down for about twenty minutes and was about to get up when I felt the cool steel of a knife slip up under my chin. The only thing I could think to do was whisper, "Damn."

"You should be more cautious, old man."

I slowly turned to the side and looked out the corner of my eye to see the fat little scout standing over me with one foot on each side of my hip. "Any last words?" he asked.

"I've come to join this group," I croaked.

"This is a pretty piss poor way of introducing yourself," he said. "I thought perhaps you were looking to take a shot at the commander. We've been having some issues with that lately."

"No, no," I gasped. "I didn't want to just stroll in. I know it's hard to join up."

"Well, I guess we'll let the commander decide about you."

He grabbed my rifle, which was laying beside me, and slung it behind him. He took my pistol out of my holster and looked at it.

"A 1911?" he asked. "It won two world wars don't you know?" After giving me a clumsy pat down, he stepped back and trained my own pistol on me. "Get going, right down on into camp."

I walked through the camp followed by my captor as his fellow soldiers jeered at me. I took stock of the composition of the force as we went. There were remnants of every unit that had been part of the Baltic Army, disgraced ex-Praetorians, local militia, and a few units of Central Command specialists. There was also a smattering of what I would call mercenaries, although I couldn't for the life of me figure out why they would join a volunteer force. There were countless thousands of soldiers from a wide variety of units. We finally made it to where the security and intelligence detail had encamped.

"I found this chap lurking in the woods," the fat scout said. "He says he wants to join up."

"Is that so?" said a severe-looking captain. "Strip him."

Three privates took off all of my clothes and gear. They dumped my rucksack on the ground and dumped out everything inside the smaller pouches and containers that had been inside. They took my wallet and dumped all my credits, ration cards, and other bits of paper out onto a blanket and examined each piece.

I hadn't noticed before but sitting cross-legged on a cot at the other end of the tent was a young man. Something in my wallet caught his eye. He walked over and picked up the picture of Diana from the pile. I took him in as he studied the picture. He was wearing a worn loyalists ranger's uniform and had an antiquated Lee-Enfield rifle in the crook of his arm. The young man's face showed a few days of stubble. Hard living showed its wear, but his eyes were kind and bright. By his expression, I could see he was pleased to see the picture. He finally looked at me. He kneeled on the ground beside me and reached in his pocket. He pulled out a photograph of his own—another photograph of Diana.

"Did you know her?" he asked. "She was my mother."

"August?" I asked.

"Yes," he said. "Are you the soldier she talked about?"

"Daniel Marconas."

"I never thought I'd ever meet you. This must be some kind of miracle."

The interrogators surrounding us did not seem to know quite what to do. They stood around with my things in their hands, awkwardly looking at the ground.

"Give him back his things," the captain said.

"Captain," August said, "I will take over this interrogation."

"Yes, sir," the captain replied.

"You're an officer here?" I asked.

August laughed along with some of the privates standing around us.

"This is my army," he said. "I'm *General* August now."

As I gathered my things, August told me how he had come to lead this band of soldiers. When the raiders who took him from Diana's homestead split from her captors, he had the good fortune of being the slaver's choice and not the cannibal's. He was taken and sold to fishermen in the Baltic. For two years, they treated him kindly considering his status. Sadly, his owners had the misfortune of being suppliers to the rebels. They were eventually caught ashore by a patrol of Central Command and killed. August was only eleven at the time, and his chain-marked ankles gave him away as a slave, which saved his life.

He was taken to the Praetorian school in the north and educated there until it was assaulted by the rebels and destroyed. He was lucky enough to survive the attack. He and a few of the older survivors carried out hit-and-run raids in the area to sustain themselves. Along the way, they joined up with the few surviving units and individuals of the Baltic Army. As their exploits spread, new recruits joined in as well.

As August and I spoke, I could see why men were compelled to follow him. He spoke honestly and without conceit, even though the reality of his achievements was truly spectacular. He had regret for his fallen comrades and surprisingly those enemies he encountered dying on the battlefield. I suspected that his early years with Diana had given him a sense of humanity that was almost lost to most who had fought this war for so long. Compassion was a strange notion to his generation, who were born and raised in a world in constant turmoil and despair. Having lived part of his life in the loving arms of Diana—and part under the dark instruction of Praetorian trainers—he was truly a remarkable man.

"I never accepted the Praetorian doctrines," he told me. "They taught us to completely disregard our feelings and prior knowledge of the world and embrace only The Architect's vision. They told us everything we would do was for a greater purpose. But I could tell the root of all of this was vanity."

"I saw you have prisoners with you," I said. "It's been a long time since I saw anyone take prisoners."

"I've started saving all that I can." The words escaped his lips along with a deep sigh.

"I'm surprised you're able to keep your men from butchering them."

"I didn't always take prisoners," he recounted. "It's a major risk. A few years ago, we located a bunker, but we found the air intake before we found the entrance. We lit a fire in it to smoke them out and mowed them down as they emerged. At first, they came out armed and firing, but after a while they were dazed and out of breath from the smoke. We gunned them down anyways. I watched the first hundred or so rebels die before I grew sick. After that, I ordered the men to close in and tie them up as they came out. It just seemed senseless to kill so many defenseless men."

"It's a shame there aren't more men who share that sentiment."

"I was spared once, as you well know. Still, I can understand the logistical problems of prisoners," August said. "We have trouble keeping them contained, and they slow us down. However, we've found many uses for them to help our cause."

"Is that why you've marked them? I see they all have an 'x' tattooed on their head."

August drew in a breath and furrowed his brow. "Yes. Partially. It helps to identify them when we put them on work details and keeps them from walking straight out of camp."

"What are you going to do with them?"

"I have no idea," he said. "We are waiting for a few companies of rangers to meet up with us, and then we are

45

moving out for the Holy City. The Imperial forces there under siege and are almost totally surrounded. The Architect has called all units to come to his relief. I guess we have no choice but to drag them along."

"You have quite a lot of soldiers here. I thought this sector was lost to the Central Command."

"Nearly two hundred thousand troops. I never intended for our unit to get so large, but they just keep coming to join us."

As we spoke, one of August's lieutenants entered the tent. "We have a new recruit who demands to meet you before he will join," he said.

"Well, bring him in then," August replied.

I was immediately suspicious of the new recruit. His arms hung at his side like he didn't know what to do with his hands. Although it was late fall, it was not particularly cold this day, and he was wearing a pair of heavy gloves. His left hand was clinched at his side and the fingers of his right hand dangled lamely, as if it was injured. Years of war makes a man wary of strangers and well-educated in the body language of aggression. I looked at the recruit's eyes and was certain he had ill intentions. Rather than a nervous look about him, I saw cold, calculating eyes.

In what seemed like slow motion, he turned his shoulders and swung his arm up. Before he had it waist high, I knew he was not posturing for a handshake—but a headshot.

I lashed out and punched him in the arm as a shot rang out. A muzzle flash blossomed from his hand as it swung to the side, and his glove burst into flames. August's lieutenant grabbed the recruit from behind. I took hold of his hand and ripped the glove off to reveal a snub revolver. He got off a few wild shots before August's lieutenant twisted his head around. The life fled from his body with one quick snap of his neck. After dropping the lifeless corpse to the ground, the lieutenant and I kneeled, panting. I looked up at August, who stood scratching his head nervously.

"That's the third time this week," he whispered.

The captain examined the assassin's body. "He's not from around here. I think you're being hunted."

As I finished gathering up my things scattered across the floor of the tent, I noticed the boots that the assassin was wearing. They were the boots commonly issued to the Praetorians. I didn't think much of it at the time. They were easy enough to come by, I supposed.

***

We broke camp in the morning and were on the move again just after the sun came up. August asked me to join his cadre of bodyguards so we could keep close. There was a lot of catching up to do. I watched August closely for the next few days as we traveled. He treated his men more like friends, yet they all showed him soldierly respect. He refused to let them salute him. He claimed it was to prevent being singled out as an officer by snipers. However, I could tell that it made him uneasy to be in charge of men twice his age. Yet all his men, young and old, treated him with reverence. I think it must have been his show of concern for their welfare. After serving in units where generals and sergeants alike treated their men like meat being fed into a grinder, he treated his troops like actual human beings.

Every morning, he woke before the rest of his officers and checked the wounded. In the regular army and Praetorian guard, medical treatment was usually reserved for officers and highly trained specialists. The rest were left to treat themselves, and the most severely wounded were euthanized. August had set up medical camps all over his area of operation so he didn't have to move them around with him in this war without fronts. Now that he was taking the whole army south, they were all with us, being dragged along on whatever scrap of vehicle could be made to run. He also treated his prisoners well. Since they could not be trusted to be released to forage, they often did not eat every day, but they were given enough to survive.

At night, he and I would tell each other stories. His stories were only of burned-out places full of death and a few fleeting memories of his life with Diana back on the homestead. All his questions for me were about the world he had never known: Before the war, before The Architect, and before The Temple. I often found myself surrounded at night by the young men and women of the outfit as they gathered to hear of things as unreal to them as a fairy tale. Things like clean running water, elections, commercial air travel, roller coasters, and ice cream. A few of the older soldiers would walk away in tears as they were reminded of their vanquished childhoods. The men my age wanted nothing to do with stories. They had been there, and they could remember all they had lost for themselves.

One night, August asked me, "What were you before the war? What did you do?"

"I was in college before the war. I never really decided what I wanted to be. I think I wanted to be a writer," I recalled. "I did write a book, but it was just a draft. I gave it to Diana."

"What is *college*?" August asked. "I've never heard that word."

"It was a type of school. You could pay to go and get educated in a specific field of study. The Architect outlawed them because many of them taught against his rule."

"What book did you write?"

"It was called 'Roses'," I said.

"Diana had that book. I read it. It was about love. It was very sad."

"Love sometimes is sad," I said. "Diana never told you I wrote that book?"

"She never told me your name. She just called you 'the soldier' and said you would never be back."

Tears welled up in my eyes, and I blinked them away. I couldn't help but think of how things might have been different if I had come back to the homestead before cruel fate—only hours ahead of me—swept in.

"So, you can read then?" I asked.

"Yes. Diana taught me to read the bible, and I got a proper education at the Praetorian school."

"Are you religious?"

"Well, it is hard to follow any one religion after all I have learned about religion and what I have seen fighting the rebels."

"You know, not all of the rebels are zealots."

"I know that," he said. "but some of the things they have done in the name of their gods make it seem like they have never read a word of any holy book."

"Then you don't believe in God?"

"I have seen too much to believe in a loving god. Still, I cannot dismiss the thought that there is some force that holds the scales to balance our evils with our good deeds. I wish that more people would follow the teachings of their own God."

"What teachings are those?"

"That men must treat other men with compassion and not like animals."

"You're a rare mind for these days."

"I am aware," he said. "My men almost shot me when I ordered them to take prisoners at first, but if the evil and sickness that takes hold of men can spread and infect others as quickly as it does, then I'd like to think the same thing can happen with mercy. I like to think that's what religion was meant to do. But it seems like the opposite has happened."

"Men *are* sometimes just animals," I said. "They eat when they are hungry, they fight when they are threatened."

"They do," August agreed. "but what animal will cut another open and let him bleed to death just because he believes something different?"

While The Architect presumably saw all rebels as the same, August came to understand that there were two distinct groups which he explained.

The zealots were fueled by religious fervor and took the most offense to The Architect's temple. Not the building itself, but the idea that their heartfelt beliefs could be combined with others' beliefs in something which was indistinct from its individual contributing denominations. While most faiths were based in similar core teachings of love, kindness, vengeance, and obedience; the discrete system of how to best execute these principles before their gods was diabolically unbending. However, though August was not particularly religious himself, he had the most sympathy for the zealots. Through his observation of post battle practice, he admired the care they took for their wounded—both their own and occasionally their enemy's—and their reverence for the dead.

The nationalists were primarily concerned with restoring the old system of nations, borders, and independent governments based on historical and often nebulous cultural associations. By his own admission, August did not understand the passion that the idea of country could instill. I explained to him that it's not the land or the culture, but more importantly the idea that people can be independent and choose how to govern themselves that appeals. Having not been part of any country, August never experienced the pride of patriotism. But he noticed the nationalist were more prone to several problems which he despised. Primarily, racism and xenophobia. As a result, August had the least regard for nationalists.

Listening to August describe his view of the world was telling about Diana's influence on him. While at that time I was filled with regret over failing to save Diana, and for leaving August to become a slave, I know that different outcomes to the course to our lives is not always better. August's life had shaped him. I couldn't help but think that there was much more about him to discover. His courage was more than that of others, but in a different way. While the rest of the world showed their might with the rifle and grenade and counted their greatness by the dead they left behind, August showed his power by the size of his heart and his courage against the hate and fear that had permeated all our lives. Still, it was obvious that August was an idealist. The strength of the impression that Diana had made on a younger August still showed through, even though the wicked world had tested him. Even slavery and extremist indoctrination were not able to sap the goodness she had instilled. It had been a long time since I had thought about Diana in earnest. Even though I carried her picture, I rarely looked at it. It's not that the loss was too much to bear or that I couldn't cope with the grief. It had been many years, and the memory was simply fading away. Seeing August and recognizing her influence on him renewed my feelings for her and reminded me that there was still occasionally beauty in the world.

One afternoon as we rested along the road, I was leaning up against a tree watching August.

"You watch him very closely," a voice said from behind me. "If I didn't know any better, I would think you had the hots for him."

I turned around to see the fat little scout who was squatting behind me. "It's just odd to see him grown up. The last time I saw him, he was only an infant. Now, he's a general," I said.

"I see," said the man. "It's a good thing I didn't do you in when I found you sneaking around in the woods," he chuckled.

"I should never have let you get behind me. It was poor field craft."

"Well, we may as well get to know each other if you're going to stick around," he said as he stretched out his hand. "Simon Gram, scout and sometimes bodyguard to August."

"Daniel Marconas, 3001st rifle regiment," I said. It was only after I had already spoken that I realized my unit had been disbanded a lifetime ago.

"Oh, so you're a shooter?" he smirked.

He dragged out his weapon from behind him and stood it on the ground beside him. It was a single shot 40mm grenade launcher.

"I don't carry a gun," He beamed as he looked at his weapon. "If you can hit something with a gun, you can definitely hit something with a grenade. I never miss. Can you say the same?"

CHAPTER 7

OBEDIENCE

As we worked our way along the frontier, there was a slow trickle of new recruits who flocked to August's army. Mostly the newcomers came in small groups of raiders and bandits looking for food and security. August had set up an extensive organization to vet and investigate all the applicants to make sure he wasn't admitting any known rebels or traitors. After it could be reasonably ascertained they were not a threat, new additions were formed into units August called "Hastati", after the Roman rank of poor or green troops, since he could not be assured of their training and effectiveness. Occasionally, larger groups would attempt to join August. Local strongmen and warlords were generally well aware of what was goings on in the world. As word of the ongoing siege of the Holy City spread out of Israel and permeated the empire, they all wanted to secure their place in the order of battle.

August's army of followers was composed entirely of volunteers. His early successes had gained him a formidable reputation, even though he was quite young to command such a large force. At thirty-three, he was older than many of his

soldiers but much younger than most Imperial officers—
especially senior and high-ranking officers. August noticed
early on that the other commanders he encountered throughout
his operations, even officers with records of colossal failure,
would often attempt to usurp his leadership because of
August's age. Although he was young, he was quite assured in
his ability. Because of this, he worked hard to maintain near
complete dominion over his force. To maintain his command,
he divided his followers under several Generals whom he
knew he could trust.

General Soho was a tall, clean-shaven man from Africa.
He wore a black beret and a well-worn camo uniform which
had been stripped of his former unit's insignia. Its only
remaining markings were a crudely-sewn imperial eagle on
each sleeve. August had recommended that his officers not
mark themselves with identifying trappings to avoid becoming
targets, and General Soho had taken this to the extreme.
August met General Soho and a small contingent of the
Central Command's Africa Corps when they wandered into
August's winter camp. Decimated by their recent engagement
and not equipped for winter, they had been disbanded by the
Central Command and left to fend for themselves. August
took them in and equipped them well enough to survive the
winter. Their addition was large enough to double August's
command at the time, and since August knew the area of

operation well, General Soho was happy enough to submit to August's leadership. Soho's loyalty was cemented after August successfully led several assaults on the nationalist rebel's strongholds along the Baltic coast.

General St Clair was a fierce looking, red haired and bearded man whose imposing stature belied the fact he was a quiet and cautious speaker. He cut his teeth as a leader in The Architect's Britannic loyalists. After being driven out of the British Isles by rebel guerillas, he landed on the Danish coast beaten and starving. Although he brought with him only a few disheartened survivors, August took him on at the rank of Colonel. Through his loyal service, August increased St Clair's command, and along with it his rank.

General Moulin was August's oldest officer. He joined August only months after August escaped the Praetorian school. While commanding separate raiding parties, they accidentally were set to ambush the same rebel convoy. Once the ambush was sprung, General Moulin was wounded in the confusion. August recognized what was happening before the two loyalist units engaged each other. He took command of both raiding parties and completed the ambush successfully. It provided much needed supplies for both groups, and the two commanders decided to collaborate with one another. Although it was never decided which of them was the ranking officer, August had a natural way of subjecting those around him without conflict. General Moulin took it upon himself to maintain many important functions for the steadily growing army, and found himself overseeing communications, logistics, and security.

At first, August held no rank or title, having been only an officer cadet when the Praetorian school was destroyed. He held his little band of volunteers together through sheer charisma and his growing reputation. But as his unit grew, he gained the attention of the Central Command. August performed well at harassing the rebels in the Baltic area, and having not much of a presence in that area after the Baltic Army's destruction, the Central Command granted him a commission. Due to the large number of followers he had attracted, his fellow officers insisted that he should settle for nothing less than the rank of General. The Central Command granted his request, and with this he would intermittently receive logistical support from the empire. But more importantly, he would receive intelligence reports.

August, with Moulin's help, ran the army efficiently. They both worked hard to build a strong culture of accountability, rather than using fear and discipline. The size of his army fluctuated as volunteers came and went according to their needs, and August would adjust the ambition of his operations accordingly. The flexible, nomadic nature of his unit kept it from being bogged down or cornered by larger rebel forces.

But not all of those who joined August were respectful of his leadership and skill. The open-door policy he adopted allowed dissenters to bleed away over time, leaving him with only true loyalists. It was an important distinction that their loyalty to August was assured as firmly as their loyalty to The Architect.

***

A few weeks after I joined August, we were passing through a dense forest when scouts reported back that our path was blocked by a large body of soldiers.

"I don't recognize them as rebels or loyalists," Simon said as he reported back to August. "If they are rebels, I think we handily outnumber them. But I can't be sure who they are with."

"Can you try to talk to one of their pickets?" August asked.

"That's the thing," Simon replied. "There are no pickets; not even scouts. It doesn't look like they are going anywhere. It's more like they are just sitting in the road, waiting."

As August and Simon were talking, General Moulin walked in with a man I hadn't seen before. He had on a well-worn leather jacket emblazoned with stripes and metals. The junior officers who accompanied him looked exhausted and emaciated.

"General August," Moulin said, "This is General Nast of the Teutonic Loyalists Legion. His men are waiting further on down the road. He's expressed interest in joining us, but I wanted you to talk to him yourself."

August nodded to Moulin, who turned and left without another word.

"Teutonic Loyalists Legion?" August asked, arching an eyebrow in concern. "I haven't heard of this unit before. Were you newly formed?"

"It's my regiment," General Nast said. "I recruited these men myself to beat back those fucking zealots, but they're giving us a hell of a time. We've been operating in this area for a few years. Now that you're here to reinforce us, we can finally push them out."

"Apologies, General Nast, but we're not here to reinforce you. We're on our way to relieve the Holy City. Were you not informed all units have been recalled?" August said.

"We operate independently," Nast said. "I don't need Central Command meddling in my operations."

"We also operate freely, but at this point there's a clear mission, and we're answering the call to relieve the city," August said. "You're welcome to join us once we vet your unit. Since I've never heard of you, there's some security concerns to address."

"I don't think we will be joining *you*," Nast said. "I need *you* to join *me*. There's seventy thousand rebel soldiers ten miles from here, on their way south. If you'll just follow my lead, we can defeat them easily."

August drew in a deep breath, but maintained a relaxed disposition. Simon tensed beside him. I had yet to see August's authority challenged in this way. Despite the rising tension, he remained calm as he replied, "If you can accept *my* lead, I will consider addressing your concerns, but that's a large force to attack without preparation and intelligence."

"Listen, young man," General Nast spat out.

"Let me stop you right there," August said as he put up his hand to signal that he would hear no more. There was an assertiveness to his tone that took me by surprise. "I understand that you may not see me as your equal because you are much older, but let me assure you that I do not make the mistake of unquestionably equating age with wisdom. This entire assembly of soldiers are my volunteers. They are free to come and go as they see fit, and yet they stay. They do not question my leadership, and I will not allow you to do so either."

"I have twenty thousand men under my command," Nast said. "I will not be told what to do by some boy."

"Ah, a whole twenty thousand," August sighed. "I can tell that we are not easily going to see eye to eye."

General Moulin came back into the tent with a slip of paper and handed it to August who reviewed it briefly.

"It looks like General Moulin has been interviewing your men. Here's a retelling of your recent engagements," August said. Then he began to read from the list.

"December 2101: Attacked rebel factory. Driven off by active defenses. Three hundred dead.

"March 2102: Attacked rebel camp, but were repelled. Thirty-two hundred dead, number of wounded unknown.

"April 2102: Ambushed by rebels at night. Eight hundred dead, number of wounded unknown.

"April 2102: Came under artillery attack while fording river.

"May 2102: Scouts engaged rebel patrol. Retreating scouts gave away the position of your main body, and rebels responded with mortar fire. Twelve hundred dead. Five thousand wounded.

"June 2102: Accepted large body of volunteers who turned out to be rebels. Four hundred of your men were killed in their sleep. No rebel losses.

"And two days ago: Engaged body of sixty to seventy thousand rebels with only thirty-five thousand men. Fifteen thousand of your men are dead as a result."

August didn't show any sign of anger at the impudence of the general, but as he finished reading off the list of failures—along with the expanding tally of dead and wounded—a flush rose to his cheeks. He folded the paper over and slipped it into a shirt pocket.

And then, August finally raised his voice. "This record does not make you look like a general. This list makes you look like a damn fool. So, before you presume to call me 'young man', let us take a minute to digest who is fit to lead who given what we now know."

"I've heard enough!" Nast shot back. "I did not come here to be insulted by a child. I'll take my men with me, and you can get the hell out of here."

As Nast turned to leave, one of his officers stepped forward. "We will join you, General August," he said. "We're desperate. I've talked to the men, and they're ready to give up."

The officer glared at General Nast and said, "We can't go on like this. It's a miracle there's anyone left. We have no food, we're almost out of ammunition, and we don't even have enough weapons to go around."

"You will definitely pay for this," Nast growled as he turned to storm out of the tent.

***

August's army broke camp and continued down the road until they met up with Nast's command. They fell in with August's men, but were to remain under guard until Moulin had completed his investigation. Moulin wanted to disarm them, but August insisted they should remain armed in case the column was attacked by rebels. Even the newcomers would need to be able to protect themselves.

After being satisfied that the Teutonic Loyalists were not rebels, or compromised by rebels, August sent word to General Nast that any of his men—including himself—who would remain were to present themselves to General Moulin's quartermaster for equipment and training. That night after camp had been made, Simon entered the officer's mess tent and rushed over to August.

"We have an issue with the new recruits," he said.

August and a few other officers rose and followed Simon. Being curious, I followed them. As we approached the Teutonic camp, the screams of an injured man pierced the air. A jumble of soldiers were brawling in a muddy pit beside a bonfire. They punched and kicked and grappled with each other on the ground. A company of Moulin's security forces had been mustered, and they fell on the fighting group, pulling the men apart and pinning them all to the ground. Those who had not been fighting joined the security force and pulled their comrades out of the mud. At the bottom of the pile was a completely sodden, mud-coated General Nast.

"What is the meaning of this?" August asked.

"He shot him," a voice from the crowd said.

The officer who had spoken up against Nast was lying on the ground, holding his bleeding thigh. Several of his men were tending his wounds.

"He disobeyed me for the last time," Nast snarled as he rose from the muck. His white eyes showed through his mud-covered face and his teeth were barred though his mud-caked mustache.

Cries rang out from the crowd, "Kill him!" "Execute Nast!" "Bash his head in!"

There were no calls for leniency for General Nast.

"Get your things *Mister* Nast," August said. "I will not tolerate friendly fire in my ranks."

Simon leaned over to me and said with a wink, "Doesn't look very friendly to me."

"You will address me as General," Nash said to August.

"As of today, you are General of nothing," August said. "For my army to survive, our officers must be our strongest link, not our weakest. If you must resort to shooting your own men to maintain your command, then you are no leader at all. Be happy that I'm letting you go alive. It seems that if it were up to your men, you would not be so lucky."

Nash turned to walk back to his tent, but his men did not part to let him pass.

"General Moulin," August said, "please have your men help Nash gather his things, then escort him out of camp."

The security team grabbed Nash and drug him away, stumbling as he spit mud out and tried to clean his face.

"I bet he's a 'general' pain in the ass," Simon said to me.

CHAPTER 8

ACCESSORY TO THE FACT

The Teutonic Loyalists were, as Nast's lieutenant had described, woefully undersupplied and under armed. Some soldiers had little more than hunting rifles and some only shotguns. It was no wonder that Nast had suffered such a string of devastating defeats. Luckily, along with the soldiers and fighting men that August's army attracted, there were also a good number of noncombatants that shadowed the army. Many of them were relations of the rank-and-file soldiers, but some of camp followers were vendors providing for the army various goods and services. General Moulin asked for volunteers to assist in procuring proper supplies for the new recruits sourced from the camp followers. I offered my services to ingratiate myself to August and Moulin.

In the Central Command and Praetorian service, all the needs of the soldiers were provided for according to their organizational doctrine, but many of the loyalist groups such as August's were left to their own devices. August's group had the benefit of being sanctioned by the Central Command, and as such would receive rations from time to time. But it had become increasingly difficult to get food since The Architect had become extremely adamant about the proper distribution of supplies. The lean years were hard on the rebels and imperials alike, so it was of strategic importance to control this resource.

The supply of food was managed by the offices of The Prophet. He devised a plan where anyone within the empire would receive a simple mark that could be scanned to verify the individual was receiving their daily ration and no more. At first, it was mandatory to receive the cartouche, and those that refused were hunted down and interred until they starved to death or gave in. However, after experiencing the strain of this effort on his resources, The Prophet relinquished this crusade and simply made it impossible to get any material goods directly from imperial channels.

After this, those who refused to receive the cartouche could not receive rations directly from imperial storehouses or from intermediaries. Although many of August's soldiers had received their mark, there was a smattering of men and camp followers who refused. August allowed them to create their own economy where they could exchange their services and goods they could fashion in exchange for the rations of others. In this way, he operated within The Architect's law, but the holdouts could provide for themselves. Luckily most of Nast's command had received the cartouche so we did not have to circumvent the law to supply them.

There was a wide variety of things available from the camp followers. Medical treatment was available through the regimental doctors, but better treatment could be procured from the private practitioners. Although General Moulin's staff worked tirelessly to provide operational weaponry to every fighting man, better guns and modifications were in constant demand. These were supplied by the arms dealers that followed the camp. Simple luxuries like candy, milk, fresh meat, and narcotics—all of which were not supplied by the Central Command—were also available in the camp markets and were a much-needed morale booster. This open, mobile economy alone attracted many recruits and helped to retain them with the army.

Also available from the camp followers was the oldest of professions: Prostitution. August did not partake of that pleasure and did not particularly care for its existence in the camp, but he made no attempt to regulate it. He recognized the role of carnal pleasure in his soldiers' lives. Unlike the Central Command or Praetorian, August forbade rape against prisoners, civilians, and among the troops themselves. He preferred his men have an outlet with willing participants.

General Moulin, on the other hand, was particularly fond of the prostitutes. He had grown quite thin from trading away his rations for other delights. He was at their camp every night and would often make multiple trips if the fancy took him. It was an unhealthy obsession, but August made no intervention as long as Moulin's other duties were well cared for. I will admit I entertained some level of interest in venturing among the women of the night. But ultimately, before I summoned the gumption, I had either eaten all I had to trade or fallen asleep.

Worldly comforts aside, the chief need of the new recruits was weapons. There was a wild assortment of weapons available. From both world wars and slightly before, there were many pistols, rifles, and—more rarely—light machine guns. There was even a vendor there who had a well-worn but functional MG34, which I found particularly intriguing. At over one-hundred and sixty years old, it was more of a relic than an implement of war. August himself seemed to prefer older weapons, as he carried a Lee-Enfield rifle which had been converted to a round more common among the imperial forces. More modern weapons were available, from the Cold War and from the former United States' crusade against the Muslim nations. When the USA capitulated to The Architect, their arsenals around the globe were raided extensively and were a great boon for the arms trade.

Then of course, there was a selection of prototype and homemade abominations the vendors offered. Assembled with little or no engineering knowledge, even the most stout-looking weapons were known to detonate from some slightly inconsistent tolerance or flaw. Although I browsed the market weekly, I was for the most part happy with the rifle I had from my time in Paris. It was an old FAMAS which I had re-barreled and upgraded with modern, plastic covers. It was not a beautiful rifle, but the free-floated barrel gave it exceptional accuracy; which I valued over all else.

August's Army was armed with an assortment of rifles from all over the world, as General Moulin had traded and bartered extensively to try and supply quality firearms. As I helped search for suitable weapons, I identified several lots which were for sale. Moulin then sent agents to negotiate a price. Most of the automatic rifles were of an old AR pattern, or from the long-since out of business H&K. A few arms from the Central Command had been supplied, which utilized the more modern caseless ammunition. The ammunition was stored in an impressively sized magazine at the rear of the gun and cycled forward by levers to be chambered for firing. These rifles had also been refitted retroactively with a counter recoil system which had been reverse engineered from a captured rebel design. Together the two systems created a deadly fast and highly accurate system. August had an open bounty for any of these caseless weapons that could be procured, and so the price in the open market had been driven up to where the common soldier could not obtain it. What August could procure, he gave to his best troops.

There were also a few rebel rifles to be found in the arms market. Probably the most innovative was a light machine gun which fired round steel balls which were suspended in and coated by a liquid propellant. The balls, along with liquid charge, were pumped from a tank that was separate from the gun. This system gave the machine gun an extremely high rate of fire, to the point there were often multiple rounds traveling through the barrel at the same time. Although innovative, it was difficult to find ammunition for the weapon, and it was prone to overheating; which would often cause it to fire without the gunner's control, and the only way to stop it was to kink the hose. If the hose was cold, it would snap. With the pump still running, this would shower the gunners with steel balls and liquid explosives. Still, a trained gun crew watching their barrel temperature could pump out two thousand rounds a minute.

Moulin also had held aside one crate of weapons usually reserved for the Praetorians. It contained several rifles which fired projectiles using no explosive propellant, rather utilizing an electrical charge. I knew of Praetorian tanks and artillery with this technology, but I did not know until I saw Moulins cache that it existed for small arms. Moulin noticed my interest in weapons and took me to see his prized possessions.

Almost as tall as a man, they were deceivingly light. The stock and mechanical components were constructed of carbon fiber and titanium. The barrel was graphene, inlaid along its length with ceramic rails and electrical components. The battery pack was contained within the butt stock, and the butt assembly could be changed out for a fresh unit should the charge diminish. Unfortunately, Moulin had no spares. The magazines procured with these rifles were also the only ones available, The rounds were not contained within a box type magazine like other rifles, but were stacked together in bundles of ten which could be combined together to form a larger magazine. The bolt would then strip off the top round for firing and another mechanism would advance the next round upward to be chambered next.

Moulin handed me one of the rounds, and I examined it carefully. A square discarding sabot surrounded a dense penetrator, the composition of which I could not ascertain. Moulin assured me it could punch through a tank at a hundred yards, though he had only fired a few rounds himself. After seeing these magnificent apex weapons, the allure of the arms market diminished for me. I would still stroll through the booths from time to time looking for large lots for Moulin or something unique for myself. A love of weapons is a hard thing to erase.

The size and composition of the camp followers changed as we moved along. Some vendors would run out of wares and leave to return home. Some would find a new source of their product and leave us for a time to restock. The families of the men and those professions which did not require stock continued on as best they could convey themselves. August did not wait for them, nor did he assist in their transportation. He did not see it as his role to intervene in this micro economy when he was tasked with other imperial business.

CHAPTER 9

A DEMON AND DELIVERY MAN

As we worked our way across the broken landscape towards the Holy City, fall rains began to pour and our assortment of cobbled together transport were no match for the mud and rough roads. The column gradually stretched out longer and longer as units became bogged down. I sat with August and his officers one night as they discussed the situation.

"We should take the best vehicles and the best troops, and leave the rest here to fend for themselves. We're not going to make it in time," said General Moulin.

"We don't have time to retrain amalgamated units," said General Soho. "If we don't arrive in full-strength, we may not be able to assure victory. There has been no communication about what other forces are able to rally."

August seemed pensive as the Generals bickered.

"We have to get over the mountains before winter," said General St Clair. "We're in no condition to travel through the mountains as it is, let alone in the dead of winter."

"I haven't received any transmissions in three days," said General Moulin. "For all I know, the city may have already fallen."

"It is somewhat concerning that we're not receiving intelligence reports anymore," August said.

August stood up, and his generals looked at him silently. Assured of their rapt attention, he said, "We have damaged equipment, winter will soon be in the mountains, and we have no communication from Central Command or the Holy City. I will not march these men all the way to the Holy City only to find it destroyed, and I will not see this army decimated by freezing to death. We will go to the Munich Control Zone and winter there. We will repair our transports, commandeer whatever else we can, and wait for spring. The garrison there will welcome our presence."

The authority in his voice seemed to quell the riotous spirit of his generals and no objections were made. The next day, we worked to consolidate our convoy and made our way down the Rhine River valley. We would need to cross over to get to Munich, but nearly all the bridges had been blown up. Some reconstruction of the bridges had been attempted, but the river was swollen from rain and there was no trust in the repairs that had been made.

One gray morning we were greeted by a column of Praetorian armor which shadowed us across the river for several hours. At noon, we reached a bridge suitable enough to cross. August, myself, and a few of the other officers met them in the middle of the bridge. A heavily armored command car drove to the middle of the bridge and stopped right in front of us. We stood there for several minutes until the top hatch opened, then the commander climbed out and jumped down.

He was probably the tallest man I have ever seen; at least a full foot taller than August or myself. He cut quite a figure in his clean black uniform and tall boots. He took off his helmet and put it under his arm. It had been a long time since I saw a Praetorian.

He was clean cut with neat teeth and cold, deep eyes. Under his helmet, he had maintained his hair slicked back. He greeted us with an expressionless face. An aura of heartlessness surrounded him. He wore an antique revolver slung low on his hip with the handle sticking out. He walked back and forth in front of us as other Praetorian guards gathered behind him.

"Who is this *August*?" he asked. "No, let me guess."

He walked close to each of us with his hands clasped in front of him. He looked down at us as he stared each man in the eyes. I was standing directly to August's left, and he came to me first. His gaze locked my eyes to his, and I could not look away. I could feel him reading my reaction like a book.

He moved to August. He must have stared at August for a full minute.

"You are August," he said in a low growl.

August said nothing.

The commander stood back and said aloud for everyone to hear. "I am General Condon of the Thirteenth Praetorian Armor Corps. I have been sent by The Architect himself to take command of this army and lead it to the Holy City for the salvation of The Temple. Rejoice, as you are now under the command of the Praetorian."

August stood calmly where he was and said quietly, but loud enough that the general could hear, "No. These are my men, and will not submit to your command. If you wish to join us for the journey, you may. We are a free company of loyalists. Our purpose is the same as yours, so let that suffice."

The Praetorian general was clearly taken aback. He stepped back up to August and looked down on him and spoke. "Who are you to command such a force for this mission? A provincial. Tell me, were you a farmer or a looter before you put together this rabble?"

August jabbed his hand into his shirt, which startled the Praetorian, who reached for his pistol and dropped his helmet. Before Condon could draw, August pressed a packet of documents to his chest. In the commotion, the guards behind General Condon shuffled up and took aim at myself and the rest of the officers. August and the Praetorian stood perfectly still, eyes locked in a silent battle of their own. Finally, Condon took his hand off his pistol and grabbed the packet of papers. He quickly read over the papers within.

"You attended the Praetorian school in Breslau," he observed.

"Yes. Before it was attacked by the rebels," said August. "I was one of the few survivors."

The general drew his pistol and aimed it at August. "Then you are a deserter, and are subject to immediate execution."

At this, all August's men on the bridge started forward with their guns ready. August and Condon stood completely still as we surged around them. More Praetorian popped out of their tanks and rushed forward. We stopped as they formed up behind their general.

Nothing happened for a few tense seconds. Finally, August spoke, "We are on the same side, General Condon. I am well aware that you know I hold a commission from Central Command. I'm sure you remember your training. It is bad policy to make a commander look foolish in front of his men." He leaned in closer to the General so that only I and a few others closer to him could hear. "Which is why I will not tell your men that your orders state you are only here to speed our journey and provide transportation for my infantry. I can read the coded transmissions from the Prophet as well, you know. I learned from the same book as you."

"How is it that you would even receive *my* orders to read?" Condon growled.

"You would be surprised what information I can acquire," August said plainly.

General Condon stood back and signaled for his men to stand down. "The road on your side of the river is washed out about ten miles down. You will need to cross your men over to our side. My personnel carriers are being cleared out and retrofitted with additional seating. Hurry up. The Architect is waiting." More loudly than was necessary, he called out, "I am glad we could reach this mutual accord, for the glory The Architect."

"For the glory of The Architect," August mimicked.

Simon looked at me with a smirk as Condon walked away. "When the Praetorian first started operating, we called them The Spicy Sausages."

I looked at him, puzzled.

"When they attack, they burn everything going in and burn everything going out." Then he made a flatulence noise.

Simon's juvenile joke cut the tension for those close enough to hear, and we returned to our forces. It took a few hours to get our men loaded onto the tanks and transports. It was a nice day without rain since the clouds had broken, so I sat on top of a tank next to August, with about twenty other men.

"You know who that General is don't you?" one of the men asked.

"Yeah, it's General Condon," another replied.

"Well, yes. But you know *who* that is, don't you?"

"No."

"He's the general who commanded the Sector Seven Massacre. Over seven thousand rebels tortured and executed," another soldier chimed in. "They raped the men and the women, then butchered them all like cows."

I looked at August. He looked troubled by what they were talking about.

Simon was sitting on the other side of August. He popped his head up and looked at the two men who were talking. "You know what I heard?" Simon called out. "I heard when they were done, they raped each other just to be thorough."

The men stared at Simon for a moment before shuffling to the other side of the tank. Simon shot me a satisfied smirk then laid back and tried to rest.

But I had heard of General Condon too. What happened in Sector Seven was only one of several barbaric events to his name. His presence brought feared to friends and enemies alike as he was known for grotesque spectacles beyond imagination.

We started moving a few hours before sunset and traveled on through the night. It was a welcome break for our men, some of which had nearly worn the soles of their boots as thin as paper. Our motorcade was rather a sad sight. Each tank and transport was piled with the tattered and tired soldiers of August's force. But with reliable transportation, we would finally make progress towards the Holy City. We traveled quickly and within another day we reached the ruins of old Zürich.

CHAPTER 10

MOUNTAIN OF SURPRISES

We stopped for half a day while the Praetorians performed checkups and maintenance on all their engines. The climb up the mountains would be hard on them, and the Praetorians wanted to replace some key components. While they worked, our men foraged for hay, dry grass, paper, or anything else they could stuff into their summer uniforms to keep them from freezing to death in the mountain passes. As the men prepped for the ascent, Condon briefed us on his plan for our trip.

"Every air transport on three continents is being sent to the east to pick up the entire Eastern Army; over sixty million troops. They are retrofitting old commercial air transports and cargo planes. Basically, anything that can fly is being commandeered. They have sent every fighter squadron and gunship available to protect the transports. Therefore, we have no choice but to travel by land and sea. My mission is to transport your army to the port of Taranto. We will travel over the mountains through a route which my officers have determined from the available satellite data, then down to the southern coast of Italy. There, we will utilize the old Ghost

Fleet. It has not been touched in years, but there should be enough serviceable vessels for all our troops.

"Are you certain there be enough ships for all my men? Have you scouted the fleet or are you just making assumptions?" asked August.

"As I just said," Condon growled, "There will be enough ships for all our troops. I have estimated that you will need only ten percent of the available vessels. They should be in good enough condition to use. No one has touched them since the plague, but The Architect's engines are very simple. As long as they float and the engines work, you will be able to get to the Holy City."

At noon we loaded up again and started into the mountains. We started having trouble keeping a handle on the prisoners the moment we got into the passes. They kept helping each other untie their bonds. If they were on top of a tank or the back of truck, they would jump off and make a run for it. If they were in a personnel carrier, they would wait until they were all untied and as a group throw open the hatch and flee.

The Praetorians were already unhappy that we even had prisoners. Most rebel armies would yield the ground without a fight if they knew they were encountering these merciless executioners. Consequently, the Praetorians became very proficient at setting traps and ambushes, which gave them an even more mystical and ruthless image. The troopers we were traveling with grand time gunning down our escaped prisoners before they disappeared into the trees. Some rebels made the poor choice of making their break in the more barren passes. None of them got away. The Praetorians were all trained marksmen. It was rather impressive to watch them take the long shots with their advanced rifles. August tasked Simon with tracking down the few that did escape the Praetorians aim, but he never did return with any prisoners. I assumed that he had taken care of the fugitives himself.

At dark, we stopped when we came to a wide valley. August had the men set up camp and make fires while he met with his officers. Since the prisoners were being so bold, we tied each one separately to a stake like dogs—far enough apart that they could not help each other—and then placed guards among them. I talked with August as he walked around gathering his officers.

"Do you know where we are?" I asked.

August nodded. "I had to beg, but General Condon's navigators gave me a map console and GPS. If you take into account weather, rock slides, blown bridges, and whatever else can't be seen on the satellites, I think we are about six days from the other side."

"The transports were a lucky break then, I guess?" I asked.

"Not necessarily. We were two days' travel from Munich. If I was hell bent on getting to the Holy City sooner, I could have marched to Marseilles. From there, we would have been able to catch a Central Command fleet and would be in the Holy City five or six days from now. We could have skipped the mountains altogether."

"There is no guarantee there would have been a fleet available. That's probably why they are taking us this way."

"The Central Command knew where to find us. They could have had a fleet ready. Which makes me wonder; why we are being taken through the mountains?"

"Do you think there is another reason?" I asked.

"The empire might be losing control of the Mediterranean. I think they are trying to shorten our time at sea which is why I am uneasy about Condon's plan."

"You don't seem to trust Condon that much. He has orders to get you there safely."

"Condon makes me uneasy," August said. "He's arrogant and I think he feels intimidated by me. No doubt he's a little salty about playing chauffeur for this army. At any rate, it's a bad combination."

"He can't kill you," I jested. "This army will evaporate."

"I have a feeling it will not." He was clearly uncomfortable at the thought. "But all of these volunteers will become conscripts quite quickly."

"Where did he come from, anyways? One day there was no reported Praetorian activity in our sector, and then they showed up across the river."

"I'm not sure why Central Command has stopped providing me intelligence directly. I'm still getting reports from my own scouts, but that is only a narrow view of the theater. I talked to one of the Praetorian troopers in my tank today," August said. "He wouldn't give me much information, but he did tell me they came from up north where they were raiding rebel production facilities and hunting for someone."

"Production facilities for what?"

"I don't know, but it has to be something important for The Architect to task the Praetorians with basic raiding. I was already in the area. It would have been easy for Central Command to request that we do it."

"Whatever it is, I'll bet it is probably in those four heavy troop carriers that Condon never takes his eyes off of."

"I've noticed that also."

"Who were they hunting for?" I asked.

"I have a pretty good idea, but I'm not sure."

"They must be pretty important to send a whole Corp."

"They're extremely important, if I'm right about who," August said.

After we collected all the officers, we gathered around a large fire near the camp.

By our latest count, we had nearly three-hundred thousand men and women in our army alone, not counting the two hundred thousand or so Praetorian tankers trucking us south. The large number of men concentrated in our army posed several problems. We presented a great target for rebel bombers and jets. Rebels typically reserved their air power for ammo drops and reconnaissance since Central Command and Praetorian anti-aircraft technology was very advanced. However, a few well-placed bombs could wipe out thousands of our men and that might be enough to tempt some rebel squadrons. Especially if they had more nuclear ordinance like the one that decimated the Baltic army.

The Architect had worked diligently to dismantle and consolidate to his control the world's nuclear stockpiles. However, since the last attack, it was clear not all warheads had been accounted for—and this had everyone on edge. The Central Command stopped using nuclear weapons long ago because of the logistical problems associated with them. They were too dangerous to deliver, and more often than not the ill-effects of radiation visited itself on the regulars and loyalists as much as on the rebels.

However dangerous the threat of attack, the more eminent problem was how to feed this gigantic army in these barren mountains. Food was probably the biggest logistical problem that both armies faced. Large scale farming existed only in the areas within the protection of The Architect's forces, and in some of the more peaceful lands overseas. The Central Command was very exacting with its appropriation of rations. But our army—being self-mustered rangers and militia, and not directly under the command of the Central Command nor the Praetorian Guards—was left with no certainty of rations being delivered. With all air transports being sent to the east, the outlook was even more bleak.

Our meeting lasted several hours, until the mountain winds became too much for us to bear. For the food problem, no solution could be found. However, one officer suggested that to combat the nuclear threat, we should divide the army into twelve marching columns spaced out twenty or thirty miles apart. This would help to minimize damage and preserve at least a portion of the army in the event we were attacked. August disliked the idea of our force being divided, but the officers were in agreement that it was the safest option.

In the morning, when the Praetorians ordered us to load our army, August was forced to defend his officer's decision to travel divided to General Condon, even though in reality they agreed.

"My orders are to transport your army in tact, not to suckle you and lay your fears to rest. We travel as I see fit," Condon yelled.

August looked rather downtrodden. I'm sure he expected some resistance from Condon. He responded slowly and calmly. "I understand you have your orders, and I don't doubt your ability to transport us, but my officers—"

Condon cut him off. "Your officers are vagabonds and deserters and worthless provincials. Who are they to decide protocol for the Praetorian Guard? You are asking me to string this convoy out over hundreds of miles of mountain roads."

"Can we reach some kind of compromise?"

Condon seemed to calm. "I will compromise you this. I will take a detachment of tanks forward. I will set your men on top of them to add a layer of protection. You will take the bulk of your army to be the center, and then my rear guard can bury you all when you are destroyed." They stared at each other for a moment. "Mount up," Condon bellowed, and then stormed off for his command car.

We let the forward guard with a tenth of our men and the Praetorians get about fifteen miles ahead of us. Then August and half of our main body departed, followed fifteen miles behind by the second half of our main body. The remainder of the army followed closer behind them. Despite Condon's desire to stay close together the shear number of men and vehicles already had us spread out over a hundred miles.

We continued our climb up into the mountains. It took endless work by the engineers to keep us moving along the road. Between rockslides, road washouts, and snow, there was enough to keep three shifts of engineers working day and night. August was confused about why Condon had chosen such an ill maintained road to travel. We didn't officially stop and set up camp at night any longer. Condon and his officers were good at estimating the time it would take for various repairs. For those repairs that were going to take more time, we stopped and let the men get some rest.

The cold and shortage of rations was beginning to take its toll. We would lose a few of the less loyal and determined every night, not to mention those who succumbed to the cold and were left along the road. On our third day in, by the grace of The Architect, unmanned supply drones delivered thousands of pallets of foot. It was enough for another three days, and some of the men's first meal in five days. The Praetorians seriously injured several of August's starving men as they rushed in to secure the landing zone from being overrun. It seemed hardly worth it for the cold, dusty cans of vitamin fiber paste. After dropping off their cargo, the last of the drones were preparing to leave just as August and the second column arrived. I glanced ahead and saw Condon standing by the last drones still on the ground. He was supervising the loading of the four troop carriers he had been guarding closely since we joined with him.

"I really wish I knew what was in those," August said with a shrug.

"Why don't they unload them and transfer whatever is in there to the drone instead of taking the whole thing?" I asked.

"They're definitely hiding something."

As the Praetorian supervised the food distribution Condon walked up to where August and I were standing. Two troopers followed him, carrying a box.

"I have a special delivery for you," Condon said.

The troopers laid the box in front of Condon and opened it. He bent down and took out a helmet and body armor and handed it to August.

"It is the armor of the Praetorian," Condon said, "A personal gift from The Architect himself. He has deemed your life too important to go so under-protected." He picked up a can of food from the box as well. It was officer's rations. Canned probably only days before. August took it and surveyed his spoils. Then he placed the armor back in the box and reached out his hand to give the can of food back to Condon.

"I will eat what my men eat," August said, "and I will not wear this armor until my men are supplied armor."

Condon stared at him, red faced. He bent over and gathered up the six or so cans of food in the box. He walked over to the mass of soldiers waiting for food and started to chuck the cans as far into them as he could. He returned to August with the last can in his hand.

"Will you eat it now, you ungrateful piece of shit?"

August calmly handed the can to me. In solidarity I passed it to the officer behind me, and he passed it behind him. This continued until it disappeared into the crowd.

"You're short a few cans," August said calmly as he stared at Condon. Condon walked up close to August and hissed, "I don't know who you think you are, just because a few peasants believe in you and call you their general."

August spoke back in a low voice "I have their faith because I can give them victory. That's worth more than some badge or medal." He pointed at Condon's uniform with stripes and bars all over it.

"You have their faith?" Condon asked. "Is that why they leave you in scores every night? Who needs faith when there is obedience? All it would take is one word from me, and my men would butcher your army in minutes."

"Well, it's a good thing you are charged with transporting us 'in tact' as you said before. Your obedience to The Architect serves me well, General," August said.

"Sometimes accidents cannot be avoided in war. Enjoy your cans of gruel," Condon said as he walked away.

I could see the hairs standing up on August's neck. "That man may be the end of me," he said.

It took almost eight hours to get the food distributed and get everyone loaded back up again. Condon's column left as soon as they could and gained a head start on August's column which was much larger. That night, a storm rolled in and dropped two feet of snow on us, so we had to stop and wait for morning. It took so long to dig everyone out, we weren't ready to move again until the afternoon. August was not getting any communication from Condon's column. He and I gathered a few scouts and we piled into a light tracked vehicle which could travel through the heavy snow to try and make contact. We found him only an hour or so ahead of us. He was snowed in as we had been. As we approached to within a few hundred yards from the rear of Condon's column a rocket propelled grenade flew in from the mountaintop above. It impacted the rear most armored personnel carrier piercing the top and exploding inside. The top and turret were blown into the sky and the men around it were thrown to the ground bloody and pierced with shrapnel.

Suddenly, from every rocky crag and bolder rockets and rifle fire tore into the Condon's stalled column. The Praetorian gunners began to return fire as the turrets of every vehicle traversed back and forth firing expertly into at the hidden assailants. August's men fared much worse. While most of the Praetorian vehicles were protected with reactive armor, August's dismounted troops were soft targets trying desperately to survive the heavy barrage. The mountain road provided little cover and even the armored vehicles could not be used as cover as the rebel fire came in from both sides of the pass. The sparse pines broke and fell as the rockets hit them and huge splinters scythed through the ranks. Suddenly from the forward part of the line we could hear distinctly, even over the continuous rifle fire, the methodical deployment of the smoke canisters as the Praetorian armor unleased a thick smokescreen.

"What are they doing?" I asked. "Our men won't be able to see anything.

"They don't care," August said. "Condon's tankers can see."

Through the thick smoke the Praetorian's thermal sighting systems turned the tables on the attacking rebels now blinded by the shroud. High up above the smoke we could see the rebel grenadiers as they ran towards the ridges above the tree line. High explosive rounds from the Praetorian gauss cannons slammed into the scree of the mountain side creating fountains of rock that shredded the retreating enemy.

As the smoke thinned and wafted through the pass our second column was approaching our position. We stopped them and told them to be alert. They dismounted and took up defensive positions along the road. August, myself, and a small party of others snuck up the pass through the smoke hung destruction, of wounded men, burning tanks, and shattered pine trees. We encountered no resistance or signs of any more enemy. It took half a day to reach the front of the column. Dozens of our tanks and troop carriers lay smoking and smashed on or beside the road. The bodies of our men lay strewn around.

"Any sign of Condon?" I asked.

"No," said August. "Condon must have pushed through."

We found him a few miles up the road. He was directing his engineers in reconstructing a blown-out stone bridge. His busted command car sat piled with rocks and had slid off the road.

"What just happened?" August asked Condon.

"We were ambushed back there, and they fled this way. As soon as they were across the bridge, they blew it up. My driver nearly drove me off the edge before he dumped it in the ditch. We should have this bridge rebuilt in a few hours." Condon yelled.

"There was a fork in the road a few miles back. Why don't we evaluate where that will take us?" August suggested.

"I came through that way when I came north a few weeks ago. It will take us north again and way to the east which will add two days to the trip, and this road will get us to the lowlands in two more days. Regardless, I want to get one more look at those bastards. No one ambushes me." Condon walked away, then turned around. "From now on, we travel together."

Condon was in a fit while the bridge was being rebuilt. In between yelling at his engineers, he insisted his radio operator try to call up any kind of air support even though he knew there was nothing in the vicinity. He poured over maps and relayed satellite images. Hours before the bridge was finished, he ordered the men loaded and ready to roll at a moment's notice. The engineers worked through the night to get the bridge back up. The temperature had warmed significantly over night, and in the morning a fog had formed as the engineers inspected the finished bridge. I stood with August and Condon as they watched.

"Are you really going to take us into this fog?" August asked.

"My tanks are fully thermal and night vision equipped. We fight in any condition," Condon said.

"That's well and good, but half of my men have little more than hunting rifles. Are they just supposed to sit on your tanks and hope you kill the enemy before my men are shot to pieces again?" August asked.

"We will have the clear advantage. With our electric drives on low, if your men can keep quiet, we may be able to get within several hundred yards of them in this fog before they know we are there."

"That's ridiculous. They know we are here. What about IEDs, landmines, and rockslides?" August asked before he was cut off.

"I am tired of your questioning. I am a highly trained and experienced commander. Your decision to divide our force has already cost several hundred men. If we had been together, they would not have been so bold."

"I am just trying to protect my men," August said.

"I am just trying to get to the Holy City before it falls to the rebels. This road is the fastest way, and somewhere along it are enemies of The Architect."

Condon's chief engineer came up to where we were standing and saluted. "The bridge is ready, sir. We have inspectors stationed on it as well to watch for failures."

"Good, Lieutenant. Get back to your command," Condon said, then yelled out, "Mount up." The tanks nearest us sounded the ready signal and everyone not in or on a tank scrambled for the nearest vehicle. We rolled over the bridge and into the mist. The fog closed in around us and blocked out everything except the man sitting on either side of us. The moisture stuck to my face and made me shiver.

We traveled through the fog without incident for many miles. The road sloped continually downward, and every brake of the vehicle felt like it was going to throw us off. We rode for two hours at an excruciatingly slow pace until the column stopped suddenly. There were about a hundred tanks on the road ahead of my position. As the fog began to clear, I could see more and more of them until the front of the column became clear, sitting in front of yet another bridge. As the fog dissipated, houses and buildings appeared across the gully. Like a ghost rising from the grave, slowly and surely a town was revealed. Those of us who were used to seeing burned-out shells of houses or piles of rubble marveled at a fully intact mountain village. Although the roofs and spaces between were covered with netting and other disguises, this place seemed completely untouched by the war.

CHAPTER 11

OLD FRIENDS

The commander of our tank stuck his head out of the hatch to listen in while August and I spoke on the radio to Condon; who was yelling at his navigator all the while.

"We have a situation here," Condon said to August. "Dammit! I said find out what the hell this place is." He said to his navigator. All I could hear of his navigator was mumbling in the background.

"It looks abandoned," August said.

"Negative, the thermal shows bodies all over," Condon said. "They're not moving aggressively though. They're just sitting around."

"Maybe they just want us to pass through and not cause any trouble," August said. "There's no way to tell until we make contact. Have the engineers check the bridge for explosives while the fog clears."

"Don't even try to give me orders," Condon spat into the radio. "We have the advantage in the fog. If we attack now, we can wipe them out before they get a shot at us."

"We don't know they are hostile. We can't go around torching innocent villages."

"This village is not on the Central Command's nor the Praetorian's charts. It wasn't on the satellite images either. It has to be an enemy village. I am pulling back my tanks and bringing up the howitzers."

"Condon!" August yelled into the radio. "General Condon!"

"Sorry, General," said the tank commander as he ducked down into the vehicle. The tanks and troop carriers jockeyed around on the road and moved aside while the howitzers advanced.

"This is insanity," August said as he jumped off the tank and ran into the mist.

I yelled after him as I jumped down to follow, along with half of the men from our tank. I ran around for about twenty minutes trying to find him. I assumed that he ran off to find Condon, so I went to the front of the column, dodging tanks all along the way. The wind picked up and the fog had nearly dissipated. The roar of tank treads grinding on the pavement was beginning to die as they got into firing position. Yelling echoed off the mountains close to the bridge. As I got closer, I found August standing in front of Condon's command car with his hand on the hood. Condon was shouting furiously at him.

Condon's face was bright red as spit spewed from his mouth. "This is my convoy. I decide how we proceed!" Condon yelled.

"You cannot destroy this town. They are offering no resistance," August yelled back.

"I am not going to drive this army right into another ambush."

I stood there for several minutes while they bantered back and forth. The town was now almost completely visible. Condon stopped yelling and looked at the far end of the bridge, just staring. I looked up and standing at the end of the bridge were three armed men. The foremost had a heavy PKM machine gun slung casually over his shoulder. The other two held scoped rifles at the ready. August stopped yelling at Condon and stared silently at the men as they walked across the bridge.

Condon's gunner popped his head out of the hatch, just barely. "Sir, the thermal shows snipers all over the far side now."

Neither Condon nor August moved. The figures were halfway across the bridge by now.

"Now you've gotten us both killed," Condon said.

"Can't you see they want to talk?" August whispered.

"Those are likely the rebels that shot up our men in the pass," Condon said as he pulled the radio to his mouth. "I'm giving the order to fire on the snipers. We can take out the first couple of blocks in minutes." Condon said.

"Damnit. Can you just wait to see what they have to say?" August said.

The figures were fifty or so yards away now. August laid his gun on the hood of Condon's car and started to walk towards them. I stood by the command car. Condon stared intently at the figures on the bridge, then put down the radio and chuckled as he jumped down to follow August.

"You should travel in better company, General August," said the foremost figure. He was an old man with a wrinkled face. A giant scar reached from the top of his shaven head down around his chin, and another from the corner of his right eye to his ear. The hand holding the gun was missing two fingers at the second knuckle. His other hand hung by his side in a black glove. He wore parts and pieces of armor from every era of the war.

"So, you know who I am," August said. "Who might you be?"

Condon stepped in front of August and walked up to the scarred man. "I see you survived my punishment at Smolensk, Colonel Raptor. Seems like a lifetime ago now."

"Sorry I didn't want to be party to your sick savageries, General," the colonel replied.

Condon turned to August with a smug look on his face. "This is Colonel Raptor, formerly of the 8th Praetorian Rifle Regiment. He's probably the last of his kind—one of the original guardians of The Architect. A primitive, weaker breed of Praetorian."

"You should watch your mouth, Condon." Colonel Raptor waved his hand at the town behind him. "One word from me, and my men will turn you into a bad memory." Colonel Raptor retorted.

"You'll lose this pissing contest, old timer," Condon replied smugly. "One word from me, and I'll turn your men and that town into a hole in the mountain."

The Colonel seemed unaffected by Condon. "I am sorry for the loss of your men, General August. There's a rebel base somewhere around here, and they obviously don't like you being here. I'm afraid I can't let you pass. The rebels have left us in peace, and I don't want to invite any trouble."

"We only need to pass through," August said. "We are on our way to relive the Holy City."

"I know exactly where you are going, General," Raptor said. "Do you think that you can travel around with hundreds of thousands of men and have people not know you are coming? I knew you were coming as soon as you reached the mountains."

"We're coming through this village whether you like it or not," Condon snapped.

"It might be the last thing you do," Raptor said.

"Don't play games with us, old man," Condon said. "I'm surprised you haven't taken a potshot at me already."

"A potshot won't do for you, Condon," Colonel Raptor replied through his teeth. "I want to carve you up like your lackeys carved me up."

"Do it now," Condon said calmly. He pulled off his glove and stretched his hand out towards Raptor. They stared at each other for only a second before Raptor suddenly brandished a long knife from inside his coat sleeve, and in one swing cut Condon between the thumb and finger. Condon reached for his gun, but Raptor was already on top of him. Condon tried to grab the knife instead, before Raptor could stick it in his stomach.

As they grappled with and kicked at each other, Condon's radio operator popped his head out of the turret and yelled, "Fire! Open Fire!" into the microphone.

August turned to me, eyes wide in panic, and yelled, "Stop him!"

I was standing closest to the command car, so I jumped up and grabbed at the radio. The operator drew it back, but I punched him square in the bridge of his nose, knocking his head back against the turret hatch.

I caught the radio as he dropped it and yelled into the mic, "Ceasefire! Hold your fire!" As I turned around to check on Condon and Raptor, the microphone cable slithered out of the turret. In his excitement, the radio operator yanked it out of the radio when he stood up out of the turret.

By then, Condon had gotten Raptor to drop the knife, but they were still punching each other. Condon tried to use some grappling techniques on the colonel, but his blows seemed to barely daze the old man as he furiously swung and kicked at Condon, occasionally landing a devastating hit that sent the general reeling.

August stood near them, trying to break up the fight and avoid a bone crushing hit at the same time. Just as August reached to grab Condon's shoulder, the colonel swung his foot around and caught August square in the back, knocking him to the ground.

The fighting stopped immediately, and both the colonel and Condon stepped back. Condon suddenly doubled over and started laughing. August rolled over, groaning. The radio operator was coming to, and I handed him back the mic before jumping down off the car to help August. He was already standing up before I got to him, and Condon was still laughing hysterically. Colonel Raptor was gathering up his weapons.

"Lieutenant," Condon bellowed to his radio operator, "order the APCs and light tanks across the bridge. Howitzers and heavy tanks to hold positions and cover them."

"Nothing goes across that bridge unless I say it does," bellowed Raptor.

"Go ahead and blow the bridge," Condon shot back. "I'll flatten your town and build a new bridge from the rubble."

August stood rubbing his back between the two of them as the tanks began to cross the bridge. "We only need to cross through, Colonel. No harm will come to your town from us."

Raptor shot Condon a furious glare. "I will tell my men to be ready for the slightest provocation."

Condon smirked, but said nothing as he walked back to his car and climbed in to wait.

We crossed the bridge slowly at first, but after half of us were through we crossed swiftly to avoid being cut off—since less of the howitzers and heavy tanks were able to cover us. As we crossed through the town, the residents lined the street to get a look. August had decided to ride on top of Condon's command car to prevent any foul play by Colonel Raptor. As if to invite trouble, or perhaps as a show of defiance, Condon rode with his head and torso out. The townspeople lowered their heads in fear as we passed. The front of the column was out of the town and halfway down the next mountain in less than an hour.

***

I saw the jets long before I could hear them over the tank treads. Little dots on the horizon, maybe twenty or thirty of them, in two lines. Condon saw them even before I did and ducked into his hatch to warn the anti-aircraft units. They swung into action only minutes before the jets screamed over our positions. They came in so low that our surface-to-air missiles seemed to pass right over our heads. Five jets were taken out in the first salvo and spiraled off into the mountainside. The rest seemed to ignore the column and continued over the mountain to the town. Moments later, explosions echoed down from the mountains. The jets peeled off, and I could hear them coming around to our right, higher up in the clouds. The anti-aircraft units sent a second salvo of SAMs after the planes, and that was the last we saw of them. One round with Praetorian air defense was enough. Condon's hatch was still open, and I heard him yelling into the radio for a damage report.

It was an hour or so before a regimental commander could give a report. The aircraft destroyed the bridge, and ten howitzers were destroyed along with it. Another fourteen howitzers were stranded on the far side. The remainder of the column was untouched except for some minor shrapnel damage to a few tanks. August assumed the rebel aircraft had meant to divide our forces by striking the bridge, but they were too late and merely inconvenienced a few units.

The town fared far worse. The bombs sparked an inferno among the old, wood buildings that was working its way through the settlement. As the news came, I could see the far away fires light up the darkening sky. Condon ordered the column to continue to withdraw away from the town, and since it was nightfall, to make camp the best they could. One more cold, hungry night in the mountains.

In the morning when I woke up, August was already up. I tracked him down and found him up in the town with Colonel Raptor. "The fire storm destroyed all of our food and supplies. These people have no way to survive now," the Colonel said as I approached. "And now, we have nothing to stay here for."

"There is little room on the tanks," August said, "but we will transport you as best we can. Anything you can get running to drive yourselves would help."

"Where will we go, August?" Colonel Raptor asked. "Most of these people are not able-bodied men to add to your army. Aside from my marksmen, you'll be lucky to find an old pistol or shotgun among them. These are old men, women, and children."

"They won't have to fight," August assured him. "The least we can do is take them out of the mountains. Perhaps they can all start again in the Holy City. I hear The Architect is very sympathetic to his refugees."

"There will be no Holy City in a few days," Raptor said. "I don't know if you are aware, but the rebels under Lord DeVonay are considering crossing the Atlantic to join the assault on the city. Once they get there, the rebel force will be tens of millions strong. Unless The Architect's Eastern Army is delivered on time, The Architect's forces will not be able to match the rebel's numbers."

"How do you know all this?" August asked.

Raptor signaled to one of his men sitting by a radio, who picked up a small box and walked over to us.

"We took this from the wreckage of one of the jets that was shot down yesterday," Raptor explained. "It's a decoder, and the self-destruct mechanism failed to fire. It's a free ear inside the rebel intelligence network. I've had someone monitoring the chatter since we found it. If the Central Command had had this weeks ago, they might have known not to send their regulars to the ends of the Earth chasing bands of raiders while the main rebel bodies closed in on the city."

"Don't you think the Central Command can decode rebel messages?" August asked. "I find it hard to believe they haven't cracked the codes by now."

"If they do, they're making poor use of it. They wouldn't lose as many battles as they have these past few months if the

Praetorian or the Central Command could intercept rebel messages."

"This could be the difference between victory and defeat," August said. "The empire could gain the upper hand and put an end to all of this."

"What is victory worth after this?" Raptor asked. "All this death, all this destruction. There is nothing left."

"With victory, we can rebuild. We can have a future again," August said.

"If you want a future, then you should pray you lose; and The Architect and that temple all burn to the ground. If you think you are fighting for a future, you are a fool. The real reason for all of this is one man's infatuation with his own vision of the world. He is a rock, and his enemies are the waves. And the waves will break against the rock until the rock is gone."

"You should have been a poet, Colonel," I said.

"Perhaps," he replied. "And we both should have been peaceful old men with lives and jobs; not standing on the side of a mountain with a gun in our hand."

"And what should I have been?" Condon chimed in as he walked towards us. "What would I have been in this perfect world that never was?"

Raptor pulled a jacket over the decoder to hide it from Condon. He was in a kind of trance of sadness as he gave

Condon a far-off glance. "You? Well, you might have been a man and not a monster."

Condon smiled smugly. "That's the difference between you and me, Raptor. I've embraced the way of the world, while you pine after a world that is long gone."

"You're a sick fuck, aren't you?" Raptor asked. "I'll bet you're one of those creeps that hangs yourself while you beat off."

Condon burst out in laughter that rang off the mountains. Once he calmed himself and recovered his smug smirk, he said, "No. I hang other people when I beat off."

Sick as he was, I found myself smiling at his crass joke. Had I never been witness to his hair trigger and violent temper, I might have thought him almost charming. The well-dressed and polished Condon certainly was a stark contrast standing next to August in his tattered ranger uniform, and Colonel Raptor in his dirty winter camouflage. Condon's jet-black uniform, perfect smile, and quaffed hair made him look like something out of another time and place set down gently on this smoking mountainside. He was a perfect representation of The Architect's will for beauty and order among chaos.

Condon gestured to an officer standing behind him. "This is Brekke," he said to Raptor. "He will help you arrange your people for transport. We move in four hours."

113

"Colonel Brekke actually," Colonel Brekke corrected.

"Not for long if you take that tone again," Condon snapped.

Colonel Brekke stomped off followed by his staff.

August and I looked at each other, he seeming as confused as I was. "How did you know they were going with us?" August asked. "I didn't tell you."

"You might think me a thug or a monster, as the colonel here calls me, but I am also a student of human nature. I knew you would not leave these people here to starve and die. I also know that you feel guilty, because you think you brought this on these people by traveling through here, when in reality the rebels could have attacked us anywhere on this mountain road." Condon paused and looked at August as if waiting for a response.

August was red in the face, but I supposed not from rage; rather embarrassment.

"You will find, General August, that I will soon be able to tell what you are going to do before you think to do it," Condon said.

"That must be a handy talent for you, General Condon," August said.

"My success on the battlefield is not only due to my knowledge of military tactics, but also my understanding of human nature," Condon said. As he turned to walk away, two

114

of his troopers dragged up a man in a flight suit. His eyes light up with glee.

"Sir, we captured one of the pilots that was shot down," the ranking trooper said.

"Very good," Condon said as he grabbed the pilot's chin and looked him over. "Very pretty." He stood back and pointed to a table nearby. The troopers jerked the pilot over and shoved him down on his knees, with his chest to the table. His head bobbed listlessly as he slipped in and out of consciousness.

Condon righted a chair and sat down across from the prisoner. He looked at the pilot in silence for a moment, then reached across the table. He gently grasped the pilot's hand and pulled it slowly towards himself. The pilot seemed rightfully surprised by this, and pulled himself together, although he looked confused. Condon laid the pilot's hands out flat on the table. He took his gun out of its holster and unloaded it, putting each round in his breast pocket one at a time. Then, Condon put the weapon on the table with the barrel facing himself. He put his hands on top of the pilot's and looked him straight in the eye. As calmly as if he was talking to a small child, he said, "You're going to tell me exactly what I want to know, or I am going to hurt you."

If the pilot was scared before, then he was surely terrified now, and he showed it. His eyes welled up and he was trembling. He said nothing. In an action so fast I could barely comprehend what was happening, Condon stood up, grabbed the pilot by the wrist with one hand, and his pistol barrel with the other. As he pinned the poor man's hand to the table, he smashed the prisoner's first pinky bone into the table with pinpoint accuracy. Condon's troopers held the man down as he screamed in pain. Condon still had his hand pinned to the table.

"That is to show you that I am sincere," Condon said. "This life is too short for me to allow you to waste my time. Where is your base? I want coordinates, defenses, and the number of personnel."

"I will never tell you," the pilot gasped.

"If I had a coin for every time I heard that, I might retire," Condon quipped.

"You'd never retire, sir," said the ranking trooper.

"That's right," Condon said with a smile. "I love my job too much." He quickly smashed another bone into the table with a series of powerful chops from this pistol.

A crowd had gathered to watch. August appeared surprisingly emotionless besides me.

"Same question as before," Condon continued. "I will find them whether you tell me or not, but I am not worried. Everyone tells me what I want to know."

"Why should I tell you? You will kill me anyways," the pilot asked.

"You will tell me because I am willing to carve the flesh from your bones while you watch. The human body can endure so much trauma, and I intend to put you through the very fires of hell if you don't tell me what I want to know." A little pile of smashed finger and blood was building up on the table. Condon scraped up a bit and looked at it. Then, he stuck it in his mouth. "Mmm, pâté de pilot." He said.

The crowd was a riot now, crying and vomiting. The pilot turned green at the sight of his own body being consumed.

"You have a lot of bones in your hand, pilot. And I have not yet had my breakfast. But if you don't tell me what I want to know very soon, *you* will be the one eating your hand." Condon growled.

Another trooper ran through the crowd to Condon. "Sir, the satellite has located an air base. One of the returning jets crashed before it could be hidden."

"Well, pilot, it seems your services are no longer needed." He looked at the beleaguered man for a few seconds with his head to the side. "You really are very pretty. It's too bad." He paused, then barked, "Dispose of him."

The ranking trooper holding the pilot down drew a long knife and shoved it through the prisoner's shoulder and into his rib cage. The man was left to collapse bleeding in the dirt as Condon and his men marched off to their tanks with Raptor and August following them.

"What luck," Condon said as he looked at the GPS his navigator handed him. "It's on our way."

"You don't need this delay just to satisfy your vindictiveness," Raptor said.

"I find it odd that you take such an interest in saving these rebels. They killed your people too."

"These people lived in peace with that base there for five years," Raptor said. "The only reason they were attacked was for letting you through."

"Condon is right, Colonel," August interjected. "If they can hit us here, they can hit us someplace more suited to themselves later. We need to ensure they will trouble us no more." August's response sent a chill down my spine. His expression was placid, and his tone cold.

Condon was obviously taken aback by August's compliance.

"We will help you plan," August said.

"Finally, some fucking cooperation," Condon gasped.

Condon, seeming satisfied, walked to his command car. Raptor and I stood there in the snow. After August and Condon had walked about twenty yards August turned around and came back to where Raptor and I were standing.

"Hide the decoder," August whispered to Raptor. "We may need it later. I'd like to talk to you about your loyalty to the Architect."

"I'll ride in one of your trucks and listen in to see what I can find out," Raptor said.

CHAPTER 12

EMPTY SHELL

Our raiding party left the rest of the column an hour before they were scheduled to depart. Condon took three hundred Praetorian tankers with backpacks loaded with all the grenades they could find. August picked five hundred or so loyalist rangers—mostly good marksmen which came from his oldest units. We traveled the main road for three or four hours. Then our transports stopped to wait for the rest of the column. We dismounted and climbed up an impossible mountain that took us nearly until sunrise to reach the summit. We were now free and clear in mountains which the rebels would not expect us to be. The rising sun lit the sky above the still-dark mountain valley.

We sat silently as the scouts probed for enemy sentries. They returned as the sun was sweeping over the mountaintop. Condon and August sat side by side as the scouts approached them. I knelt behind August, watching over his shoulder.

The first scout back reported, "We have found no guards or defenses around the runway. There are two guards in front of the hangar doors."

Condon shook his head and said nothing. I could see the wheels turning in his head. It was an hour before the next scout came back. By this time the sun was fully up, but clouds rolled in and grayed the valley.

The second scout panted as he knelt before Condon. "There is a shaft and emergency exit on the north side of the mountain. If we attack the front, they will surely use it to come out and flank us."

"Thank you, Private," Condon said.

The other two scouts returned shortly, but had little to report. Condon and August discussed strategy for a short time. Ten men and a load of explosives were to work their way around the mountain to the emergency shaft while the rest of us descended the mountain. August's riflemen would remain on this side of the valley and cover Condon's Praetorian as they snuck across the runway to the other side of the valley, creating a killing field for any rebel that might make a run for it from the hangar doors.

We moved out as soon as the explosive detail was out of sight, down into the dense forest. I stayed close to August as he worked his way down the hill. We stopped about a hundred yards from the runway while Condon's tankers continued down to the tarmac. In an effort to conceal the runways from satellite and aerial surveillance, the rebels had strewn them with fake rocks and bushes and bits of gravel and brush. The wrecked aircraft which had given the base away was covered with tarps and snow. The Praetorians darted between the obstacles to avoid detection by the hanger door guards. In minutes, they were across and hidden in the trees on the other side. August relaxed and sat down on the ground.

In little less than an hour, we heard a massive explosion on the other side of the mountain. Smoke rose over the facility. I looked through my scope down to the guards at the door. One was scanning the valley excitedly and the other was talking into the com box on the side of the door. He yelled to the other, then they both disappeared into a manhole. We waited for an hour. I worried that we only created a siege, but that faded as smoke began to waft from beneath the hangar door.

"Now we have them," August mumbled. The doors began to open, and rebels poured from the gap as well as manholes nearby.

The base was more complex than we had thought. From the hanger door and from ports and manholes all along the runway hundreds of rebels charged out to escape the smoke filled bunker. I carefully selected targets through my scope and although they were mostly less than a hundred yards away I lead them slightly as I squeezed off round after round felling the running soldiers. Between reloads I glanced at August who was crouched down behind a rock watching intently with his rifle slung behind him.

"You're not shooting?" I asked.

"That's what the soldiers are for," he said. "I'll shoot something if the need arises."

Not long after we began shooting at the men running around the airstrip, there was a mechanical noise behind where August and I were sitting. We looked back to see a pillbox rising out of the earth as bits of twigs and chunks of matted pine needles fell off the domed top. August grabbed me and pulled me up right next to it just before the gun port opened and a machine gun unleashed a tide of bullets into the men all around us. August and I watched in horror as our men were shredded by the gunfire.

I grabbed a grenade from my pouch to throw into the pillbox, but August grabbed my arm to stop me. We were crouched in front of the gun port. August stood up, and with gloved hands, grabbed the barrel of the machine gun pulling it out of the hands of the gunner. He then plunged it back into the port, flawlessly smacking the gunner squarely in the face. We climbed up on top of the pillbox and opened the hatch to find the squirming gunner holding his face. I raised my rifle to shoot him, but August stopped me again. He jumped down into the pillbox with his captured machine gun and tied up the rebel.

Then he reemerged and signaled to two of our men still alive nearby. "We're going down in the base," August said.

They looked at each other without a word and August started off down the ladder with the machine gun slung on his arm. The two soldiers and I followed him down. We got to the bottom of the ladder and entered a dimly lit, concrete tunnel.

August examined a power box beside the ladder. "Retract/Extend," he read aloud, then hit the switch. The pill box above us retracted back into the earth, and soon the light at the end of the ladder was gone. "Ok, let shut them down," August said.

Our pillbox was the last one in a long line of defenses which flanked the runway. August took off running down the tunnel, flipping all the switches along the way; smashing them with his gun to keep them from being used again. The retracting pill boxes cut off the gunners who had our men pinned down outside. Finally, we came to the exit of the tunnel. The rebel gunners—seemingly confused about the sudden retraction of their pillboxes—filed into the tunnel. August closed the door to the corridor and one of his men tied it securely with a roll of aircraft cable laying nearby.

We found ourselves in a junction area between the pillbox tunnel and an elevator. Guessing from the direction and distance we had traveled I assumed we were below the forward staging area close to the hanger doors. The four of us

124

entered the elevator and rode it up two stories along with all the munitions which the rebels had left piled in the back. When the elevator door opened, we walked out onto a platform next to the hanger door which overlooked a bustling scene of panicked rebels. A thin film of smoke hung in the air as the life support systems attempted to fight the damage from our explosives. The onslaught from our riflemen outside had compelled the rebels to close the hangar doors again.

Rebels were running around, trying to ready the aircraft for a desperate escape. We crouched behind August as he surveyed the area. He stood up and walked back into the munitions elevator, where he examined a bomb that was waiting to be moved to the hanger floor. He grabbed the handle of the cart which held the bomb and struggled to roll it out of the elevator onto the platform. He knocked the nose cone off with the butt of the machine gun, which made me flinch.

Then, August fired a burst of rounds into the air as he put his finger on the crudely made pressure switch in the nose of the bomb. "Lay down your arms and open that hanger door, or I will blow us all to hell." He yelled. The other two soldiers with us rushed out and stood beside August, training their guns on the stunned rebels in the staging area. Most of the rebels just stood there, staring at each other. One rebel soldier off to the side began to raise his gun towards August. Before he could take aim, I jerked my weapon to my shoulder, found him in my scope, and shot him in the chest. He fell with an echoing thud.

The rest of the rebels laid down whatever they were holding. We directed them out of the hanger door with their hands up as it was being opened again. The Praetorians had shot down most of the men on the runway and were closing in on the door as the rebels emerged. They were clearly surprised to see the defeated rebels walking out as they closed in. From the platform August surveyed the rebel surrender as his men from the outside took prisoners before the Praetorians could massacre them.

"That's an eight hundred pound bomb," I said, "That would have brought down this whole mountain."

"Not this bomb," August said. We walked around behind it. The back was missing, and I could see clear into the front of the bomb. It was completely empty of explosives.

CHAPTER 13

BELLY OF THE BEAST

"Very impressive, General August," Condon said as he strolled through the hangar doors. I walked with August, Condon, and Simon as we inspected the rest of the facility. As soon as we walked into the auxiliary hangar, Condon threw up his hands and started cursing. He stomped off towards the corner of the room. There, partially covered with tarps, were pieces of one of the drones into which Condon had loaded his secret cargo. Lined up next to the wall were covered bodies. Condon walked down the row of bodies, pulling off tarps, to reveal several deceased yet still handcuffed rebels.

"Do you know who these men are?" August asked.

"They were suspects for an individual we are looking for," Condon said. "An enemy of great interest to The Architect himself, whom he has described as 'The Arcani'."

"Ah," August said. "Rebel leaders."

"Exactly," Condon said. "But not just any rebel leaders. The principal leader of the rebellion. My unit was charged with routing out and detaining suspects. There has been heavy

Arcani communications coming from the Germanic, Baltic, and northern France area. Your area of operation no less.

"Congratulations. Looks like you might have killed him?" August asked.

"Apparently not. Communications continue to be transmitted," Condon said.

"Well, there could be more than one. Don't you think? I thought 'Arcani' was a generic name for their leaders?" August asked.

"There's more to it than that. We've identified up to twenty-four distinct leaders split among seven identifiable groups, some of which are on other continents. But there's one central figure, who seems to have loose control over the groups, if not direct control." Condon said.

"Have you captured the Lion or the Eagle?"

Condon shot a glance at August. "How do you know about the spymasters?"

"I have my own intelligence officers. I may know more than you about the rebel organization."

"I highly doubt that. Your little group of provincials could hardly match the long arm of The Prophet," Condon said as he walked away.

August walked over to one of the bodies. "This man, his name is Klaus Meyer. His codename is 'Kalb'. He's the spymaster for the Baltic rebel forces. He probably knew more about the rebel operations than you'll know in a lifetime. But he's not who you are looking for."

Condon stopped cold in his tracks, turned around, and walked back to where August was standing. "I don't know how you know that but let me assure you we do not need your help to find anyone. It is only a matter of time before they are all revealed."

"I was under the impression the Praetorian could find anybody easily," August jabbed. "It sounds like you are at a loss to track down this shadowy figure you are hunting."

"The Arcani has some way of scrambling his signal or some manner of relaying messages which we've not yet discovered. We're monitoring every channel for his communications. It's been extremely challenging to triangulate any of them," Condon said. "Once we pick up his code name the message origins are hundreds even thousands of miles apart. But we will find him eventually. There are bigger things at stake right now."

"Let me know if you want my help," August said. "I'm sure I have information which could be enlightening."

One of Condon's lieutenants walked up, leading a bound, bearded old man wearing the tattered rags of a uniform. "Look, General!" the lieutenant exclaimed. "We've recaptured Old Johnny."

The old man fell to his knees as he approached the dead bodies of the Arcani suspects lying on the floor and recited, "In the center and around the throne, there were four living creatures covered with eyes in front and in back."

Condon kicked the old man in the ribs, sending him toppling to the floor. "More Bible jabber, Johnny? Can we get some Nostradamus for once?"

"Who is this man?" August asked.

"This is Old Johnny, my oracle," Condon said.

"I had no idea you believed in occult."

"Well, ever since I found Old Johnny, he has opened my eyes," Condon said as he motioned for the lieutenant to take the old man away. "In his own way, he's warned me of several ambushes, which I was then able to turn around. I was sending him as a gift to The Architect."

Although the old man seemed blind, he turned to face August and said, "Then I saw the heavens opened, and there was a white horse; its rider was called 'Faithful and True'. He judges and wages war in righteousness."

"Oh, look," Condon said smugly. "He likes you."

I could tell August was curious. He stared at Johnny as the old man was led away.

***

On our last night in the mountains, I couldn't sleep. August was asleep for what seemed like the first time since we joined Condon. Where he got the strength to carry on as he did, I will never know. Even the best soldiers had to abandon their vigilance and surrender themselves to sleep to survive.

But August spent his days entertaining the questions and fears of his men and officers, and his nights pouring over intelligence reports from his scouts and from Raptor's captured decoder. He also confided in me that he suffered terrible nightmares which—brave as he was—shook him to the extent he could not sleep afterwards. That night, however, he slept peacefully.

As the sun rose the next morning, I walked out of the tent to find the cloud cover fighting against the dawn. I walked up through the snow to reach a peak just east of our camp. About halfway up, I came across another set of tracks through the snow. I did not know whether to expect friend or foe, so I held my rifle at the ready as I climbed. To my surprise, I saw Condon sitting cross-legged and completely naked on a rock he had cleared of snow, his uniform folded neatly beside him. His hands were on his knees and his face was raised to the rising sun.

"What are you doing?" I asked. "You will catch your death up here."

He did not turn to answer, and kept his face to the sky. "Have you ever watched the sunrise?"

"Of course," I said. "But never naked in the snow."

"Then you have not known what it is to be alive. Here it is just you, the Earth, the sky, and the elements."

"That's not exactly my idea of feeling alive. I would prefer a table of food surrounded by good friends. Those were the days when I felt alive. Even if it was an army mess tent."

"But you see now how superficial that all was. All gone now. Gone to the devil. But you are still alive, are you not?" Condon asked.

"I suppose I am," I said.

"You see, I am a misanthropist. Because I have come to see the utter worthlessness of most human interaction; and ultimately human life."

"I can see how someone growing up in this world might feel that way. You don't remember the days before."

He laughed. "Do not patronize me, old man. I grew up in the Holy City. I have seen the ideal world and the pinnacle of man's accomplishment. My hatred for people is simple. No matter how good a person's life is, they will always want it to be better. When in truth, all they need do is appreciate the simple things. The ingratitude of most people is disgusting to me."

He paused for a moment as the clouds parted and a stream of light shot through them, bathing us both in light.

"Do you know when a person is most beautiful?" Condon asked. "They are most beautiful when they are dying. Because, without question, they will never be more beautiful than when they truly appreciate being alive. In the moments before that last carnal spark fades, all that matters is being alive."

"I never thought about it that way," I said.

"Of course you didn't. You come from a time when material possessions were paramount and the fabric of life seemed less fragile.

I said nothing. The clouds closed again, and it was dark once more.

"I assume you have killed men before," Condon said.

"I have. I don't even know how many."

"Have you ever watched them die? I mean, *truly* watched?" he asked.

"I have been a marksman for most of the war. Most of the men I killed, I saw only through my scope."

"Do yourself a favor. Next time you must kill a man, take a minute to appreciate them as they die. You will love your own life a little more."

"I think it's the fear that you like more than beauty."

"I know that you and August both think I am sick and demented. The truth is; I am a chameleon. I change to be whatever is necessary to survive. For all his ignorance, Colonel Raptor is correct. Were he and I to meet in another place or another time, we might have even been friends."

"What about you and August?"

"I doubt August and I could ever have been friends. He strikes me as quite judgmental. The holier-than-thou kind of person. He would have been out trying to be a do-gooder and save the world while people like you, Colonel Raptor, and I were out carousing."

"He was raised by a very devout woman," I said.

"Then he was sheltered as a child, and that's what makes his heart weak and ignorant now."

"You forget he has the same training as you, and I think you will find that he is much wiser than you give him credit for. I assume that you think his compassion is his weakness."

Condon broke his gaze from the sky and fixed it on me. "His men may love him, but the enemy does not fear him. While it is not a problem as we travel, when we engage the enemy we will need them to lose heart. It's extremely likely we will be outnumbered."

"Well, I'm sure you can create enough fear for the both of you."

"Oh, you can be sure of that. I've already prepared a few demonstrations for our rebel foes to consider," he said with a smirk, then turned his face back to the sky and said no more.

I left him on the mountaintop and walked down to the camp. Just as I reached my tent, August was coming out.

"Where have you been?" he asked.

"I have been in the mind of a madman," I said.

"You found Condon on the mountain, then?"

I looked at him quizzically.

"He does that every night," August continued. "It's how he sleeps. While you and I struggle to fight off the cold, he sits out there and embraces it."

"How does he not die?"

"The mind is a powerful thing," August said.

We both stood silently watching the mountains until we saw Condon descend and return to his camp. I do not know to this day whether to think of Condon as brilliant or think him mad. I had to admire him for finding his own peace in turbulent times. It is no wonder he was so at ease with all his duties; heinous and mundane. He took everything wrong with the world and embraced it. While the rest of us wrestled with our guilt and bad fortune, and lamented the state of affairs in which we had come to find ourselves, he accepted his lot in life. He was a perfect chameleon.

CHAPTER 14

INTERCEPTION

The next night, I sat with August in his tent as he reviewed dispatches. Messengers came and went as he issued orders to his men, attempting to better organize his forces for the coming battle. Simon came in about midnight and called for August to join him outside. August looked concerned and followed Simon immediately. I rose to follow after them, but August motioned for me to stay.

"Remain here and let anyone that comes know I'll be back soon. I have a few matters to discuss alone with Simon," he said. As August left the tent, the wind whipped through the flap and scattered some of the papers laying on his field desk. There was no one else there, so I picked up his papers to get them off the damp ground. A stack of seven papers clipped together had fallen near his desk. As I picked them up, I noticed the top paper was signed 'Ovis'.

These dispatches were devoid of the usual classified markings which were plastered all over Central Command and Praetorian papers, so I was intrigued to see if I could determine who Ovis was. It was probably improper to read a general's correspondence without him, but years of war and my age had dulled my sense of propriety, and curiosity got the better of me. The first letter read:

Delivery Instructions: Relay to Coalition Operations Group EP

GS,

I would like to congratulate you and your officers on the recent discovery of Imperial spies within your ranks. You have suffered much by their betrayal, and I am glad that those you did not capture have been expelled from your camp. However, I have discovered troubling news that some of your soldiers have been involved in sex trafficking; which as you know is a serious distraction from the task at hand, and hurtful to our cause. Our cause is supposed to be the more righteous and allowing these disgusting practices to continue will only tarnish our image among the populous and play to the hands of our enemies. I request that you stamp out this trade within your camp and request that the perpetrators show the proper remorse for what

they've done. Please continue our good work
both martial and humane.

     Peace to you,

     Ovis

It dawned upon me that this letter was not Imperial or loyalist. It was meant for a rebel commander. Why else would they be worried about Imperial spies among them? The Prophet often dispatched liaisons to the various loyalist bands that patrolled the Empire, so it would be of no concern for a loyalist commander to have Imperial intelligence agents around. I decided to see what else the stack of letters contained. The second letter read:

     Delivery Instructions: Relay to Coalition
Operations Group SM

     GH,

     Allow me to start by saying I am also
saddened by your recent loss of men and
equipment at the Battle of Izmir. The traitors
within your organization who claimed to be
among the faithful have done you a great
injury, and though many of your soldiers have
become prisoners because of this, I will free
them once we take the Holy City. Please

continue our good work both martial and
humane.

Peace to you,

Ovis

I continued through the stack of papers.

Delivery Instructions: Relay to Coalition
Operations Group PE

Lion,

Your bravery in maintaining the
resistance within the Holy City itself—right
under the nose of our enemy—is continually
inspiring. Despite the heavy losses you have
suffered, you continue to keep the faith. But I
am afraid I must issue a warning to you. Some
of your operatives have come under the
influence of one who is not a true believer. He
slanders our religion, and while he fights The
Architect as we do, I have received
intelligence that he has sabotaged some of
your efforts. His aim seems to be to further
the cause of the Nationalists over those of us
who serve gods rather than nations.
Furthermore, there are some among your

organization who continue to participate in sex trafficking. Our cause must be that of the righteous, and tolerating these actions undermines our position. Please resolve this issue before I arrive in the Holy City, or all involved will suffer the consequences. Please continue our good work both martial and humane.

Peace to you,

Ovis

The fourth letter:

Delivery Instructions: Relay to Coalition Operations Group TH

GC,

The situation within your command is very dire. I have received word that there is one among you who is advocating compliance with The Architect; who has recently reached out to you offering amnesty. I have heard that she is trying to convince others that she can see the future, and that in her vision The Architect is victorious. I do not know the future myself, but I can tell you this: I have issued orders for the traitor and her followers to be delt with. Do not concern yourself with saving them should they become ill. I understand that at face value this may weaken your forces, but in the end it will make you stronger. Do not give up your position until I arrive. Please continue our good work both martial and humane.

Peace to you,

Ovis

The fifth letter:

Delivery Instructions: Relay to Coalition Operations Group SA

GV,

The atrocities your troops have committed are an outrage. You have lowered yourself to the level of our despicable enemy, and for that I am considering removing you from command. When I make my final determination, you will not know the outcome until it is too late for you. With that in mind, be extremely careful of how you conduct yourself and the actions of your troops until my arrival. There are those among you who were not party to your crimes, and I will see to it that those without sin are separated. I will not tolerate cruelty when the world is already cruel enough. Please continue our good work both martial and especially humane.

Peace to you,

Ovis

The sixth letter.

Delivery Instructions: Relay to Coalition Operations Group PH

LD,

The Architect has called all his forces to relieve the Holy City, and thus a door has been opened for you that must be taken advantage of. Although you have been weakened by the prolonged campaigns in the Americas, you are still a sizable force. Without your presence in the Holy City, victory will not be assured. Please make haste to mobilize your forces for transport. I have issued a request for all ships of the coalition to come to your aid, and you may yet procure

some which have been hidden from
destruction in the Americas. Together, you
and I will bring our enemy to their knees.
Please continue our good work both martial
and humane.

Peace to you,
Ovis

The seventh and final letter:

Delivery Instructions: Relay to Coalition
Operations Group LA

GP,

When reports of your engagements reach
me, I am continually disappointed. You
attack, but then retreat. You are attacked, and
although you are victorious, you do not press
the advantage. You are the one of most well
equipped and numerous armies we have ever
fielded, and yet your accomplishments are
less than those of weaker more poorly
equipped units. I can only assume that you are
poor in leadership, and that your officers are
blind to opportunities for greater victories.
Should we be victorious in the end, there will

be no place for cowards. Please continue our
good work both martial and humane.

Peace to you,

Ovis

I was so engrossed in reading that I did not noticed
August and Simon as they entered the tent. As I looked up
from the last letter, I turned around to find them standing
behind me. Both had their arms crossed.

"I'm so sorry," I said. "The wind blew your papers, and
curiosity got the better of me. Who is Ovis?"

"You've never heard of Ovis?" Simon asked.

"No," I said. "I assume he's a rebel, but from his tone in
these letters it sounds like he's *the* leader."

"His name keeps showing up on rebel dispatches that we
capture," August said. "Simon has been trying to track him,
but he's very elusive."

"I just know he's right under our nose," Simon said as he
pounded his fist in his hand.

"Have you turned these over to Central Command or the
Praetorian?" I asked. "This could be the key to catching the
Arcani!"

"Condon is not interested in anything I give him," August
said. "I gave a stack of letters to him a few days ago, and he

burnt them right in front of me without looking at a single one. Such an arrogant bastard I've never met."

"How are the messages delivered?" I asked.

"From what we can tell," Simon explained, "Ovis writes his orders down and one messenger takes them to another. This individual makes several copies of each dispatch and sends them separately with a different courier to ensure duplicitous delivery in case one of them should be captured. If the distance is too long for messengers, then they relay the orders with an analog radio. The technology is so archaic that none of The Architect's forces are monitoring for analog signals anymore."

"That's pretty smart," I said.

"I couldn't have thought of better myself," Simon said.

I handed the letters over to August, who shuffled them a little then handed them to Simon.

"I think I'll call it quits for tonight," August said.

I retired to my tent wondering if they would ever catch Ovis.

CHAPTER 15

THE BUTCHER OF BELLINZONA

The climb down the mountain was a welcome change from winding through the cold passes. Travelling downhill was much easier on us, and it was slowly getting warmer. Mountains passes soon gave way to green valleys, and although the air was still cold, it was nothing compared to the frozen terrain behind us. As we approached the ruins of old Bellinzona, carrion birds circled in large numbers. This was typical in the aftermath of a battle, but August was unaware of any that had recently taken place.

August, Simon, and I were riding near the front of the column, a few tanks behind Condon's command car. We wound through the valley as we approached the city. The birds above us circled in increasing numbers. As our transport rounded the bend in the valley floor, the putrid smell of rotting flesh wafted over us on the breeze. The valley beyond came into sight and row upon row of rebel soldiers were revealed, impaled through the rectum on wooden spikes. The impaled were so numerous, and so evenly staked out, they looked like an expansive field of corn or wheat.

"What happened here?" August murmured.

The commander of our transport had been riding with his head out of the cupola. He glanced over and said, "We received intelligence that a rebel army was making its way through the valley. General Codon intercepted them."

"This seems like a colossal waste of time and energy to spend on dead bodies," August said.

"Dead bodies?" The commander asked. "These are the survivors."

As we approached the end of the impaling fields, an enormous mound of dead rebel soldiers had been piled two stories high with earth moving equipment. Pools of blood soaked the tread tracks where they had churned up the ground. Birds hopped up and down the pile of bodies, stopping now and then to peck away and pull at the decaying flesh. A gap had been left for the road to pass through. Beside the road was a sign. "See you in Jerusalem," it said. It was a warning to any rebels who might pass through this way. As we passed through the mound of decaying bodies the smell overwhelmed many of the men sitting atop our transport and they wretched and heaved as they vomited over the side. Upon closer inspection, I noticed the bodies of the rebel soldiers had not only been piled together, but many had been completely dismembered. Limbs and head were chopped from the torso and many more had their stomachs sliced open, with their entrails hanging out. On the other side of the mound, a little way down the road, were twenty neatly-dug graves; each one with a Praetorians helmet resting at the head.

"You only lost twenty men?" August asked the commander.

"We only lost twelve men in the battle," The commander said. "General Condon had the other eight executed as malingers."

"How many rebels were killed?" August asked.

"What a stupid question," the commander said. "All of them, of course. We didn't really keep track."

He recounted the battle to us in great detail, and with great relish. Condon had traveled north from Balkans several weeks ago to begin his missions in the north. As he traveled his scouts had reported the same seventy thousand strong rebel force which General Nast had asked August to engage. They had made their way unmolested through the mountains and were making their way to the Holy City to reinforce their rebel brethren there. A detachment of Condon's force, which had damaged vehicles, presented itself in a compromised position—knowing full well the rebels were approaching. The rebel scouts had presumably reported back to their command that there were Praetorians for the easy taking. Knowing that even damaged Praetorian tanks would be a threat, the rebels ordered a full-scale attack with all forces. The overzealous rebels advanced rapidly, and as they did the rest of Condon's force emerged from hiding and closed in around them trapping the rebels in the narrow valley.

Between their advanced weapons and extensive training, the Praetorians inflicted a great number of casualties. The tanks, which generally fired a single solid projectile or a high explosive round, had brought with them special rounds which contained a canister full of steel balls. This ordinance scythed down great swaths of the rebel lines in the narrow valley. Mobile howitzers and mortar carriers rained down shells and phosphorus, burning and smothering the trapped and panicking rebel troops. As the onslaught continued, the rebels broke ranks and scattered. The Praetorian's mechanized infantry dismounted, and with their long gauss rifles, expertly picked off the terrified and fleeing enemy.

Against better judgement, the rebel commanders asked for quarter. To their surprise and relief, Condon accepted their surrender. As soon as they were disarmed, the hellish reality of what they had surrendered to began to unfold. Condon ordered them to cut apart the bodies of their own dead. Having no means to resist and still holding on to hope that they would be interred rather than slaughtered, they complied. Once that work was done, in lots of ten, they were forced to select one among them to be impaled by the others. After several rounds of this grotesque game, Condon became bored and ordered his own men to complete the gory task.

Eight Praetorians were caught refusing to defile the bodies. Angry that these soldiers were not occupied executing his orders Condon had them stripped of their armor and personally executed them in full view of his other soldiers. It was his right to do so as their commander, and afterwards the remainder of the rebel prisoners were impaled at an astonishing speed.

Although we were aware of Condon's reputation, seeing his handiwork firsthand was still unsettling for us all. August was silent as we steadily motored on through the carnage.

"What have I done?" he asked Simon.

"This isn't your fault sir," Simon said.

"I should have saved those men."

"It's not your place right now."

August shook his head. "I should have engaged them when Nast told me about them. I could have driven them off and saved them from this fate."

"Judging by their insignia," Simon said, "I think these were mostly nationalists. We may have just had to fight them again when we got to the Holy City."

"No man deserves this fate," August said. "No man should wish it upon another."

"General Condon won't last forever," I chimed in. "You can only kill so many of your own men before there's an accident in store."

"Judgment day can't come soon enough for that creature," August said.

As we passed by the graves of the executed Praetorians, I recognized Colonel Brekke and several other Praetorians kneeling in mourning to honor their fallen comrades.

CHAPTER 16

THE OLD GUARD

We reached the outskirts of Milan by nightfall. This territory was notoriously uncontrolled and contested, so rather than pushing through, Condon called for camp to be established and for pickets and a defensive perimeter to be set up. Condon met with August as the troops set about making camp.

"Even if the city is unoccupied, it could be filled with traps," Condon said. "Tomorrow, in the daylight, we'll begin to probe it out before moving the main body through. There haven't been any reports from this sector lately."

"Why don't we just go around?" August asked.

"If there are any enemies in the city and we bypass them, they will be at our back," Condon said. "I can see you've never moved a truly large army before."

"It's a good thing you're here to guide us, then," August said facetiously.

"I've sent in scouts to see if there's any activity above ground, but the enemy could be subterranean as well," Condon said. He did not seem to acknowledge August's haughty comment.

August left Condon's headquarters and returned to his tent. I tried to catch a few hours of sleep, but just before sunrise August woke me and his other bodyguards to meet him at Condon's tent. We arrived just as Condon's scouts were debriefing on their findings.

"There's plenty of activity in the city," a scout said. "Looks like several regiments of mechanized infantry, but they are all packed up and ready to leave. They've been packing all morning."

"Are there any unit markings or insignia?" Condon asked. "You've had all night to look at them. Who are they?"

"Sorry, sir, but it was very dark. There's no moon and there's cloud cover, and we were unable to get too close," the scout said, wavering.

"This is a useless report," Condon said.

"Very sorry, sir," the scout said.

"Get out of my sight," Condon barked.

The scout scampered out of the tent along with the rest of his squad.

Someone's in there but sounds like they are prepared to leave," August said.

"I want to know who we're facing," Condon growled. "If they're rebels, they're not going anywhere."

"Do you really want to fight a major battle today?" August asked. "We've still got a long way to go."

153

"Once we're across the Po, we will be in extremely dangerous territory. I cannot afford to have several regiments of mechanized enemy infantry harassing me as we try to cross," Condon said.

One of the scouts returned to the tent. "Sir! The enemy is approaching. They've mounted up and the whole unit is coming this way."

At the scout's urging, we all ran outside for a better look. We had camped to the west of Milan with our back to the Ticino river, and fallow fields lay between us and Milan. Dust from the approaching enemy billowed into the air as their vehicles tore over the dry ground. I looked through my binoculars and saw every manner of technical, motor bike, heavy truck, and all-terrain vehicle bouncing over the ditches and hedges. Condon climbed on top of his command car, looking through his binoculars, as our troops were scrambling to array themselves to repel the oncoming forces.

"Tell our men to hold their fire," Condon yelled at his radio operator.

"But they're in range, sir," the operator said.

"I said fucking hold fire," Condon yelled again.

"What's going on?" August asked.

Condon groaned, "They're Praetorian Dragoons, not rebels."

"Dragoons?" August asked.

154

"Yes, they just ride around looking for a fight," Condon said. "They're amalgamated units from all the old-fashioned, leftover Praetorians and other miscreants."

"You didn't know they would be here?" August asked.

"Obviously I didn't know they would be here. No one ever knows where they will be. It's fucking insufferable," Condon barked. "They won't communicate, they won't follow orders; they're basically a bunch of old psychos waiting to die."

"Do you think they're waiting to go with us?" August asked.

"I hope not," Condon said. "I'll strangle every last one." Condon turned around and kicked the cupula of his radio operator's seat, and the operator poked his head out.

"Give me the flare gun," Condon said.

The operator handed him a single shot grenade launcher which had already been loaded with a flare, and Condon raised it up and fired one shot skyward intending to signal the Dragoon commander his location. The oncoming waves of Praetorian Dragoons responded by firing hundreds of their own flares. As they came to within a few hundred yards of our position, they began whooping and hollering like banshees.

"Idiots," Condon said as he reached down into his command car and pulled out a gauss rifle. "Lieutenant! Hand me the banners." The Lieutenant pushed a box up through the

155

hatch and Condon rummaged through it until he found his Imperial flag. He tied it to the rifle and raised it high over his head.

By this time, the Dragoons were right in front of our lines, spinning out and running their vehicles in circles, stirring up choking clouds of dust. Some were walking towards our lines loaded with bags and boxes of things to trade. Condon was growing impatient when a four-seater all-terrain vehicle pulled up in front of his command car.

A man stepped out and walked towards Condon. These Praetorian Dragoons were nothing like the polished soldiers we'd been traveling with. They were covered in mud and blood smears. They wore long slickers over their clothes and had a wide variety of weapons and head gear. The man lowered his bandana as he approached, and to my surprise I recognized Captain Ajax.

He noticed me just as he was walking by, then stopped in his tracks and clapped a hand on my shoulder. "Daniel! You're alive. I thought for sure you would have kicked the bucket by now, you old softie."

"Sometimes it pays to be a softie," I said, then turned around and pointed to August. "Remember that baby I picked up? This is him. General August."

"Well, I'll be damned," Ajax laughed. "All grown up and commanding armies."

"If you've had quite enough of this little reunion," Condon interrupted, "let us get down to army business."

"Ah, always was like you to get straight to business, little Condon," Ajax said.

"General Condon, if you please, General Ajax," Condon reminded him.

"General?" I asked.

"Yeah, it pays not to be a softie sometimes," Ajax said with a wink.

"What are you doing here?" Condon asked, his tone growing ever more impatient. "We are on our way to the Holy City. I assume you are doing the same."

"Oh, no. No," Ajax said. "We're just passing through. We were doing a little raiding in Spain, but now we're on our way to Romania. I figure we might find a little trouble there trying to catch some of the rebels moving south."

"The Architect has recalled all units to his aid. Will you not answer the call?" Condon asked.

"Oh, we'll get there eventually, but no reason we can't fight our way there," Ajax laughed. "What's the hurry?"

If Condon's glare could be weaponized, Ajax would have died on the spot. "The city is under siege and the defenders are soon to be extremely outnumbered," Condon said seriously.

"Well, you hurry along and save a few rebels for me. I'll be there when I get there," Ajax said. "It was good to see you, Daniel."

"What's the status of this sector?" Condon asked as Ajax walked away.

"Not much to report. Since you stomped out that bunch at Bellinzona, most of the rabble around here is pretty scarce. Word on the street is General August is a cold-hearted butcher," Ajax said.

"You cannot be serious?" Condon asked.

"What are you talking about?" August asked Ajax.

"Well, you see, when you don't leave enough survivors to tell the story, people just make up their own. Word on the rebel side is that General August is commanding a joint force of loyalists and Praetorians, and that it was you who set the ambush at Bellinzona. You're well known in the north for these tactics." Ajax's broad grin showed he was aware of the pain it caused Condon to have his victory attributed to August.

General Condon was red in the face and his grip on the rail of his command car was turning his knuckles white. "August wasn't even with us then!" he yelled. He sank into his vehicle and cursed incoherently.

Ajax walked up to August and put his arm around the younger commander. "Let me give you a little advice. The next step of your journey is extremely treacherous. To get to the Ghost Fleet, you will have to cross through the lands of the Severots; listless, faithless, mercenaries. They control everything from the river Po to Naples. You won't be able to cross through their land without their notice."

"I'm somewhat familiar," August said. "But I assumed Condon had a plan for that. A tribute, perhaps?"

"Don't make that mistake," Ajax whispered. "Condon's plan is likely to push through and dare them to attack him. He's so arrogant, he thinks he's invincible. If you follow his lead, he's going to get everyone killed. You'll need to find a way to control this situation."

"I appreciate the advice, but I'm learning to deal with Condon. When he's already mad, I like to push him just a little bit further. I like to think it will make him feel that much better once he calms down."

"I like your style," Ajax said. "Normally, I wouldn't bother giving advice to anyone. But now that I know you're with Daniel, you're like family. Good luck to you."

By this time, Condon had cursed out everyone in his tank and signaled to his troops to mount up. Ajax returned to his ATV, and with a wave he signaled for the Dragoons to move out. They disappeared in a cloud of dust as they sped across the empty fields.

Once the troops were loaded, we proceeded through Milan to the Autostrada del Sole. From there, it was fast traveling until we reached the river Po. August and Condon argued furiously about whether to cross or to camp on the north side of the river, but the day was still young and Condon insisted that the crossing take place at once. Only one bridge was still in place, so the operation was time-consuming. By three in the afternoon, half our troops had made it across.

A scout from Ajax's Dragoons made contact and informed us that a rebel body was located in the vicinity of Venice. Condon wanted to send a detachment to engage them, but August had already contacted Ajax, who had agreed to stand by and protect our rear until we were further down the peninsula. Needless to say, being cut out of the loop on serious tactical decisions made General Condon furious, and he refused to talk to August for several hours.

Our army made it safely across the river before nightfall. Scouts were deployed to look for the Severots, if any were about. We also set out pickets and several redoubts were hastily constructed by Condon's engineers. It was a restless night as we waited for the sun to rise.

CHAPTER 17

THE SEVEROTS

The next morning, as we were all sitting around the campfire, Captain Raptor was talking to August. The night was uneventful but the scouts reported that Severot patrols had been seen galloping around the location of our camp so it would only be a matter of time before we encountered them.

"Who are the Severots loyal to?" August asked.

"That depends on who is paying them, and how much they are paid," Raptor said. "If they are not on our side, we will know by tomorrow."

"With your men, Condon's, and mine, should be able to make a run of it and get to the port," August said.

Raptor shook his head. "We will never make it. When they are paid, they are well paid. Besides the Praetorians, these are some of the best equipped soldiers in the world. And they're horse mounted. They will ride circles around us."

"I've never fought against mounted troops before. How could they be any match for tanks and machine guns?" August said.

"I commanded mounted troops when I fought for the Central Command. You'd never think horses would be as handy as they are in modern warfare. They can go where a tank can't, hide in plain sight, and don't break down."

We didn't make it very far down the peninsula before we encountered the Severots. We heard them long before we saw them. Our column was entering a long valley with a stream that ran back and forth under the road with hills rolling up a hundred feet or so on either side. I felt the air around us vibrating from the thundering hooves. We couldn't see them, but could tell they were on the other side of the hills on both sides of us.

Condon stopped the entire column. If they wanted a fight, they already had the upper hand. Our men dismounted and sat nervously with their backs against the tanks. Suddenly, the Severots galloped up to the top of the hill on either side and stopped. Luckily, they didn't fire on us. They just stood there on their horses, looking at us. August stood up and looked through his binoculars to find Condon at the front of the column.

"He's talking to one of the horsemen," August said.

"Is it getting hostile?" I asked.

"I can't tell. Looks cordial so far. I feel like I should go up there. Condon may pick a fight."

"I would just stay put. He knows we are trespassing. If there is a fight to be picked, we already picked it by being here."

About twenty minutes later, the commander of our tank opened his hatch and held out the radio. "It's for you, sir," he said to August. August took the radio. I could hear Condon's raised voice from where I sat.

"We have been informed that we are trespassing," Condon said, "and they want us to turn around or march straight to the coast. I asked to see their commander, and they offered to take our command group and a small bodyguard to see Kratian Kray and discuss letting us pass."

"How long will it delay us to go to the coast?" August asked.

"Indefinitely," Condon said. "There is no guarantee we can transport the army without using the Ghost Fleet."

"Then we have no choice," August said. "Tell them I am coming up."

"Hold your position for now. They want us to move out of this ditch so we can set up camp. They seem like a rather considerate bunch of heathens."

We moved the army down into a wider part of the valley. The men kept tight to each other and close to their guns as they set up camp. August picked a hundred men, among them myself, and went to meet up with Condon. We loaded up in heavy armored transports and followed slowly behind our horsemen guides. They led us through rolling hills of grapes and barley along well-maintained roads. Every now and then, we came across burned-out vehicles, skeletons, and other evidence of the Severots' campaign to preserve their autonomy. But for the most part, the land was a beautiful oasis compared to the northern theatre.

We arrived at Kratian Kray's headquarters a few hours before dark. It was the most beautiful building I had ever seen up to that point in my life. The giant, fortified villa sat prominently on a hill. Olive groves surrounded the property. As we passed through the outer defenses and into the villa compound the stout fortifications gave way to marble colonnades, gardens, and terraces We were asked to dismount the vehicles when we reached the gate of the central palace, but they let us keep our weapons as we entered. We were led through a maze of terraces and alleyways until we entered a large courtyard hung with torches all around. The sun had set, and the torches cast the villa in a flickering, orange glow. Half the courtyard was filled with armed Severots. In front of them, reclining on a couch, was Kratian Kray in all his splendor; bedecked with robes and jewels and other bits of treasure.

"Welcome to Elysium," he said cheerily as he stretched out his arm.

August passed his gun behind him for me to hold. I took it and slung it over my shoulder. There were two chairs in front of Kratian's couch with a table of food in between. Beautiful girls stood close by with pitchers of wine.

"Please sit," Kratian said. "I had thought you might try to sneak through my domain, young August. I'm sure your rising fame and now heavy following have given you a swollen enough ego to think you can go wherever you like. Or perhaps, our dear Mister Condon has simply decided that he can fight his way through anything, as he is renowned for completing his mission with the utmost determination and disregard for human life or decency. At any rate, we have a predicament.

"I have a written and sworn bond with The Architect that I will not collaborate with nor allow the rebellion to use my lands. In return, The Architect has agreed that none of his forces—either by land, sea, or air—will ever enter or threaten my lands. I keep the rebellion out, The Architect keeps his men out, and that makes this one little corner of the world that the Central Command doesn't have to worry about.

"However, ye bold rovers have broken that pact, and now someone must pay. It brings neither profit nor pleasure to me, and certainly no advantage to The Architect, for me to kill you all. Therefore, I am resolved to hold you and your army here—as my guests of course—until The Architect sends me my annual tribute along with a novel sum for your release. What do you say to that?"

Kratian grabbed a handful of nuts from the table and laid back, staring intently at August and Condon. The generals

165

looked at each other, as if waiting for the other to talk. It was an awkward moment between the two of them. Each seemed to wish to answer, feeling they had the authority, but both were at a loss for words at Kratian's boldness.

"I see you may have something to discuss," Kratian laughed.

Finally, August motioned to Condon that he would speak. In a rare show of deference, Condon waived him on.

August cleared his throat and said, "Surely, as I gather Your Grace is well informed, you have heard that the Holy City is under siege. We are enroute to relieve them, but to get there in time we must go to the Ghost Fleet."

"I have heard as much," Kratian said, "but the presence of your bold volunteers will have little effect on the outcome, especially since the city is defended by the mighty Praetorian Guard," Kratian said as he pointed at Condon.

"The Architect has recalled all forces to lift the siege. It would appear that there is a clear threat."

"Have you ever been to the Holy City, General August?" Kratian asked. "Apart from being an architectural and artistic masterpiece, it is also a military and engineering marvel. Every road, tunnel, and building is designed for military purposes. I'm sure your Mister Condon knows this well, having been many times to the city to receive his medals for victories against the peasants he so aptly slaughters."

166

Condon was turning red at Kratian's jabs. He looked like he was about to speak, but held his tongue as Kratian's bodyguards crowded closer around us.

"At any rate," Kratian continued. "I can think of little reason why I should let you go with no punishment for having offended my lands with your very presence."

Condon took a long, deep breath and said, "Perhaps Your Grace would excuse my arrogance, but you have just heard all The Architect's forces have been recalled to relieve the city. If that is not a cause for concern, then please tell me what is. You have already delayed us at least one day. I would ask you, for all our sakes, that you delay us no more, Your Grace." Condon's eyes were narrow and black in the torch light. His tone was cold and flat, but calm.

"I see your loyalty to The Architect has you eager to rush to his aid," Kratian said. "Were you quite this eager when you killed your parents to run away and join the Praetorian?"

August jerked his attention to Condon at this, and watched the Praetorian and Kratian lock eyes. August could clearly feel the conversation deteriorating, and the rest of our party who could hear looked nervous. "What General Condon says is true," August spat out. "The rebellion has massed troops around the city and are preparing—"

Kratian cut August short. "I still see no reason to let you pass. What do I care if the city is lost? I have my lands and my men. We will reign here no matter who reigns in Jerusalem."

"Because your tribute will stop," August said. "Do you think the rebels will uphold your contract with The Architect after all the trespassers you have executed?"

"I will continue to beat them out of my lands, as I have done for years," Kratian said. "Architect or no Architect the rebels here pose little threat to me."

"The rebels in the immediate region may pose little threat, but if the Praetorian and Central Command are defeated, who will keep the rebels from all over the world from running through your land? They won't treat you with kindness, I promise."

"General August, I have five million of the finest mounted troops alive. We do not fear rebel nor loyalist here," Kratian said.

"Your Grace, I am not suggesting you fear anyone. I am trying make plain the urgency of our mission, and the benefit for your people if you let us go."

"I see little benefit for myself or my people just yet. You are doing quite a poor job," Kratian said.

"Let me try my hand," Condon said. "By holding us here, you are bound to offend The Architect. And if the city stands, with the rebellion out of the way, he will turn the full might and power of the Praetorian upon you—for which you and all your men are no match. Do you think he will be grateful enough to pay you for our passage after having nearly cost him the war?"

"Ah, spoken like a true draconian enforcer," Kratian said. "Your words are angry, but I will not entertain your arrogance by being cross with you."

And then, August took us all by surprise. "Come with us."

"Excuse me," Kratian scoffed. "You've not yet drank anything, and I fear you're already drunk."

"Come to the Holy City with us and earn The Architect's gratitude. Why ask for a ransom when you can earn a reward? Help protect your lands, your means of income, and your relationship. And in the process, you can become a hero of the Empire. The Architect's rewards would be boundless."

Kratian laughed. "First I was only to release you, and now I am to go with you. Who will protect my lands while I am away?"

"There isn't a major rebel army for thousands of miles," August said. "They are all on their way to the Holy City."

Condon was presumably surprised at the suggestion but offered is encouragement. "The Ghost Fleet will accommodate you and your horses, providing they can be loaded," he said.

Kratian reclined and stared off into the sky, clearly in thought. "Can you see me entering the Holy City as the great savior of the Empire, Mister Condon?"

"Of course, Your Grace," Condon said.

"I will undertake it," Kratian said. "I will have my men ready in three days. Return to your troops and await me in the port."

"Just like that?" Condon asked. "You go from being our captor to being our ally?"

Kratian had gotten up to walk away, but stopped to turn around as Condon spoke. "As you well know, these are strange times, Mister Condon. I have sat for too long behind my walls while the world crumbles around me. But who will remember me after I am gone? It is time that I do something. I can't wait to see my old friend Lord DeVonay." He patted one of his soldiers on the back and then motioned to his entourage to follow. "I will see you in the port, General August," He said as he walked away.

"How did he know about the Army of the Americas?" I asked August.

"This man is no ordinary mercenary," Condon chimed in. "He's a major player in smuggling, assassinations, robbery, and all-around back stabber. He likely knows about lots of rebel movements we don't."

"I can't believe he's going with us," August said.

170

"Be careful what you wish for." Condon growled. "He's three steps ahead of us already I'm sure."

We were invited to stay in the villa for the night, but Condon insisted that we get back to the men and avoid any treachery. I felt he secretly feared Kratian in some way for his intimate knowledge of his history. Condon looked troubled the entire evening as the officers and his lieutenants discussed the upcoming loading operations. I briefly caught him alone while dinner was being served.

"Did Kratian shake you up?" I asked.

"That's none of your business peasant," He said quietly.

"We all have pasts. They can be hard to escape."

Condon looked me straight in the eye, much like he had done that day in the mountains. "He reminded me of a memory I had almost forgotten. I have not thought of my parents in many years."

I thought better of pressing the issue, but curiosity got the better of me. "Did you really kill your parents?"

"Yes, but it's not what you think. It was an accident. By the time I was captured, it was determined that I did it on purpose. They put me in a Praetorian school as punishment."

"That must have been terrible for you," I said.

"To be completely honest," He smirked, "It was exhilarating."

171

CHAPTER 18

SKELETON CREW

It took two days to reach Taranto from where Kratian had halted our advance. I smelled the salt before I ever saw the sea. To be honest, I was excited to see it again. It had been nearly thirty years since I had seen the sea up close. I remember looking back at it for a last time as my unit marched over the hill and away from port so many years ago. It had been quite a sight with the setting sun shining off the water, silhouetting the anchored fleet that stretched out towards the horizon. That day was probably the proudest day of my service. My green unit was all decked with new uniforms, guns, and equipment. Regimental colors waved bravely in the sea breeze. It was exactly as romantic as I had imagined it, sitting back at home dreaming of the service and trying to forget my heartache.

If I knew then what I know now, I would have shot myself in the leg. Maybe both legs just to make sure I would not be subjected to a life constant conflict. Then again, it didn't matter. This wasn't the kind of war anyone could escape from. Maybe at first it was, but inevitably it seeped through every aspect of life on Earth.

I reminisced for a minute on that proud moment long ago when I marched out with my newly formed unit gloriously seeking battle. Then I turned back to look at the long column of August's army moving down the road. Patched uniforms from a hundred different units were scattered throughout. The only unifying emblems were burnt, torn, and dirty pieces of green cloth with an eagle sewn on it. I don't know what anyone else saw, but as I looked at our tattered men, all I saw was ruined lives wasted on war and a desperate fight for survival.

When we arrived at the outskirts of the port it was just after sunrise. We didn't know who held the city, so we sent in scouts and skirmishers to look around. August and I watched with our binoculars all morning but couldn't see any activity other than squatters and vagabonds. It wasn't until midday that the first scout returned. "It's deserted," The scout said. "There are no enemy."

As we inched through the city, the signs of pandemic were evident. There were skeletons everywhere; in the streets and in every house. Bones clogged the drains like logs. This was the port of the Ghost Fleet. Several years ago, the Central Command's fleet returned from an action in the tropics. While they were there, some of the men who had gone ashore contracted a terrible disease that spread like wildfire. By the time the fleet made port, the ships were already full of dead bodies. The few men who returned to shore to get help only spread the sickness further. The Central Command sealed off the area and gassed the whole town in an effort to contain the disease. It did not work as anticipated. The ships that were not at anchor—pilotless and full of disease—were swept out to sea and landed on many shores. Not knowing what hell was aboard, when the ships were found washed ashore, they were boarded by scavengers, who unknowingly spread the disease further. By the time it had run its course, it ravaged nearly a quarter of the population. Full of rotting corpses and disease, the fleet was left to rust at anchor or sink in the roads. The bay was filled with a thousand floating crypts left to decay. Once we reached the wharves, we could see the deck of every ship docked there littered with bones. The skulls rolled back and forth in the scuppers as the waves rocked the ships.

"We should not be here," August said.

"The disease has died out," Condon said. "If you lived through the time of the sickness, you are immune to it now."

"If you are planning on taking those ships, it will be like robbing a grave," August said.

"Don't be so sentimental," Condon snapped. "If it bothers you that much, you can swim for all I care."

We spent the day fixing the wharf so that Condon's tanks could be loaded, and another party spent the day ferrying men out to the ships so that they could clear them of bones. Though

174

no one had thought of it when the decision was made to recommission this fleet for our service, all the ships were still full of equipment from that ill-fated expedition. It was a welcome bit of good fortune for our bedraggled troops. Most of the rifles and small arms had been carted off by scavengers and gun runners, but we found tents, cookware, medical supplies, water containers, and crates upon crates of toilet paper—which some of the younger men had never even seen. The other grace of leftover supplies was uniforms. Though the diseased had died in theirs, they left behind rucksacks which held extra clothes. Most of the men had no problem reappropriating these for themselves.

By noon, the Praetorian battle station *Poseidon*, which was lying further out from the port, sent in enough sailors and marine mechanics to get the ships running and loaded. It took the longest to load Condon's tanks, and when he arrived, Kratian's horses. Luckily, the Praetorian quartermaster had planned on how to load the ships, so loading was ordered and efficient. Still, it took four days and nights of jockeying ships from their anchorage to the wharf, picking up men, and then sailing back out to the sea lanes.

Condon's calculations had not originally accounted for the Severots. Once everyone was loaded there were about thirty thousand light infantry remaining on shore, as well as August, Simon, and myself, for which there were no more serviceable ships. It was decided that we would be transported aboard the *Poseidon*, along with Condon and his highest officers. After everyone else was loaded and began forming up the convoy for our voyage to the Holy City, all the ship's landing craft were sent back to the wharf to pick up the last of the men.

It took over a half and an hour to get within sight of the *Poseidon*. It started out as just a bump in the water, like an island sticking out of the sea. With no coastline to compare it against, its scale was lost. As we drew closer I could only have dreamt of such a thing built by humans. I saw aircraft carriers when I was being ferried from America to Europe at the beginning of the war. I estimated that the battle station was the length of ten aircraft carriers. It had no superstructure, and was more or less cigar shaped except for the flight decks and heavy guns sticking out of it. The *Poseidon* dwarfed the other escort warships which cruised around her as our launch drew near.

"Looks like a great cigar," Simon said. "You swim round and light the propellers, and I'll smoke it from the bow."

"I've never seen anything like it," August said. "It doesn't even look like it's from this world."

"This battle station is over one million tons of the finest engineering ever to float on water," Condon said. "Forty pairs of twenty-inch MAC guns, three hundred anti-aircraft batteries with both SAM launchers and cannon, twenty-four rotating torpedo batteries, two hundred aircraft, thirty ballistic missile silos, and all rigged to become one giant EMP bomb upon self-destruct."

The smooth, black hull was a patchwork of life boat hatches, gun ports, and missile and torpedo tubes. We passed through a gate in the anti-torpedo hull—which came to just above the waterline—and into a narrow canal between this and the main hull. A platform slightly above the waterline was lowered as we approached. A contingent of Praetorian marines filed out onto the platform as soon as our bow touched, and the Admiral came out to greet us with his chief officers.

"Welcome aboard, General Condon. I am Admiral Hess. Strength and Honor."

"Strength and Honor," Condon replied.

"This dispatch arrived for you three days ago, General," The admiral said as he handed Condon a folded piece of paper.

Condon took it and read it. "Have you read this yet, Admiral?"

"No, General. Only the operator has seen the dispatch."

"It seems Field Marshal Yaseen has been assassinated while organizing the Eastern Army for transport, and I am to assume his command and finish the job."

"You are to be congratulated, General," the Admiral said, "That post will give you command of the largest part of The

Architect's forces. Your authority will be second only to The Prophet himself."

Condon turned to August. "Get your riff raff cleared away and loaded. I have work to do."

Our men were already being loaded as the rest of us left the platform and headed to the bridge. The interior of the battle station was a city in itself. We walked through the central staging area to a giant lift that could probably have lifted a whole city block. About five stories up, the lift stopped and the sailors and marines got off.

"This is the enlisted men's quarters, General August. Your man can get off here" the admiral said, jerking a thumb in my direction.

"He's not my man, he is an officer of my unit," August said.

"Very well," the admiral said.

After two more stories, we got off the main lift and onto a smaller one, which took us straight up into the bridge. It was not a traditional bridge as I had witnessed on other ships— with windows all around and steering wheels and gauges—but rather a huge, circular room with giant video screens giving a panorama of the sea and sky surrounding the entire ship.

"Switch to thermal display," the admiral bellowed.

The screens around the room went blank for a moment. Then red, blue, and purple ships faded into the view as the thermal cameras calibrated. The admiral took us to a large map table in the center of the room. A couple of taps on the screen zoomed into a satellite image of the area surrounding the Holy City.

"Gentlemen, the situation at the Holy City has reached critical mass," the Admiral said "We stopped receiving directives from The Prophet directly and have lost communication with the Central Command within the city. We do not yet know if this means the city has fallen or whether communications have been knocked out. We continue to receive scattered communications from loyalist elements outside the city. The rebels have set up a double siege line, one encircling the city defenders and another keeping reinforcements out. They are being resupplied from the southeast."

The admiral tapped on the screen several more times and zoomed to the south. "Approaching from the south is the entire rebel army from the Americas. They landed at Oran and Tunis before the battle station *Thor* and the aircraft carriers *Hammer* and *Crucible* could intercept their fleet. They have been running sorties against them night and day, but they are still approaching quickly along the coast. Our mission is to land just north of the city and move south to breach the siege lines before the rebels are reinforced. If Lord DeVonay makes it to the city first, that will bring the entire rebel force to over one hundred million men." The admiral paused as gasps and mutters floated among the gathered officers.

"Just nuke them already and be done," Condon said.

"All nuclear ordinance is being reserved as a last resort. We're not trying to destroy the world. We're just trying to win the war. Besides, the rebels have captured some of our nuclear sites in recent days and there is a real threat of retaliation if we bomb them."

"Set us ashore in Sinai instead then. I will hold them at the Suez Canal.

"I don't doubt your prowess in battle," Admiral Hess said, "But your force is no match for an army that size. It's not just an army. It's a whole nation."

"I don't like this plan." Condon said. "Let the Eastern Army figure out how to get here themselves."

"General Condon, I have orders, as soon as your troops are landed, to dispatch you by jet directly to the Eastern Army, along with the rest of my air units, to airlift them to the battle."

"I really think I should stay and coordinate the reinforcements already in the vicinity," Condon said. "Someone else can be sent east. Surely there is someone already qualified out there. I am ready for battle now. I'm not interested in getting myself in the middle of a logistical nightmare." Condon's bloodlust was clouding his judgement.

"General, my orders are very clear that you are to go east. Since that is the last order I received, I cannot approve or assist you in any arrangements otherwise."

"Very well then. Can you not dispatch me immediately?" Condon asked. "I have no desire to wait around and watch this mess unfold if I cannot be given the chance to change it.

"I wish I could, General, but the main lift has been damaged by a missile attack and the repairs will not be completed before tomorrow at the soonest."

"Who is coordinating our forces around the city?" August asked.

"Until recently," Admiral Hess said, "it was the Central Command. Now, no one in the vicinity is coordinating. I have issued orders to those that will listen to stand down infantry and armor attacks, but to sustain artillery fire. However, I do not have contact with every unit. There seems to mostly be small unit commanders, and no one above brigadier general. It is an absolute mess. The rebels should never have been able to put us in this position."

"Do *you* know how millions of rebels sneak up on the city?" August asked Condon. "The Prophet's satellite system has three-hundred and sixty satellites in orbit. Not one of them saw?"

"We knew something was amiss," Condon said. "The other reason I was dispatched to the north was to investigate

181

why we kept losing satellites as they passed over that area. Some of those armored cars I sent back on the air transports had samples of guidance systems for portable surface-to-space missiles the rebels have developed."

"Did they take out all of the satellites?" August asked.

"No. Only twenty or so," Admiral Hess said. "The rest of the story is so simple, it's almost brilliant. The rebel forces were on a strict order to move only at night. During the day, they dug in and covered their positions with foil blankets, which reduced their heat signatures enough that the satellites couldn't detect them. On top of that, they put up camo tarps. Together, this made them invisible by day.

"Why didn't the thermal catch them at night when they were moving?" August asked.

"The blankets," Hess said. "They wore them as they travelled."

CHAPTER 19

EMPIRE'S MOST WANTED

Admiral Hess, against Condon's wishes, invited August to stay on the bridge with him. There were quarters there which were available for visiting officers, and since August held a commission from the Central Command, Admiral Hess offered him a berth. Simon and I were told to go some levels below the main bridge where the other minor officers were bunked. We were shown to a cabin which had eight bunks and no windows deep within the hull. A ventilation fan blew damp, salty air through the space.

August's other bodyguards bunked with us, and we got settled in while waiting to be called for dinner. We stowed our kit as best we could in the cramped space and laid down to try and rest. I turned off the light and a small, dim red light turned on to illuminate the cabin while we slept. The battle station resonated with the vibration of the massive *Therion* engines several stories below us as the ship started to get under way. A few hours later a bump against the bulkhead made me open my eye. Suddenly the door burst open and six Praetorian sailors stuck their rifle barrels through the opening. A petty officer turned on the light in the cabin.

"Simon Gram," the officer said, "you are under arrest for treason. Come quietly, or I will kill everyone in this cabin."

I and the others in the room tried to not move a muscle as the Praetorians trained their guns on us. I was not quite awake and had only just begun to process the situation when Simon rose slowly and glanced at his grenade launcher laying against the wall by his bunk. Between the guns being trained on him and tight quarters, the thought of resisting must have been fleeting. He raised his hands and walked towards the door. The sailors jerked him out into the hallway and handcuffed him.

"I'm generally into this," Simon said to the officer. "What's the safe word?"

"The safe word is 'night, night', funny man," the officer said as he bashed Simon's head against the bulkhead. He slumped to his knees and was carried away.

I watched down the hallway as they disappeared around a corner, then I left the cabin and made my way to the bridge. It took some convincing to have the guards at the bridge door fetch August for me, especially since he had not called for me and I otherwise had no business on the bridge. Eventually, they let me in, and August showed me to his cabin.

"They've arrested Simon," I whispered.

"I know," August said. "When we entered the ship, facial recognition scanners identified him. They matched his face

184

against images imperial spies took at a rebel camp a few weeks ago. They think he is a go-between, or double agent, or something."

"Do you have any reason to believe this?" I asked August.

"Well, it's complicated. He has a brother on the rebel side. I've told him not to visit, but since he's out of my sight a lot, I can't really control him," August said.

"What will they do to him?" I asked.

"They've told me he's being taken to the brig tonight. As soon as the interrogators are finished with some of their other prisoners, he'll be questioned and then executed. Admiral Hess has offered to let me confront him myself first."

"Surely he's not guilty of spying? Can you convince them to spare him?"

"I'm not sure, but it's unlikely anything I can say will save him."

There was a knock on the cabin door, and August opened it.

A petty officer from the Poseidon's crew stood in the doorway. "Follow me, sir. I will take you to the prisoner." He turned around and walked down the hallway.

Before following, August leaned in close and whispered, "Pay attention to where we are headed. You may need to remember later."

We followed the petty officer out of the bridge to an elevator. I watched the levels as we descended into the hull. We stopped abruptly on the seventh deck. The elevator transitioned to a monorail and took us laterally down the length of the hull. A second indicator on the elevator indicated we were at section ten when we stopped and exited the cab. We walked through a maze of white-painted halls with lights which turned on and off as we passed. Two left turns. One right turn. We walked down a long hallway and the third door on the right was opened by the petty officer. Keypad code: three, three, three. Not a very imaginative code, but easy for me to remember. We stepped through the bulkhead door and into a dimly lit brig with dozens of empty cells. In the first cell sat Simon with his head in his hands. The petty officer stopped and stood at attention while August spoke to Simon through the bars.

"Is it true, Simon?" August asked. "Did you go to the rebel camp? They have pictures of you, they tell me."

"Am I the only bearded fat man in the world?" Simon asked without looking up.

"I haven't seen the pictures, but they assure me that it's an exact match," August said.

"It's probably this stupid hat," Simon said as he pulled off his hat and threw it on the ground.

"I don't have to tell you that your future doesn't look bright at the moment."

"You sound like my dad," Simon said, "but I really appreciate the pep talk."

"I'll do whatever I can to help you because I don't believe that you're a spy. But you will have to explain what you were doing at the rebel camp."

"Well, if you can't save my life, can you at least get me some dinner? I'm too fat to die hungry."

The petty officer smirked. August looked at him questioningly, and he nodded.

"I'll see he's fed his last rations," the petty officer said.

We exited the brig and I committed our route to memory again, to make sure I had it right the first time. August left me at the elevator to return to the bridge.

"Take three of my guards and go get Simon out. When you have him, go to the nearest porthole, give him a life vest, and dump him out." August said.

"Are you serious?" I asked. "He could be lost at sea."

"He'll be dead if we don't get him out of there," August said. "There are over a thousand transport ships behind us. One of them is sure to pick him up. It's the best chance to save him."

"I'll try, but I'm not sure that he will fit."

"Tell him to suck it in like his life depends on it," August said as he walked away.

I was curious why August had tasked me with this mission. We had only just met. Still, I was somewhat thrilled at the thought of dumping Simon overboard. He was a little too cocky for my taste and a swim might do him good assuming we could get away with it. I went back to my bunk to find the other guards sitting around cursing. I told them what had happened, and that I needed three of them to come with me and help free Simon. Not satisfied that only three of them could go to Simon's aid, all seven of them resolved to go along. Four sailors' uniforms had been found in the cabin, and four of them disguised themselves. They took the other three of us, myself included, as feigned prisoners.

I directed them to the elevator and we traveled down into the hull, to the monorail, and then into the hallway which led to the brig. As we approached, three Praetorian interrogators were approaching the brig from the other direction. Their faces were pale from living in the shadows, plying their gristly trade. They wiped blood from their hands, evidence they were done with their last interviewee. As we neared, they stopped at the door, eyeing us incriminatingly.

"I had no idea we had other clients," the first one said.

"Let's play a game to select our next contestant," said the next one.

He motioned to my comrade holding me to use the keypad and open the brig door. There was an uncomfortable hesitation, as I had neglected to tell anyone else the keycode, and it would be exceedingly odd for a prisoner to know it. As a ruse I began to struggle against my pretend captor, who then clubbed me lightly and pushed me to the floor. My fellow conspirators also began a ruse of resistance. The interrogators were unimpressed and opened the door for us.

"Let's get these animals caged before someone gets hurt," said the third interrogator.

I walked through the bulkhead door ahead of my captor. I glanced over my shoulder as the last interrogator stepped though. One of August's bodyguards whipped out a knife and cut the interrogator's throat, covering his mouth as he started to gurgle. The other two interrogators were quickly overcome and met a similar fate. After being released from my bonds I took a set of keys from one of the interrogators' belts and tried frantically to find the one to Simon's cell.

"It's probably that one," Simon said, pointing aimlessly at the ring of keys.

"You're not helping," I spat.

Finally, I found the matching key and opened the door. There was a storeroom at the back of the brig with blankets and mattresses and boxes of supplies. We dragged the dead interrogators to the corner and covered them with the items there. A hose had been provided for the space, along with a drain in preparation of the gristly work that sometimes took place there, so we cleaned the area as best we could. One of August's guards, still dressed as a sailor, stood in the hallway and watched for others. We were several decks below the waterline and there were no portholes from which we could eject Simon. We decided to skip the elevator and took the stairs three stories up. There, we found an unlocked crew cabin that had a suitably sized porthole. There was a window which could be opened at the top of the porthole, but the thick armor of the hull necessitated that a long tube about eight feet long had to be passed through to exit the hull.

"Get in," I said to Simon.

"Get in, yourself," Simon said. "I know we didn't start off on the right foot, but you don't need to dump me overboard."

"August said so," I said. "A transport will pick you up."

"Okay, which one?" Simon asked.

"There's a thousand out there. One of them is sure to see you."

Our lookout popped his head into the cabin. "There are sailors coming down the hall."

"Now or never," I said. "Unless you want to go back to the brig."

"Fuck you," Simon said as he grabbed a life vest and struggled headfirst into the tube.

"Don't forget your beacon," I said as I handed him a flashing light to alert the ships behind us. He reached behind him and grabbed it violently and then shimmied about halfway through before calling out. "I'm fucking stuck!"

I could barely reach his foot enough to touch it and I could not push him out the rest of the way. I looked around the room and the only thing long enough to push him out was one of the rails of a dismantled bed frame laying on the floor. Another guard and myself grabbed the bar and pushed against Simon's foot. Suddenly he was ejected out of the porthole and was gone. Over the hum of the station's machinery and the sound of the surf we heard a faint splash.

"I really hope they pick him up," I said.

"Either way, if we ever see him again, he's going to be pissed," said another guard.

CHAPTER 20

POSEIDON, THE GREAT DEFENDER

There was no fooling ourselves into thinking our progress towards the Holy City was going unnoticed. Before we entered the Severot's territory we had captured rebel scouts and seen surveillance aircraft marking our location throughout the trip. Why the rebels waited to attack until we were being escorted by one of the most heavily armed battle stations ever constructed was a mystery, but not a complete surprise. By nightfall we had almost cleared Crete. I was on an observation deck above the bridge getting some fresh air when a massive salvo of surface to ship missiles was fired from the island. The glow of the rocket engines reflecting off the exhaust trails dotted the horizon. The Poseidon was running along between the island and most of the fleet in anticipation of an attack, and the battle station's sensors picked up the incoming threat before any of the missiles hit their mark.

Giant clouds of chaff erupted from ports in the hull and made an impenetrable wall a mile long and almost a mile high. The missiles weaved and bobbed. Some crashed into the ocean while others became so unsteady, they simply disintegrated in flight as their self-destruct devices activated. Then, the battle station's active defenses opened up. Anti-missile laser turrets, as well as chain guns, shredded the incoming second salvo as the chaff settled to the sea.

After putting up this defense, it was the *Poseidon's* turn to attack. The deck trembled as the twenty-inch dual batteries on the port side emerged from giant armored doors in the hull. The enormous muzzles trained on the island preparing for a full broadside. The lights on the observation deck dimmed as the main battery's capacitors charged. I was suddenly nearly blinded as the MAC guns fired in quick succession. Milliseconds later the island erupted in fire as explosive shells tore into the bunkers where the missile fire had originated.

A shot from the *Poseidon's* first salvo must have struck a magazine, as multiple large explosions erupted, followed by one final explosion that lit up the night sky as bright as day. In spite of the spectacular results of the first salvo a second broadside was loaded. This was a mixture of high explosive and white phosphorus. Again, I was nearly blinded as the guns fired. The phosphorus burned brightly, and along with the exploding missile batteries, bathed the island in a hellish glow.

There were several officers on the observation deck and they yelled at me to get below deck as they rushed towards the hatch. Seeing stars and with my ears ringing I descended several flights of stairs to the bridge. As I stepped off onto the

193

gangway I was nearly run over by General Condon who was running past trying to get to the bridge floor. August came out of his cabin and together we stood close to the railing to stay out of the way as various officers raced to their battle stations. Below me I could see a radar display. Suddenly, the screen came alive as several squadrons of bombers and jets headed straight for our mostly defenseless transport ships to our south. The *Poseidon* had an answer for them as well. The starboard anti-aircraft batteries opened up. On the thermal displays in the bridge I could see the weapons filling the entire sky with a maze of exploding shells. Then surface to air missiles picked off aircraft at a steady rate.

Three ships that were the farthest to the south were hit. But after seeing the absolute destruction that the battle station was wreaking on their compatriots, the remaining rebel aircraft began defensive maneuvers and their accuracy was severely diminished. Most of their ordinance came nowhere near any of the transports and fell harmlessly into the sea, or sometimes exploded under the surface, causing great boils and waterspouts.

Although Admiral Hess was certain we had destroyed the facilities, we wasted no time getting out of range of the island. Fortunately, there were no more incoming sorties from the south showing up on the radar. August and General Condon joined Admiral Hess on the bridge floor.

"We should remain in the area to look for survivors," August said to Admiral Hess.

"There were only three transports hit," Admiral Hess said calmly, "They are of no consequence. Statistically."

"We should still try to recover anyone we can," August insisted, "There are also probably pilots in the water who will need assistance."

Condon slammed his fist on the console next to him, "You cannot be serious."

"I am dead serious," August barked back.

"I do not care one bit about your worthless soldiers and even less about our enemy," Condon said.

"I'm not talking to you," August replied, "I am having a discussion with the commander of this vessel. I don't believe Admiral Hess asked for your opinion either."

Admiral Hess was preoccupied with looking over the various reports and slips of paper his officers were handing him. He rolled his eyes at the mention of his name. "I am not loitering here with this entire fleet," He said, "Nor am I spending one ounce of energy to recover our enemy. I've issued orders to the vessels that I can communicate with to shoot any rebel survivors on sight."

"Let one ship remain in the area to look for survivors of the ships that have been sunk. The rest of the flotilla can continue on," August proposed.

"Do you presume to give orders to an officer as decorated at Admiral Hess, who is twice your age, and infinitely more qualified than you will ever be?" Condon asked.

"Endorsements aside, I think I can handle this situation without help from either of you," Admiral Hess chimed in, "The destroyer *Abaddon* is in the rear. I will have her sweep the area before she moves on."

"I thank you sincerely," August said.

Condon plopped himself down in a chair and was about to interject when the *Poseidon's* bridge came alive with red strobe lights and a deafening alarm.

The sonar operator turned in his chair to Admiral Hess. "Sir, we've detected sixteen— No twenty— No, upwards of thirty submarines!"

"What is their location?" the admiral snapped.

"They are directly under the transports off the starboard bow. I believe they are lining up for a shot at the battle station," the sonar operator said, his voice cracking.

Condon stood up from his chair. "Admiral, can you launch your depth charges that far?"

"Yes, but they aren't a precision weapon. We're as likely to hit our own ships as we are the submarines. Admiral Hess said pensively.

"Should you not protect this station?" Condon asked.

"I also need to deliver most of this army intact," Hess said.

"It's mostly provincials. It would be a small loss compared to this battle station. You have my permission to fire at will," Condon said.

"I do not need your permission, General Condon, and I intend to let this battle station's defenses do what they were intended to do. The torpedo belt will protect the hull initially. We need to signal the transports to clear the area."

The signal men began to operate the signal lights above the bridge. Many of the Ghost Fleet ships had been stripped of communications gear, and our only hope was that someone aboard could interpret the battle station's signals. It had been nearly impossible to find enough seamen among the land army to man the ships. As it was, many ships had only a handful of sailors, and some no sailors at all. The signal Hess sent was simple. He repeatedly sent the "Juliet" signal, which to most mariners would be immediately interpreted as, 'I am on fire and have dangerous cargo; keep clear.'

The bridge crew breathed a sigh of relief as the transports made hard turns to the south, putting distance between themselves and the battle station. We could see on the sonar overlay that the submarines were now exposed. The rebels must have seen that their cover was blown, and though not all were aligned to take their shot, those that were fired their torpedoes in quick succession.

It was only seconds before the super-cavitating torpedoes slammed into the *Poseiden's* torpedo belt. The ship groaned and shook as the explosives ripped into the anti-torpedo hull. By this time, the remainder of the rebel submarines had gained firing position and fired their torpedoes. With the anti-torpedo hull severely damaged several torpedoes found purchase in the main hull. Damage indicators lit up on the bridge's control panels.

Our ships had mostly cleared the area, and unwilling to wait any longer, Admiral Hess ordered all starboard depth charges to be fired together. It was not immediately clear on sonar if the depth charges had the desired effect, but shortly after they were fired, we could tell that some of the submarines had been broken in half and others began to roll or list. Those there were farthest from the battle station peeled off in retreat. Admiral Hess watched the sonar closely for a few minutes until the damage control officer got his attention.

"Sir, we're taking on a lot of water. They're working on an isolation solution, but some of the main bilge pumps near the brig were damaged. We're also dragging a large section of the anti-torpedo hull which has come loose. It's acting as a sea anchor and significantly reducing our speed."

"Send out divers and blow away the hull we're dragging.," Admiral Hess said.

"We risk further damage to the hull if we do that, sir," the damage control officer said.

"If we can make it to the coast and we haven't stopped the flooding by then, I intend to beach this hulk," Admiral Hess said. "We can't afford to lose speed."

"Very well sir. I'll mobilize the dive teams," the officer replied.

A noticeable starboard list developed as the flooding intensified. Admiral Hess checked his course and ordered a steady speed to be maintained until the damaged portions of the outer hull could be removed. He ordered the signal "India" to be sent to the now-scattered transports—a message to 'Come alongside'. Most of the ships responded quickly, but a good number continued to lag behind the convoy. After about two hours, the demolition charges were rigged and ready to blow. The bilge pumps had not all been fully repaired. The list was so pronounced by this time, walking on the deck was becoming a conscious effort. The ship rumbled as the charges exploded. Almost immediately, the list lessened as the blown-away section separated. Admiral Hess ordered all engines full speed ahead. The now-compromised hull groaned and racked as the battle station picked up speed.

It was nearly a full day before the coast came into view. Some of the bilge pumps had been restored, but not enough to prevent the inevitable. Admiral Hess and his navigators spent some time trying to find a suitable location, and eventually settled on a sand bank several hundred yards from shore just south of Tel Aviv.

The stricken battle station was slowly maneuvered parallel to the coast, and using the stern and bow thrusters, the ship was brought alongside the sand bar. Although we were in the Mediterranean, and the tides are of a very low amplitude, Admiral Hess waited for the highest tide before pushing the *Poseidon* over the sand bar. By low tide, the battle station came to rest gently on the sand. All our ships had caught up to us and were jockeying their way into various ports up and down the coast. The *Poseidon's* boats began to ferry men off the battle station. Condon and August agreed on a rally point to set up camp which was large enough for our army and on the beach, under the protection of the *Poseidon's* batteries. Even beached and flooded, the battle station was still formidable.

CHAPTER 21

SCOUT'S HONOR

August's force's had started out as a few hundred thousand provincials in the north, and had swelled with the addition of the Praetorians, Raptor's mountain survivors, and the Severots. Moulin and the other generals set about preparing for the coming battle including rearming and better equipping as many men as they could. The provisions and equipment provide by the Ghost Fleet were a much needed moral boost. In addition, the *Poseidon* had an extensive armory, and rather than let it go to waste or to the bottom of the sea, Admiral Hess ordered his quartermaster to distribute the entire contents to August's best troops, and to train them in the Praetorian rifle's use. The new weapons required some getting used to, as they were much longer and lighter than the rifles common among the volunteers and Loyalists. While the Praetorians were well-practiced at the manual of arms, they grew impatient with their students and would beat them if given the chance. Although no lives were lost, some blood was shed. By the end of the first day of training, there was no love lost between August's volunteers and Condon's Praetorians.

We sent scouts inland to attempt to try and ascertain the status of the different elements currently vying for control of the city. Without Simon, who August trusted most of all, the reports which came back from the other scouts were somewhat dubious. Simon had not yet been located and August was beginning to fear the worst. There was a cadre of dozens of scouting teams. Previously Simon would hear their reports and filter out the ludicrous and irrelevant to boil down the information into elements which had a common basis. Not trusting that any one team would return the whole truth and nothing but the truth, Simon conglomerated their findings into a more tempered and cohesive picture.

In Simon's absence General Soho attempted to fill the void and even though he was adept at filtering the mundane from the meaningful the reports which were returned did not always align well. I sat with Soho taking notes as the scouts returned to debrief.

"They city has fallen," Said the captain of the first scouting group to return, "We have found many fragmented loyalist groups but they are so disorganized we could not even approach them. We were fired upon by multiple loyalist sentries."

"How do you know the city has fallen?" Soho challenged.

"Well, it's surrounded by rebel and we've heard there is no communication from Central Command."

"I told you that before you left," Soho said as he put his head in his hands.

The second scouting group to return was only marginally better. "The Temple is still standing as well as The Architect's palace," the captain said.

"And you have seen this with your own eyes?" Soho asked.

"From the sector we probed The Temple can be clearly seen."

"What about The Architect's palace?"

"There are loyalist units in the southwest of the city who can confirm that The Architect's palace is still being defended," the captain mumbled.

"And you talked to these men?"

"We talked to the someone who was in contact with those loyalists three days ago."

Soho did not reply as his face contorted and he struggled with his frustration. There was more of the same as the day continued. The reports varied widely from, "The city has fallen," to, "the rebels are retreating." Then, of course, there was everything in between. The only thing that all the scouts could agree on was the level of mismanagement and disorganization that was plaguing the loyalist forces around the city. Dozens of warlords and low-level commander had assumed positions just out of range of the rebels outer line of defense. Presumably, they were waiting for the chance to relieve the city. Soho relayed his findings to August who was visibly disappointed by the lack of clarity.

"Here's what I can confirm from multiple accounts, General Soho said, "The strongest loyalist units are all concentrated in the north. Specifically in the north west. There are between twelve and thirty European Loyalists units like ours stretched out from Rehovat to Jericho and an unknown number of African Loyalist units from Rehovat to Hebron. However, the Army of the Americas has been sighted in Sinai so our forces in the south are scattering to get out of their way. They're leaving behind them as many mines and traps as they can assemble to slow Lord Devony's progress, but the rebels will likely clear corridors quickly."

"Has anyone been able to contact Central Command or a Praetorian Unit?" August asked.

"From what we can tell they are holding out just fine behind the city's inner walls."

"Why aren't they communicating?" August said.

"There seems to have been some kind of electrical storm. Much of communications equipment around the city has been destroyed."

"I find it hard to believe that the rebel lines are so tight that no word can be passed between The Architect's forces on the inside and the outside."

"We've done some probing of our own. The rebels have hundreds of miles of trenches, redoubts, pickets, minefields, barbed wire. They've wasted no time constructing their fortifications. They've even sapped down into the bunkers and tunnels below the city." General Soho said as he passed August a map with his rough approximation of the rebel fortifications scribbled on it.

"What are the loyalist on the outside doing about it?" August asked., "Has there been any major actions?"

"Just skirmishes. Everyone is trying to hold out until the Army of the Americas or the Eastern Army arrives. Whoever arrives first will tip the scales."

"I don't know if we can wait for that," August said, "We need to get things moving ourselves. When the big armies get here there will be no negotiating. If we can avoid a major action we can save many lives."

"Your goal is noble General, "General Soho said, "But there is no way to avoid what is coming. The Architect will not relent and the rebels have been fighting for decades to get to this point. They are at his doorstep now. They will fight to the last man I know it."

"I have one goal now. I must stop this bloodshed before the whole world burns."

"The world is already burning August. Anything we do now will only fan the flames."

205

I'm afraid you're right Soho," August said as he sat down and raised his eyes to the sky, "I'm afraid you are right."

Reports continued to come in, but nothing that would otherwise reshape the picture which had been painted. A deeply entrenched rebel force surrounded a confident Praetorian and Central Command mercilessly defending the city center. Around the rebel's fortifications a loosely confederated mess of loyalists sat helplessly as the rebels continued to shell the city day and night. Confident that he had a good enough evaluation of the battlefield August ordered Soho to recall all the scouts. They would be needed to support our advance as we made our way towards the city.

CHAPTER 22

IN THE NIGHTMARE

On the last night we were encamped by the sea, before we advanced the thirty miles to the Holy City, the troops carried on about camp with much enthusiasm. It helped them to feel like a real army to have the proper amenities of war, which the Ghost Fleet had provided. Even with the enthusiasm, the air was tense. We could all tell the soldiers were anxious about what the coming days might bring. That night August, myself, and a few of the officers sat around a fire of broken-up pallets and boxes to escape from the chill of the desert night. The dirty, old wood gave off a sooty blue smoke which the sea breeze blew away into the cloudy sky. The night was so dark we could barely make out the ships riding at anchor.

"What's the plan for tomorrow?" Raptor asked August.

"I wish I knew," August said. "Condon has been trying to reach the Central Command and The Prophet all day and can't get through. For all we know, the city could have fallen even though we've confirmed reports that The Temple still stands.

We are about to walk straight into the biggest concentration of rebels in the world."

"If we wait to hear from the inside for too long, and the city has not fallen, we may be too late," Raptor said.

August frowned into the fire for several moments before responding. "I have brought these men so far, I would hate to waste them against unbeatable odds."

We all sat silently for a moment. Now that the journey was nearly over and our hour of trial was near, everyone's courage was slipping, and August seemed to be running out of faith. We all sat and stared into the fire for a while. Around midnight, our silence was interrupted by gunfire over the next dune, in a part of camp we couldn't see. We all shot to our feet. The sky over the dune glowed brighter and brighter with fire light. The gunfire grew more intense.

"Get to your commands," August said. "Stay organized and get your men over that dune." The generals took off into the night, yelling orders and trying to find their lieutenants August and I gathered a few soldiers that were standing nearby and rushed to the top of the dune.

On the other side, thousands of tents and a few tanks were burning at the edge of camp. August's lieutenants organized his men and formed lines at the top of the dune to either side of us. From the sound and the muzzle flashes we saw the fighting was heaviest to our right where we had established our supply reserves. Another hot spot was far off to our left, near where the prisoners were being held. General Condon was already advancing on the left so August gave the order for our line to advance to the right and down the dune. He ran in front of the troops, but they would grab him and pull him back. We advanced at a brisk pace weaving our way through the rows and rows of tents until enemy fire started to rip through the lines. The burning tents and equipment gave some illumination, but it was anyone's guess to pick a target they were sure of. The rebels had infiltrated deep into our encampment and now the maze of smoke and fire was proving to be a handicap for us and the enemy.

From the top of a rocky outcrop, which had been more or less the center of camp, the rebels were pouring fire into the surrounding area. We dropped to the sand and fired at the flashes of gunfire in the black night. As we suppressed the incoming gunfire, we got up and advanced until we encountered stiff resistance again. I never got my night vision goggles fixed, so the best I could do was look through my scope and hope to catch a muzzle flash from the enemy. I fired a few shots, but never could tell if I hit anything. By the time we got to the base of the outcrop the Praetorians had rallied their armor and from behind us several mortar carriers unleashed a barrage that cleared the hilltop. We climbed the hill and as we crested the top we could see in the area beyond a fiery hellscape of flaming tents. In the spaces between men were fighting hand to hand smashing each other with rifles and throwing each other into the surrounding fires.

August's ranks reformed into a more or less solid line and advanced down the hill into the fighting below.

General St Clair's division had been camped near the perimeter to the south and as we fought our way through the melee we met his flank. The fire was spreading rapidly through even more of the encampment and August sent a detachment to try and create a fire break before the entire area was engulfed in flames. We held our position until Praetorian tanks with searchlights rolled up behind us. We made gaps for them, and they churned past our line and took off into the night, firing their machine guns as they went.

As soldiers filtered away to help with the fires, I heard someone running down the line, shouting, "August. August. General August!" He grew louder until he finally reached us and August flagged him down. He fell panting at August's feet. "The raiders tried to free the prisoners, and now General Condon is executing them."

August said nothing as he took off down the line towards Condon. I followed as best I could, but August tore across the sand ahead of me. As we neared Condon his figure was outlined against the burning tents, standing with his hands on his hips as his second in command and a few other troopers went down the lines of bound prisoners, shooting them as they kicked sand and squirmed against their bonds.

"Stop!" August yelled. "Stop this!"

Condon spun around with his hand hovering over his revolver. August stopped dead in his tracks as the Praetorians stopped what they were doing and knelt with their guns trained on August.

"Stop this. What are you doing?" August gasped.

"It is against The Architect's policy to take prisoners," Condon said. "These men were nearly freed by their compatriots along with the tens of thousands of prisoners which were just recovered by the enemy. When you give people hope, they always take advantage of it."

"These men are not to be killed. They are defenseless," August said.

"What were you going to do with them tomorrow?" Condon asked. "Tie them to their posts and hope they were good little prisoners while we were away fighting?"

"You have no right to execute my prisoners."

"Maybe that's true. I guess we were never clear on who the ranking officer was in our little collaboration. But now that I am to command the Eastern Army, I'm sure we can agree I am in charge here. I have grown tired of your antics, and deem you unfit to command. You have gathered the men as The Architect has requested. Now, I will take them into battle."

"By what right? You cannot take this army from me." August said.

"You're obviously losing your mind and are no longer fit to command. I have heard you have nightmares," Condon said.

"Yes. It's why I can't sleep," August said. "Everyone has nightmares."

Condon chuckled. "Look around you, August. Look at this world. *This* is the nightmare."

It was a true and chilling thing to hear. General Condon, shrouded by smoke, lit by the flames of burning tents, and surrounded with bodies of the slain, was truly a nightmare.

"There is no justification to kill them," August said, "They are not a threat to you or me or anyone."

"Justification?" Condon questioned. "I don't need justification to kill anyone, anywhere, ever. Since the day I was born it has been my natural right to take life whenever I feel like it. I am blessed with a gift, you see, when I take a life I feel absolutely nothing."

"That's not a blessing. That's a curse."

"You aren't made for this world August. There's no place for those who cannot see how frivolous we all really are.

"I've never once felt like I or anyone else was frivolous. Someone somewhere is always counting on us," August said.

"You think you are unique?" Condon laughed.

212

"I think I am the only me. I think that only I can feel what I feel and be who I am to be."

Condon knelt down beside a prostrate prisoner. He grabbed him by the hair and pulled his dirty face up next to his own. Putting a knife to his throat "Do you think that this man is unique?"

"I don't know that man by there's no way he is not unique."

"When I look at his man I see a nameless, faceless, analog for every other worthless being on this plant," Condon said

The prisoner was trembling violently, and tears began to streak his face.

"What's your name? August said.

"Michael," he croaked.

"There you see," August said, "He's not nameless anymore."

"Goodbye Michael," Condon hissed as he slid the knife across the prisoner's throat.

"You bastard!" August yelled as he rushed towards Condon.

Condon stood suddenly and squared his hips to August as he reached for his gun. But as he drew, a shot ripped through Condon's head, and his revolver flew out of his hand and landed at August's feet. Condon's body slumped to his knees, then fell to the ground. revealing directly behind him, the smoking barrel of his own second in command, Colonel Brekke.

The officer stepped over Condon's body and approached August. "Our obedience is to The Architect, not to General Condon."

"Thank you, Colonel," August said. "There will be some explaining to do."

"He obviously died in the raid," the Colonel said. The other Praetorians nearby looked at each other nodding in agreement. Then, the troopers unceremoniously dragged Condon's body away.

"Are you okay?" I asked August.

He stared off into the night as the casualties were carried off. "I guess you can only kill so many of your own men," August said.

***

We lost some equipment and a few hundred men in the raid; a small number in the overall scheme of things. The Praetorian tanks trickled back into camp just before the sun came up. A few had been lost to landmines, but for the most part the enemy's route was a running massacre through the desert.

As we prepared to move out that morning, I searched for General Moulin. As I passed by the Praetorian's camp, I saw Old Johnny wandering aimlessly, talking to himself.

I walked over to him, and as I approached, he turned to face me. "Then I saw an angel standing on the sun. He cried out in a loud voice to all the birds flying high overhead, 'Come here. Gather for God's great feast, to eat the flesh of kings, the flesh of military officers, and the flesh of warriors. Feast upon the flesh of horses and of their riders, and the flesh of all, free and slave, small and great.'"

A shadow crossed over us as carrion birds soared above us in the desert sky, circling over the night's casualties.

"We had better take him with us," August said as he walked up behind me, "This world is not kind to those who cannot look after themselves."

"He's survived this long," I said.

"He's survived this long as Condon's pet. Let's see if we can make him human again."

Old Johnny turned to August. "The armies of heaven followed him, mounted on white horses and wearing pure white linen."

"Okay, Johnny," August said. "Let's get you some breakfast."

CHAPTER 23

OUTSKIRTS

Admiral Hess, upon learning of Condon's death, took it upon himself to gather the Eastern Army. He left that morning by jet, leaving the ship's captain to command the stranded battle station. Colonel Brekke took over Condon's Praetorian Armor Corp. Since there was no communication coming from the city, he pledged to coordinate with August until he reestablished contact with The Prophet. Kratian Kray and his Severots withdrew north to await official orders from the Architect himself. He wanted to make sure his presence was noted to ensure The Architect's utmost appreciation.

We approached the Holy City from the northwest. We passed through the wreckage of what were once, only a few months earlier, green fields of corn, wheat, and rye that fed the great city. They laid trampled and scattered with the waste of war. We met the first loyalist outpost in the late afternoon. As we marched along an abandoned highway, a man on a motorbike came out of the bushes ahead of us. August, Captain Raptor, and I were walking at the head of the column. As we approached, he rolled down the embankment into the road.

"You must be the guys from the north," he said. "We've been expecting you."

"We started out in the north, but we've picked up a lot along the way. Now you could say we are from all over." August said.

The scout reached out his hand to August, "Corporal Ateatamol, Ninetieth Legion, serving under General Tano."

August took his hand. "I'm August."

"Well, come with me and I'll take you to my commander."

"How far are we from the city?"

"It's another twenty miles to the outer wall, but we'll hit the suburbs just up ahead."

The bike trooper took us down the highway to the suburbs, abandoned neighborhoods of great manor houses and estates that once housed the merchants, tycoons, and high officers of The Architect's empire who flourished before the war. The Architect appointed good men to manage his empire. His ministers were doctors, engineers, and economists. He refused to hand control of his creation to charismatic politicos feeding off public momentum. It was a good strategy when all was well, but once the pockets of unrest opened, there was no one to sooth the masses with a golden tongue. The houses stood empty with their common contents strewn in the yards— the better items likely stolen by raiding rebels.

Our guide told us about the desperate position of the city. The rebels were well-organized and greatly outnumbered the imperial forces; with more rebel units coming in every day. Every night, the rebels would make a bold attack on the outer wall. The Praetorians always made them pay dearly, even though the defenders were most likely running out of munitions.

"Here it is," Corporal Ateatamol said as he pointed to one of the manor houses. "This is our headquarters." He took us through the front door guarded by two gunmen and up to a study guarded by two more. There were several men standing around a table piled with maps, computers, and damaged communication equipment.

They turned as we entered, and Corporal Ateatamol saluted the tallest of them. "Sir, this is General August, Colonel Raptor, and the General's aide, Daniel Maconas. They've come to assist our effort to relieve the city and they've brought reinforcements."

"That's bloody fucking awesome," the tall one said. "I am General Tano. We are most glad to see you here. Let me fill you in on what's going on."

"Your scout filled us in on some of the situation," Captain Raptor said. "Sounds rather bleak."

"Bleak is an understatement," Tano said. "We are outnumbered, have little munitions left, and the Central Command isn't communicating with us."

"If you're not getting your orders from the Central Command, then who is in charge here?" August asked.

"Whoever wants to be," Tano shrugged. "How many men do you have with you?"

"We're a sizable force," August said. "Three hundred thousand loyalist under my direct command, two hundred thousand Praetorians temporarily under my command, and an unknown number of Severots who are standing by. Probably several million."

General Tano's eyebrows shot up. "We have roughly a three million loyalists scattered around the outskirts of the city, all under different commanders. If you have as many men as you say you do, that gives you the largest cohesive force. I only have about thirty thousand left under my command."

"How are you communicating with the other units?" August asked.

"By messenger," Tano said. "About a month ago, the rebels fired an EMP above the city. It was a design we've not seen before. Multiple warheads with cluster munitions entered the atmosphere and then exploded, showering the city with black magnetic dust. It turned the whole sky dark for a day while it settled. It didn't damage the vehicles, but it shorted

219

out and destroyed most of the communications equipment. A few older, analog devices still work, and we've been trying to bring in new equipment. But we're having a hard time coordinating a communications network."

"Do we know how many more reinforcements are set to arrive?" August asked. "Admiral Hess has just left to rally the Eastern army, but I'm not aware of any other large units who are available."

"If the Eastern army can get here in time, that would be a miracle. I was not aware they were still in play." General Tano sat down and put his hands in his head.

August walked around the table, studying the charts and maps. He traced a line on one of the maps with his finger. "What is this marking drawn across the outer rebel positions?

Tano glanced at the map and said, "That is a pipe that will take you under the rebel defenses to a hill above the city. You can survey the situation for yourself, if you like. Corporal Ateatamol can show you the way. But be careful. You will be right between the enemy lines. We've been trying to think of a way to exploit it, but it's too small to move a large force quickly."

August nodded. "I'll take a small party and take a look."

He selected a dozen of his best men, along with myself, Captain Raptor, and Colonel Brekke. We followed Corporal Ateatamol to a burned-out water pumping station. He looked around to ensure no one was looking, then hopped down into a bomb crater, lifted a few bricks off a piece of sheet metal, and pulled it aside. Beneath was a pipe with a jagged hole, slightly bigger than a man, in the top of it.

Ateatamol dropped down through the hole and disappeared. Colonel Brekke insisted that the Praetorians he brought with him lead the way so that they could check for explosive devices. The lead Praetorian dropped down into the pipe and his mates lowered down additional armor for him. He moved aside as the rest of us dropped down and waited as he assembled his armor. We could stand inside the pipe, but just barely. Some of the taller men were hunched over to keep their helmets from scraping on the pipe above.

Ateatamol pulled the sheet metal over the hole and we were in complete darkness for a moment before we all turned on our weapons' lights. We moved slowly through the piping, stopping occasionally to listen for activity ahead of us. Eventually the pipe sloped uphill until it reached a section that was so steep, we had to pull ourselves along hand over hand. Fortunately, a thick, slimy rope had been previously installed for that purpose.

After about an hour of traveling through the pipe, Ateatamol told us to be quiet. We waited as he went on ahead to find the exit. After a few minutes, a beam of sunlight shot into the tunnel. Ateatamol motioned for us to follow as he

221

exited the pipe through an old, rusty metal door. We emerged from the base of an empty water tower into an alley.

"We must move quickly," Ateatamol said. "If we are caught, they'll kill us for sure."

We snuck along the alley until we came to a door on the side of a row house, entered, climbed the stairs, and exited the building through a hole in the roof. From here, we had a perfect view of the whole city. The outer wall was crushed and blackened by the shiploads of ordinance that had been discharged on it. About two thousand yards out, the rebels had dug trenches, constructed redoubts, and set up barricades between buildings. From there, the great city sprawled towards its center and the great temple, an enormous spire of steel and stone towering over the city.

I had never seen The Temple before with my own eyes. It dominated the entire landscape and was three times as tall as all the broken and mangled buildings around it. Even though the white stone facade was cratered and scorched after weeks of attacks, the grandeur of The Temple was not diminished. It was perfectly square, with sides sloping gracefully inward as it rose above the stumps of former skyscrapers around it. At the top, it abruptly flattened, and on that platform was a low dome. Above the dome was a polished sphere which resembled the sun.

"Sol Invictus," August whispered.

"What makes you say that?" I asked.

"I just thought of it," he said. "Diana had some books on the Roman Empire. I don't think it's an accident The Architect chose to include the sun as his totem."

"It's supposed to be a temple to all gods," I said. "It's the whole reason for all of this."

"Now that I've seen The Temple, I know it's not about the building. Maybe it started out that way, but one building is no reason for all this suffering."

"Well, it's about religion."

"It's about vanity," August said. "It's time to end this."

I surveyed the scene again thinking about what August had said. Smoke from fires around the city wafted through the city ruins. The sun reflected off The Temple illuminating it and making it a radiant centerpiece in an otherwise ruined cityscape. As a building it was simply beautiful. As a symbol, to me, it was a perfect embodiment of The Architect's abiding power over the chaos caused by the primitive rebel brutes. I reminisced for a moment on my youth. Agnostics and the religious faithful worked and played side by side confident enough in their own beliefs that they never dared to risk everything. How far we had all descended into anarchy grasping for some moral and absolute victory. Never once had I thought to look at The Temple as anything other than The Architect's attempt to cement the peace between the secular

223

and the pious. I assumed that August, intelligent as he was, may be overconfident that his view of the world was more just. Perhaps seeing the monumental accomplishment of another had awoken some spark of jealously which he had not previously experienced. I found myself embarrassed at thinking less of him for a minute. The feeling was fleeting as I looked around to find myself alone on the roof. The others had already descended to return to the tunnel. I took one last look at The Temple. A cloud cast The Temple in shadow and for the first time I saw it as other might see it. A dull grey building standing all too proudly above the destruction it had wrought.

I ran quickly to join the others, and we worked our way down the alley, back to the pipe, and eventually back to our own lines. As Ateatamol was covering up the hole in the pipe, August said, "Corporal, can you send word to the generals around the city and have them come here to meet us?"

"I can try, but I make no promises," Ateatamol said.

August turned to me. "Please call all of our generals together for a meeting at Tano's headquarters. I have a plan."

CHAPTER 24

THE BEST LAID PLANS

August's generals and several loyalist commanders from around the city gathered by nightfall, while several dozen runners were recruited to carry August's plans to the disjointed units surrounding the city. As the senior officers gathered in Tano's manor house headquarters, August bid them all to sit around him.

"We need to establish communications with the besieged," he said. "Since we can't risk visual signals and they aren't responding to our coded messages, the only way to do this is to break through. Colonel Brekke has informed me the Eastern Army is enroute, and as long as the weather holds, they will arrive sometime tomorrow. We need to clear a landing zone for them, and from what intelligence we can gather, the rebel lines are thinnest on the East.

"If we can maneuver enough of our forces there, we can break through and create a gap. And in that gap, the Eastern Army can touch down. If we can coordinate the loyalist forces to the north, east, and west, hopefully this will allow our defenders on the inside to concentrate on repelling the Army of the Americas on the south.

225

"I will stay here and command the western forces. I've promoted Colonel Raptor to General. He will move to take command and control of the loyalist forces on the eastern side of the city, oversee the breakthrough, and coordinate with Admiral Hess when he lands.

"How do you get such in depth intelligence?" General Crease, who had been waiting for the opportunity to break through for weeks, asked. "We've heard no such thing about the Eastern Army."

"August is in contact with the Praetorians," General Tano said. "His army traveled here with their assistance."

"I came here to listen to what you had to say, but now that I see you are just a boy, I will be going," General Chang said. He grabbed his hat and stormed from the room as his attendants followed. General Lebeuf followed him without saying a word.

"Let the Eastern Army make their own landing zone," said General Crease. "They have all the air transports and all of the gunships. If we had any air support, we could have broken the siege weeks ago."

Lord Halifax, the oldest and most seasoned of the Loyalist commanders, sat in silence as the others debated. He was given his title by The Architect. He was not a nobleman by blood, but when The Architect had enriched his officers to the point where no amount of money would entice them further, he had commenced with handing out titles. Lord Halifax leaned to whisper to his staff. They nodded, and he stroked his grey mustache. Still, he did not join the debate.

August continued his plea. There were seven remaining generals in the room. August appealed to them to critique his plan so they could perfect it, or offer up another plan. The suggestions ranged from the overly cautious to the wildly ambitious.

General DeSaxe liked August's plan, but would not commit without Chang and Lebeuf. General Zhukov wanted August to give over his forces to an older General and to quit trying to assume command. General Walid did not think that the Army of the Americas was that big of an issue because their leader, Lord DeVonay, was more a figurehead than a real general. General Shaw wanted to execute a series of probing attacks to draw out the rebels, in hopes they would open one of their flanks. General Bankole had heard that additional Central Command reinforcements were due from Siberia, and insisted they take no action until that was confirmed. The remaining Generals were in agreement that they must hold their positions—as they had been doing for weeks—and that this council should reconvene after either the Eastern Army was landed or the Army of the Americas was within range of the city.

All said their piece except Lord Halifax. He rose to his feet with slow, deliberate precision. The other generals turned their attention to him.

"I don't know who this General August is. I've never heard of him before. I don't know whether August is a first name or a last name or some kind of idiotic codename, but I do know this: General August has brought to us the first fresh idea since the siege began, and he has called the first meeting of all of the premier generals that we've ever had. So all of you gutless, spineless, sacks of shit who won't move a muscle without an order from The Prophet or The Architect had better pull your heads out of your asses and follow his plan. I will arrange the order of battle, and I will send you all more detailed orders."

The other generals' eyes widened. Some leaned forward and opened their mouths as if to offer protests, but in the end they all remained silent and hung their heads while Lord Halifax continued.

"DeSaxe, you will go to Chang and Lebeuf. Tell them that if they do not follow my orders, I will see them and their entire officer staff hanged. I am putting them under General Raptor's command and they are to follow his orders to clear the landing zone. The rest of you, return to your posts. Do not rest until your forces are ready for rapid deployment and be ready to execute my orders without fail or hesitation. This time of sitting around idly is over. Now, go!"

Lord Halifax returned to his seat as the other generals—excluding August's own and Tano—were ushered out by their chattering staffs.

"Thank you, Lord Halifax," August said.

"Don't thank me," Lord Halifax said, "Because if your plan fails, or in any way compromises our ability to break this siege, I will hold you personally accountable."

"I think that seems fair, but I am very confident in this plan."

"I know you are confident, but are you capable? There's a distinct difference, and since I don't know you, I will coordinate your plan if I am to commit my own troops." Lord Halifax struggled to stand again, and his staff helped him up. "Next time, find a place to meet with better chairs. I'm going to need a new ass now."

After Halifax left, August and his generals set out to prepare their forces for the battle. The messengers were sent out, carrying the weight of Lord Halifax's name along with August's plans. Most of those who returned by the end of the day said the commanders they met with agreed to follow Lord Halifax's direction, at least until communications could be restored with Central Command or The Prophet.

Loyalist forces around the city moved into position as Lord Halifax issued orders based on August's plan. The rebels, confused by the sudden impetus, responded by moving some of their troops as well. A delicate ballet of cautious movements unfolded throughout the night as each side tried to maintain the status quo of the stalemate which had characterized the last few weeks of the siege.

CHAPTER 25

GOLDEN IDOL

August called me into his tent later that night. Although I was tired, I wanted to see what he needed. In recent days as I came to know him better, I was confused about how I should treat him. I could, if I tried, consider him a son, but only in a broad sense of the word. He was more distinctly my general and employer. I determined as I walked that for the time, he would have to be my general and I would come when he called. Maybe once the war was over, we could develop a more familiar relationship. For now, I would follow his orders. August was solemn as I entered the room. A man I did not recognize was sitting in the corner.

"Daniel," he said, "when I was standing here tonight, I realized something. It doesn't matter if we win tomorrow or not. The war will go on. The rebels may retreat, but those that live will fight on. As long as The Temple stands, people will rise against it." He walked over to a chest of drawers in the corner of the room and pulled out a roll of paper. He unrolled the drawing on the table; it was a plumbing schematic for The Temple itself.

"Where did you get this?" I asked.

"It has come a long way from someone who's waited a long time for the right moment to use it."

August jabbed a finger at a label on the diagram. "Look right here: 'Old City - Main Water Supply'." The tag was located on the largest pipe under the foundation of The Temple. "That's the main water supply from the reservoir to the treatment plants all over the city. It's a gravity pipe, so it's likely still pressurized. It was built before The Temple. See all the little circles in rows and columns: Those are the bearing piles for The Temple. It is so heavy, and the soil so poor, that it has eighty-foot bearing piles down to the bedrock. If someone were to remove the dirt from around the piles, they might buckle." He looked me straight in the eye. "We can end this war tomorrow."

He motioned to the man who had been sitting in the corner of the room behind me, who came forward.

"This is Kazim. He's one of Tano's soldiers, but he knows General Raptor from before the war. We've been communicating with him and others using the decoder. He was an engineer before the war and a munitions expert since. He says it would only take one hundred pounds of explosives to blast down to the pipe. All we need to do is rupture the pipe, and the water pressure will do the rest of the work. If the water can wash out enough dirt to make the piles buckle the foundation of The Temple will fail. I need someone I can trust completely to do this. Will you do this for me tomorrow?"

I nearly collapsed in a chair. The disbelief in what I just heard was paralyzing. Not only was August discussing treason, but he also expected me to carry it out. I was certain he was overconfident or that seeing The Temple had somehow altered his sense of duty and respect for The Architect.

"Why me? I asked.

August looked away from me for a moment then spoke. "Although you delivered me to Diana before I could remember. I have dreamed of you. When mother told me stories of you, they were of a man with flaws and courage in equal share. But that is never once how I imagined you. To me you were the strongest soldier. The fiercest fighter. The most vigilant protector. My own personal hero. When I was taken from Diana I prayed you would save us both. I imagined for years that you were still trying, and as I hoped endlessly for you to find me, I believe I slowly became what I hoped you to be. Strong, patient, resilient, determined. When I first saw your face, even before I knew it was you, I could tell that you were a man of great courage. Even as my guards stripped you and humiliated you, I did not see in your eyes shame or hubris. I saw only purpose. Out of all the men under my command there is not one I trust more than you to do this."

I was moved. Although we had not been reunited long, I was glad to hear that I was making an impression on him as he was one me. "How would we get in?" I asked. "We can't walk into the Holy City with bags of explosives."

"I've taken care of that," Kazim said. He walked over to the table and pointed to a drain line on the plans. "This drains the lowest level of The Temple. The Architect new the dangers if the soil became saturated. It's four feet tall and two miles long, leading directly to the canal. There's a security grate every five hundred feet, but I can carry a pipe-cutting saw to remove the grates. However, I cannot carry the explosives as well. I have asked General August for help, and he has suggested that you might be trustworthy. Will you undertake this?"

"Are you a rebel?" I asked. "Are you a spy, or just a traitor?"

"I'm a dreamer," Kazim said, "I dream for all of this to be over."

I sat there and said nothing as they both stared at me. I fought for years to defend The Temple and everything it stood for. It was built as a symbol of unity to bring the religions of the world together. It was a gift from The Architect to all the people of the world and all the gods in heaven. The moment I saw its towering spire reflecting light onto the broken world below it, all the senselessness and butchery and cruelty that had been my whole life since the day I enlisted seemed to be justified. Destroying The Temple would be like destroying the whole idea of everything I thought I had been fighting for.

As if August could read my mind, he walked over and put his hand on my shoulder. "Whatever it may have stood for when it was built, that is gone now. You've seen what this war is. It's all I have ever known, but you know how it used to be. This could all be over tomorrow. We could have peace again."

"Why can't it stand?" I asked. "If we win, it will be destroyed for nothing."

"No," August said. "If we win, the remnants of the rebels will escape to breed more rebellion. It will never be over. I don't think mankind will ever understand the power of symbols over men. To you and others like you The Temple is a symbol of progress. But to the rebels, it is a symbol of oppression. If we lose tomorrow, it will be destroyed anyways. If we win *and* The Temple has fallen, the rebels may feel like they have won as well. Then, perhaps a truce can be reached."

I stared down at the schematic in silence.

August squeezed my shoulder. "I asked you because I trust you. If anyone else knew this plot the diehards would drag me out and tear me to pieces. You said you like to finish things. Let's finish this."

I could not find the words to answer him, so I nodded.

"How will we escape?" I asked.

"Once The Temple is destroyed you can hide inside the city until this is all over. If you can bring down The Temple you've done more than enough."

***

The next morning I met Kazim at his tent at three o'clock. The troops had just left to form up for the day's battle as we slipped into the sewer near the camp and followed it to the canal. As we floated our equipment downstream to the drain entrance, passing under the enemy lines, we saw rebels on every bridge as we passed under their lines. Soon we were inside the city's walls.

The sun was not yet up, but we already heard gunfire from skirmishes around the city. Praetorian Gauss cannons hummed as they powered up around us. Rebel artillery began to target locations around the city. Bits of concreate and brick steadily rained into the canal as the heavy shelling further punished the few standing buildings that remained.

By the time we reached the drain, the sun was casting long shadows through the remnants of the stricken city. We cut through the first gratings quickly to get into the drain before we were discovered. A sodden pallet was nearby and I grabbed it to cover up the damage we had done to the drain as we entered the pipe. We reached the next gate quickly. Kazim

236

worked fast with the cutter and we were through the gate in minutes. We crawled on to the next one, which was much the same as the first; and then the third, and fourth. By this time, we were several hours in and it was eight in the morning. My knees were raw and my back cramped from crawling through the pipe. We eventually found a drain shaft that went straight up and took turns standing. Explosions from artillery and mortars echoed through the city above us and rang down the shaft.

If we rested too long, we would get stiff and the rest of our mission would be more painful than it was already going to be, so after about ten minutes we started crawling again. We reached the fifth gate, then the sixth, seventh, eighth, ninth… By the time we reached the tenth gate, the saw was dulling and throwing a lot of sparks. The fumes from its smoking blade were almost unbearable, gagging and choking us. By gate twelve, we had to stop and change the blade—which took longer than either of us would have liked. After gate fourteen, the pipe became steeper and filmed with sediments, making the crawl slippery and filthy.

Every movement was a conscious effort. What started out as a hundred-pound pack of explosives was now a monster which seemed to grab me and drag me back down the pipe. The first fourteen gates took us nine hours to cut through. The next seven took twelve hours. After six the next morning, we reached the end of the tunnel below the last gate. What had not been shown in the plan on August's table was the twenty-foot vertical pipe that lay between us and the last gate, which would bring us out into the foundation of The Temple. My body was numb in some places and on fire in the rest. I could not stand up straight in the shaft without propping myself against the wall.

Kazim was no better off. "We must climb," he said.

Luckily, the side of the main pipe was covered with smaller inlet pipes. These made the climb easier, but by no means easy. We rigged a bit of rope to the saw. Once we both climbed to the top, we threaded the rope through the bars of the grate and I jumped down with the rope tied around my waist, hoisting the saw up to Kazim.

Kazim cut the grate bar by bar, carefully tying them off before they fell loose so they would not fall and spear me. While he worked, I took several canisters of expanding foam and filled the bottom of the drainpipe completely full so that the deluge we were planning would not escape without consequences. Once enough of the bars were cut away, I tied the rope to the pack of explosives and started the arduous climb once again.

Once I was out, together we hauled up the explosives. While Kazim located the water pipe, I looked for a way out of the foundation. There was an inspection hatch that led up into some kind of storage space. I went back and helped Kazim dig down several feet to increase our chances of rupturing the pipe. We then placed the bomb, set the timer, and covered the hole. In that dark, dirty foundation, not even I could have found that bomb again. We took off for the hatch and left our little seed of treason planted in the soil.

Kazim climbed up through the hatch first, then helped me out and said, "We have sixty minutes to get out of The Temple and far enough away that it won't fall on us."

We wandered around the storage and mechanical spaces of The Temple. The schematic we had brought with us was useless as we snuck through staircases and hallways, getting nowhere. Every other door we came to was locked and every hallway led to more hallways.

Our time was running out. The fatigue of the long crawl through the drain made every hallway seem like a mile and every stair a mountain. We finally came to a pair of doors that were taller and heavier than the rest. As I opened one, we were blasted with a powerful golden light. I pulled back from the opening, shielding my eyes as they burned from the incandescence. We both stood in the doorway, blind after our hours in the dark.

As the daze wore off, we walked into the inner sanctum of The Temple. The walls of The Temple rose for dozens of stories, covered in golden panels depicting the history of every

239

religion—ancient and new, dead, and alive. The morning sun streamed through an oculus thousands of feet up and bathed The Temple in daylight. Kazim fell to his knees and spoke in his native language.

"What's wrong?" I whispered.

"I am begging forgiveness for what I have done," he sobbed.

At that moment, regret gripped me. I felt worse about what we were doing than I ever had for anything. Worse than for all of the terrible things I had done—my many misdeeds and cruelties—in all the years of the war.

But the very thing that froze me in place, the pending destruction of The Temple, reminded me we had no time to linger on such regrets. I looked at my watch. We had fifteen minutes. I grabbed Kazim by the collar and yanked him towards the main door.

He pulled away from me. "I must stop the bomb," he said, and he ran for the door from which we had come.

"You will never make it!" I screamed after him, but he was already gone.

I turned around and ran as fast as I could out the main door of the sanctum and through the colonnaded ringing The Temple. Massive columns towered hundreds of feet above me. I could see a door at the end of the hallway. I ran but didn't seem to get anywhere. The scale of The Temple made the doors seem close, but for all the urgency with which I sprinted, they remained distant. I finally reached the doors, rushed through them, down the long flight of stairs, and into the street.

A Praetorian Gauss cannon crew was on the road ahead of me. The battery commander turned as he saw me exit The Temple and he walked towards me pistol drawn. I ran right towards him. He yelled at me to stop. I suppose he thought I was a suicide bomber or an infiltrator of some sort. I still wore the tattered frontier drab I always did. At about ten yards, he fired and shot me clean through the upper thigh. I fell and rolled onto my back.

The Temple loomed over me as I lay there staring up at it. The sun was like a halo behind the spire. A low thud shook the ground. The Praetorian gazed at The Temple in horror as he stood over me. A rumble like distant thunder began to vibrate the street, then water blasted from the ground-floor windows on every side of The Temple.

A muddy sludge gushed down the steps and into the street towards us. I felt faint from the loss of blood as the water flowed around me. It deepened as it soaked my back and took away the sting of the hot pavement. The Temple slumped to the left, the spire wavered, then began to fall over. My vision faded as The Temple's marble obelisk swung slowly towards the ground.

CHAPTER 26

THE PROPHET

It was dark when I woke. Dead bodies surrounded me, luckily most were still fresh. Still, the smell of spilled blood and disembowelment filled the air. The bodies around me were simply pushed into piles with tractors and covered with lime. I could see how the machinery mashed and mangled the lifeless corpses of all walks of life. It seemed I was lucky enough to have been discarded by hand sparing my unconscious body from the grind of steel and pavement.

My leg throbbed and ached. The bullet wound seemed clotted, and as far as I could tell the projectile had passed all the way through just under the skin missing bone and artery. As I pushed and pulled the bodies off myself, I took in the world around me. Fires burned all over the city and lit up the smoke-filled sky with an orange glow. Feet scuffled everywhere in the dark. The ground trembled with pounding feet and rumbling tanks. I crawled into the shell of a burned out building to address my wound and wait until morning.

As the sun rose, it illuminated the broken, leaning stump of The Temple towering over the rubble. The spire broke off several floors above the surrounding buildings.

I decided to climb The Temple ruins to get a good view of the battle. Wounded and cut off from my unit, I had no intention of taking part in the coming fiasco. Perhaps I was a coward for that, but I felt I had done my share of fighting. To be honest, with The Temple destroyed, I was struggling with my loyalties. I had survived the entire war, and I was not about to die at the very end. As August had said, I've done more than enough.

I made my way into the maze of crushed marble slabs and mangled steel beams. The sanctum's golden panels had been stripped from the rubble. I was surprised there were no scavengers digging for remaining bits of gold. I trudged across the debris, then up the mangled flights of stairs still left inside. My leg throbbed, and the progress was slow.

I finally reached the floor where The Temple broke off. The last part of the stairwell had collapsed right before the landing. I reached up, grabbed the floor above, and struggled to pull myself up.

As soon as my shoulders were above the floor, someone grabbed me under my armpits and hoisted me up.

Two dusty Praetorians held me from either side, as an officer glared at me. Then, he smirked as if he recognized me. "I think The Architect will be glad to know you are alive."

It was the Praetorian battery commander who had shot me. I was in the wrong hands and presumed I was in a

243

spectacular amount of trouble. The soldiers dragged me to an impromptu observation and command post at the edge of the platform. Communication consoles and wire ran everywhere. The broken parapet was lined with pale men holding scopes and binoculars. My captors tied my hands behind my back and lashed me to a twisted bit of broken column. It was a few minutes before a bald, old man in a Praetorian uniform approached. His hands were folded behind his back and his ghostly, pale face held a scowl that could kill.

"We thought we lost you in your flood," he said. "The Architect will be anxious to meet the man who destroyed his masterpiece. However, I suppose I should thank you. You provided the perfect command post from which to control this final battle. From here, we can see the entire battlefield. And just in time to replace my bunker."

His pale face and mention of a bunker brought it together for me: This was, most likely, The Prophet himself.

"I am sorry about your bunker sir," I said. "I assume the rebels overran it."

"You assume correctly," he said. "Emboldened by the fall of The Temple, they pushed very hard to take it. A costly mistake, to be sure." He sighed as he surveyed the rubble strewn below us. "It was my idea, you know."

"What was?" I asked.

The Prophet spread his arms out and looked down. "This was. This building. The Temple. I urged him to do it. Even when the rebellions began, with The Temple nearly finished, I urged him to continue its construction." The Prophet said.

"Why would you do that? Perhaps this could all have been avoided." I said.

"I will spare you the inner workings of my mind, but in short: This needed to happen. This war. This great cleansing. All the weak, are nearly gone now and we will renew our species with strength and dignity. The final purge is about to begin. All the forces of good and evil and everything in between meet today in the final clash to end all weakness. Hundreds of millions of men will test themselves against one another. You should count yourself lucky. You've chosen the perfect place to witness the final cull."

I thought I saw the darkest of men's souls as Condon butchered and tortured with glee. But I realized in that moment he was only a minion, at best. Condon paled in comparison to the old man standing before me. This man, who served The Architect of a new world, was himself the architect of its destruction.

***

Smoke from the burning city obscured the sun as it rose high in an otherwise clear sky. Dust billowed in the south as the Army of the Americas arrayed their forces to assault the city. Their artillery was already pounding the staging grounds for the Praetorian within the city. As more and more buildings in the southern part of the city began to catch fire and burn it obscured their movement as they entered the outskirts.

Loyalist artillery harassed the rebels fortified in the north as August's forces assaulted the western rebel positions. Small arms fire all around the city grew louder and louder as more units joined the fight.

The day before I embarked on my mission the rebels had broken through the western defenses and pushed almost to The Temple. They swung their forces from the east to the south in preparation of joining Lord Devonay's assault. The loyalists, regulars and Praetorians outside of the city, according to August's plan, took advantage of this move and pushed into the city's eastern side in an attempt to establish lines with the besieged. The rebels in the North, pinched between August's army on the outside and the Praetorian on the inside, dug in deep. In most places only a few hundred yards separated the two armies. The breakthrough in the east succeeded, but just barely, and the remaining loyalists and Praetorians there were trapped between enemies to the north and south. They were unable to reinforce the Praetorians inside the city although now a line of communication was established. The only thing they could do was hold and hope for rescue from the Eastern Army.

By a stroke of good fortune, and strategy; August pushed the western rebels from their defenses in the outskirts. They retreated south to close ranks with the Army of the Americas and prevent themselves from being pinched between August the Praetorians inside the city as their northern allies had been. Through careful planning by August and expert execution by Lord Halifax, the outnumbered forces of The Architect were positioned well—if they could hold. The rebel forces were split in two. A small assembly on the northern side of the city was completely enveloped. The rebels in the south consisted of the mostly intact Army of the Americas, flanked by what remained of besieging rebels on the east and west.

I surmised the rebel's only hope was to take the city and set up new lines before the Eastern Army arrived. They fought hard into the night but failed to make any meaningful gains. August redeployed most of his forces to harass the left flank of the southern rebels, but he did not press the advantage he had gained. The remainder of his force held the northern rebels in check and prevented them from taking any meaningful actions.

The Praetorians inside the city, encouraged by Colonel Brekke's presence in the west, made deep, piercing blows into the Army of the America's center. They established several long fingers of penetration, but while they were inflicting heavy losses, they were also taking heavy casualties. It was only a matter of time before they would have to withdraw back into the city.

The Prophet was on the radio all day, through the night, and into the next morning; stirring the Holy City's Praetorians to engage with more aggression. By noon, his white face was red with rage. His final culling had become another stalemate.

CHAPTER 27

DOUBLE EDGED SWORD

By noon, The Prophet had determined, through various channels, that for some unknown reason the Army of the Americas was standing down despite their overwhelming numbers. They had withdrawn a little ways to the south to create a gap between themselves and the murderous Praetorian onslaught they had endured.

"Well, since there is a break in the action it seems there is time for you to meet someone," The Prophet said to me.

"Who do you mean?" I asked.

"Today you will meet The Architect," he growled.

The click and grind of jackboots on the fresh rubble was nauseating as the Praetorian dragged me and a few other prisoners from The Temple ruins to The Architect's Palace. We were taken through the gates, where a Praetorian officer came out of a mobile command center. The Prophet gave a brief introduction of each of our crimes. Then he pointed at me and said to the guards, "Take this one to the main hall. Kill the rest." I was sprayed with blood from both sides as my fellow inmates were executed posthaste. The Prophet walked briskly into the palace as the guards dragged me close behind.

More guards lined the walls, each armed with two belt-fed machine guns affixed to their arms and armored from head to toe. They looked more like machines than men. They stared at me through their dark tinted visors.

The ceiling of the palace consisted of enormous bays painted with giant murals of The Architect's accomplishments; the purchase of the Chinese army, the treaty of Russian membership in the Empire, the surrender of Germany and the United States, all painted in stylized grandeur.

When we got to the door at the end of the hallway, it opened and we walked into a long, narrow room. At the end was a window that stretched from the floor to the high ceiling. A single figure stood in front of the window.

They walked me to where he stood and kicked me onto my knees. One guard stood behind me and held my collar. The figure turned around and as he did The Prophet threw up his hands in frustration.

"Who the fuck are you?" He yelled.

"I am the steward. The Architect has charged me with maintaining the city as he prepares for what is next."

"Where is The Architect? The Prophet demanded.

"He has withdrawn to the north to rally the loyalists and await the Eastern Army," the steward said.

"He is abandoning the city?"

"The Eastern Army is again delayed,"

"We have fought them to a standstill. There is no reason to withdraw. Why am I arguing with you? You are a fucking serf," The Prophet bellowed.

"Be that as it may, I am charged with this city until The Architect can return. I request that you prepare our defenses as best you can."

"I'm not going to sit here and be overrun. I'm taking what's left of the Praetorian and withdrawing. You can have Central Command to cover our retreat. They are nearly decimated anyways," The Prophet said. He seemed to have forgotten about me, but as he turned to walk away, he was reminded.

He looked at the guards holding me. "Cover his face and take him to the courtyard. Kill him quietly and burn the body. Flush the ashes down the sewer. I don't need a martyr."

They put a bag over my face as they dragged me up to my feet. Just then, the doors behind me creaked open and the footsteps of a crowd of people rang out on the floor. The footsteps grew nearer, then stopped.

"Well, well. What are you doing here so soon?" The Prophet asked.

"There will be no more bloodshed today," August said as he took the bag from my head. General Raptor and several others were standing behind him.

251

"August," The Prophet said. "I have long anticipated your arrival."

"It is an honor to be in your presence," August said. He seemed different. He was stern, unafraid, majestic. The Prophet seemed curious about him.

"I've been watching you, August," He said. "You're a remarkable man. In a world where you were exposed to nothing but violence, you learned something that your training was designed to extinguish: Compassion for your fellow man. It's extraordinary."

"Some people remember how a human is supposed to feel, Your Grace. All men have at least some small amount of compassion, even if they don't show it."

The Prophet stared at August in silence. His brows knit together as his eyes threatened to bore into the very soul of the younger man standing before him.

August broke the silence. "The rebel commanders have agreed to a ceasefire. However, they have some terms."

"I would expect nothing less. Let us hear them," The Prophet said.

"First, they want the assurance that all rebels and their commanders will receive full pardon."

The Prophet nodded. "Reasonable."

"Second, they want to make sure The Temple is never rebuilt."

"The Architect is an old man now, General. I am sure he will have no desire to rebuild it."

"They also demand the complete disbandment of the Praetorian."

"But who will protect me?" The Prophet asked.

"I don't think you will need to worry about that. Which leads me to the final condition: You and The Architect are to be turned over to them, immediately…" August paused as The Prophet's eyes opened wide. "…for execution."

"Even if I did agree to that, do you think my guards would allow it? I am their father, their leader, their master."

"I have already spoken to several Praetorian generals. They are assembling in the grand square for disarmament," August said.

The Prophet looked out into the square below and watched as his Praetorian filed in and lined up including the guards from the hallway.

"This is my world, August, The Prophet said. "I have hundreds of eyes and thousands of ears. I have millions of men that will fight to the death for me and The Architect."

August shook his head. "Not anymore. They are tired."

The Prophet was clearly on edge now. His power slipping away before his eyes. "Leave us!" he yelled. No one in the room moved. August turned his head and motioned their compliance. The Praetorian holding me began to drag me off.

"No," August said, "Leave him."

My guards dropped me to the floor. The room emptied and the steward pulled the doors shut as he exited with the rest. The Prophet walked around for a moment and then began to look out the window again.

The Prophet sighed and his shoulders slumped.

"Do you know what you are to The Architect, August?" The Prophet asked.

"I suppose you're going to say I'm just like him," August said.

"Oh, no," The Prophet gasped. "You are the yin to his yang. You aren't like him at all. You are his antithesis. You've spent your whole career trying to destroy what he has created."

"I've been his loyal soldier for many years now. I've won many battles in The Architect's name," August said.

"Loyal? There's no bother hiding it now August. Do you think everything that has happened to you recently has not gone exactly as the Architect has planned? Is it not convenient that General Condon was so handy to provide transport for your army?

"It was extremely helpful. It would not have been possible to rush to your aid without his help.

"Do you know what General Condon's mission was?"

"He told me he was ordered to provide us transport," August replied.

"Yes, but why was he where you just happened to be?" The Prophet asked.

"He was hunting Arcani," August replied.

"Yes, he was," The Prophet said. "Did he catch his prey? Did he bring me exactly what I was looking for?"

I glanced back and forth between the two men, unable to comprehend in the moment what The Prophet was implying. A smirk appeared on August's face as he realized the man standing in front of him had, in essence, captured *him*.

"Yes," August said. "I am Arcani."

"No, no," The Prophet said, "You are not just any Arcani. You are the most important rebel leader they have ever had. From what my spies tell me, you coordinated the entire European rebellion without ever having set foot in a rebel camp. The prisoners you kept in your camp were not prisoners. They were unwitting messengers who came and went from your army carrying your orders. Where is Simon? I was looking forward to meeting your spymaster after his miraculous escape. How beautifully he coordinated this deception. Tell me: Is it you or he who is named Ovis?"

It all made sense to me now. The letters in his tent. The protection of his captives. The unlikely stalemate on the battlefield today that averted the most horrendous massacre.

They were all *his* soldiers. Loyalists and Rebels alike, answering to one man. Where better for the most powerful enemy of the empire to hide than in the belly of the beast. Right at the head of one of their own armies.

"Did Condon know?" August asked.

"Of course not," The Prophet said. "He was merely a pawn. A truly blunt instrument bent on destruction for its own sake. Still, Condon was my creation. When he killed his parents, he was young and terrified; but I knew that he would make a most demented supplicant. I offered him amnesty in exchange for his complete obedience. It was a small price to pay for such a promising, empty vessel. In time, he came to accept and even embrace his fate."

"Were all Condon's actions your orders?"

"Oh, not all of them. As all good artists do, he developed his own style and flair. Rest his soul."

"How did you figure out I was Arcani?" August asked, "I never communicated directly with any rebel commanders. There's no way you could have traced me."

"Patterns, August," The Prophet said. "But I can't take all the credit. The Architect maintains a healthy fascination for strategy. He has studied your battles in particular as I study all battles. It became clear to us the tactics you deployed were the same tactics some of the rebels deployed. I also noticed that the battles you won against the rebels were never against the zealots. You only attacked mercenaries and nationalists. It became abundantly clear to me what was going on when it was reported to me that you bypassed several zealot strongholds to attack a heavily fortified bunker full of nationalists."

"If you were so sure I was Arcani, why didn't you just have me assassinated?" August asked.

"The Architect tried. He issued orders for your death to a number of miscreants, but they all failed. Then, I had another idea. I thought that if I might bring you in alive, you could help me not just end the war, but win it." The Prophet turned and gazed back out the window. In the distance, clouds of sand and dust billowed as rebel tanks jockeyed around the city outskirts. "I assume it is on your recommendation that they have agreed to surrender?" The Prophet asked.

August shook his head. "I reached out to my contacts in the rebel ranks. There's a consensus among them that if this battle continues, both armies will be annihilated."

"That's exactly what I want," The Prophet's voice boomed through the chamber. The Prophet strolled up to August and locked eyes with him.

"Here's what is going to happen now," The Prophet said. "You're going to complete the surrender of the rebel forces, making whatever promises you need to complete the disarmament. I will take the remaining Praetorians and go into

257

hiding. Once the rebels are disarmed, we will return and wipe them out."

"Why would I agree to that?" August asked. "Who's captured who? It appears you think you have the upper hand in this matter."

"Let me show you why I have the upper hand," the Prophet said with a cruel smile. "I've brought something to show you." He reached into his coat and pulled out a letter. He handed it to August. I looked over his shoulder as he opened it to read.

Delivery Instructions: Relay to All Coalition Operations Groups

Gs,

Seventy thousand of our noble rebel brothers have been brutally massacred at the City of Bellinzona. Dismembered and impaled for sport at the hands of the Architect's minion, General August of the Architect's Belgica Loyalists. Make all preparations to destroy this villain as he travels through the mountains, to the lands of the Severots, and across the sea to Jerusalem. A demon such as this we cannot allow to be victorious.

Peace to you,

Ovis

"You see," said the Prophet, "I've been doing a little letter writing of my own."

"How could this possibly be advantageous to you? I thought your goals was to capture me, not destroy me," August said.

"Indeed, but you also made a very enticing bait which many of the Architect's enemies wasted themselves on. A bunker captured in the mountains. The Corsican batteries destroyed. The rebel submarine fleet decimated, and the North African air squadron shot to pieces. I assume you thought they were after Condon. But no. They were after you August."

"It doesn't matter what the rebels think of me. They are so close to victory now. A little misinformation cannot stop the tide which is rising against you and the Architect."

The Prophet was pacing back and forth now obviously pleased at having the chance to reveal is deception. "On the contrary August, a little misinformation goes a long way. There are already rebel plots to capture and kill you. Your only chance to survive now is to help me destroy the rebels."

"Id rather die at the hands of the coalition than give you one more ounce of aid," August growled.

"Guards!" The Prophet bellowed. His Praetorians returned to the room. He pointed to me and they grabbed me again. The Prophet pointed to August and they flanked him with guns at the low ready. "If you do not agree, I will kill you right here and now, and the final battle will continue. We may not win, but then again we might," The Prophet said. "I'm willing to take that chance."

"You will never win," August said. "You're trying to kill an idea. Religion is alive in spite of your best efforts, as it has been for thousands of years. There's nothing more resilient. Religion transcends nations, time, and even blood."

"We're not trying to kill religion, August," The Prophet said. "We're trying to create a *new* one. I will take you to my communications headquarters and I give you until sundown to extract an unconditional surrender from the rebels. If you do not, I will expose you to your own soldiers and let them tear you limb from limb."

"The rebels aren't offering their surrender. They're offering a chance at peace," August said.

"If you are not successful, I will kill your man here." The Architect pointed at me.

"I'm not letting him out of my sight," August said as he put his hand on my shoulder.

"Then behold the sight of his death." The Architect motioned for one of the Praetorians to execute me. I grimaced and squeezed my eyes shut as the soldier raised his rifle.

A shot rang out and echoed through the expansive room. I opened my eyes just as the Praetorian dropped his gun, swayed, and fell on the floor. A pool of blood grew around his head in a crimson halo.

Two other Praetorians lunged at The Prophet and ushered him towards the exit at the back of the room, using their own bodies as shields. Three more identified the location of the shooter far up on the roof through an open skylight. They opened fire on the assailant but fell one after another as the shooter picked them off in quick succession.

By the time the shooting stopped, The Prophet was gone. A rope dropped down through the skylight and down slid a fat, little man with a funny hat.

"Simon! You missed!" August snapped. "He was right there."

"Well, excuse me, but I thought I should shoot the people with guns first," Simon said.

After dumping Simon in the sea, I didn't think I'd ever see him again. "You're alive!"

Simon glared at me. "No thanks to you."

"I thought you couldn't shoot?" I asked.

"No. Ass-hole. I said I never miss," he snapped back.

"Let's get out of here," August said. "This place is about to be swarming with guards." He let in Colonel Raptor and the rest of his men who were beating on the door. A medical team brought up a stretcher for me.

"Take him to get his leg looked at," August said as the medics helped me onto the stretcher.

"No," I refused. "I want to stay with you. If this battle happens, there's no telling how it will turn out. I may never find you again."

"You're severely wounded."

"I've been hurt worse than this." I said as I attempted to roll off the stretcher and stand. "It's clean through and the bleeding has stopped."

"Lay down. Lay down!" August said. He turned to the medics. "Keep him near me if you can."

CHAPTER 28

DOUBLE AGENT

Although August was too busy trying to stop the battle from continuing to explain in detail, the revelation of his identity left me wondering one thing. How? How did an orphan and Praetorian officer cadet become the leader of the global resistance? August knew I had questions and he briefly explained to me how it had happened. The root of it was simple: A continual supply of accurate information.

By supplying information on imperial troop counts, troop movements, battle plans, and various other useful bits of intelligence to a wide range of rebel leaders, he had built a network of trust among the resistance, even though none of them had ever met him face to face. Simon had acted as an intermediary and used the cadre of prisoners to communicate between forces. Although August's communications with the coalition of rebels were only one way, he witnessed his desires carried out by coalition forces. August received Imperial intelligence reports relative to his area of operations since he carried an Imperial commission, as well as information from his own loyalist scouts. He took this information and provided it to the rebels, whom he now referred to as "the coalition".

Being careful to protect his own force while dealing maximum damage to the Praetorian in particular, this information was invaluable to the coalition. August was never a diehard loyalist, and his time at the Praetorian school only enhanced his disdain for the globalist empire. He reached a breaking point when he witnessed for himself the callousness of The Architect's efforts to regain his dominion.

After being captured and pressed into service, he initially made all attempts to be a good student and learned the field craft willingly and adeptly. However, the nihilist indoctrination never took root in August; it could not overcome the moral compass which Diana had instilled in him.

Although August initially took up the loyalist cause after the Praetorian school was overrun, he changed when he witnessed their brutal handiwork first-hand. After the destruction of the imperial Baltic Army, the rebel coalition had been able to take much of Northern Europe—especially some of the major cities where they found a new source of sympathetic recruits. Out from under the thumb of The Architect's forces these cities breathed new life into the rebellion. Old Berlin, rechristened Germanica by The Architect, was particularly helpful in supplying new equipment and able bodies.

August and his raiders were assigned to help assist the 78th Praetorian Division to retake the city, but he arrived late. What he found was so profoundly evil that he resolved to never again allow something so horrific to happen. The rebels, seeing that they were vastly outnumbered and outgunned, retreated from the city. The Praetorians, unsatisfied that there was no one to fight, decided to punish the citizens of the city instead.

When August arrived, the streets were filled with rows of men, women, and children who had been lined up and executed. Although an exact count could not be taken, he learned through reports later that over two million citizens were killed. Hardened by this experience, but unable to abandon his command, he sent word to the rebels in the area that the Praetorians were feasting and having a bacchanal time not far from the decimated city. The rebels slipped in among them at night, planted charges throughout the camp, and blew up almost the entire division. Those that fled were picked off by rebels hiding around the camp.

Although August was unsure of its origin, the coalition coined the moniker 'Ovis' for him and spread word of their victory. August continued to provide intelligence to certain rebel factions and the legend grew.

In August's dangerous game, simplicity was his best ally. Short, concise messages relayed through a chain of couriers all in the dark about the bigger picture. August rarely proposed battle plans directly to his coalition contacts. He would supply information presented in a manner that would show his intended target as an opportunity too good to pass up. He would also provide guidance which was not related to any particular goal, such as the messages I had found in his tent on the mountain. These messages were meant to maintain his mysterious relationship with them and to build rapport.

If coalition commanders who he had previously assisted did not heed his warnings or conduct themselves in a manner which he prescribed, he had a solution for that. As commander of a large loyalist force, he had the muscle to punish any rebels who would not obey Ovis's orders. The coalition quickly learned that if you do not heed the word of Ovis, you would suffer at the hands of General August and his loyalists. It was in this way that August balanced precariously between the defender of the empire and its destructor.

Now that it was clear to The Architect and The Prophet that a traitor was in their midst, it was difficult to determine if they would expose him. If they did, August speculated that it would have unintended consequences. Although he did not know who they were specifically, he learned there were many others within The Architect's ranks who were less than loyal— either for selfish or noble reasons. Exposing August could ignite a firestorm of defections which could not be extinguished. Alternatively, even if there was not a massive mutiny, the news was sure to reach the coalition and the moral boost would be a much needed injection for the beleaguered insurgents. August was unsure if being implicated in the massacre could be rectified, but dispatched Simon to try and repair the damage as quickly as he could.

August fully expected that every attempt would be made to exterminate him quietly, but he had only one goal now: He wanted to save as many lives as possible.

Up until then, the coalition forces and The Architect's forces had slowly eroded each other's numbers at a steady rate. The loss of life was terrible, but it was nothing compared to what was to come if August could not stop it. Once The Architect's Eastern Army and the coalition Army of the Americas joined the battle, tens if not hundreds of millions of men and women would go head to head for possession of the Earth and everything that remained. It was sure to be a nightmare for the defeated and victors alike.

CHAPTER 29

SKY ON FIRE

For about a half an hour, there was a deafening silence around the city as The Architect rallied his forces and the coalition formulated their next move. August set up a command tent on a hill in the destroyed Forest of Martyrs overlooking the western edge of the city. He tried furiously to get the word out that a ceasefire was being negotiated and that no units should take any action other than in defense. Communications among units had been somewhat restored, and August's radio operators were still unaware that August was in fact trying to command both the coalition rebels and the loyalists at the same time. They were quite puzzled by his orders to contact coalition units about the ceasefire, but they carried out his commands, nonetheless.

Simon was gone as quickly as he had appeared and was absent for some time that day. Late in the afternoon, there was a commotion outside August's tent. He looked up from his maps as the flap opened wide and Simon entered, followed by Lord DeVonay—commander of the Army of the Americas.

Lord DeVonay was one of the last people alive to hold a genuine royal title after The Architect purged many lineages, trying to stamp out nationalism. He fled to the Americas and was an instant success among the rebellious inhabitants there for his eloquent calls for disobedience. After the governments of the Americas capitulated, both North and South America degraded into an almost feudal society as self-styled warlords gathered the support of those looking for security.

Aided by his genuine title, Lord DeVonay eventually built a sizable force to resist The Architect's stranglehold. While the loyalists and Central Command had controlled much of the coastline, the interior was firmly held by Lord DeVonay's forces and his feudal allies. After The Architect recalled his forces to defend the Holy City, Lord DeVonay made a daring move to break out and was successful in landing an enormous force to move against The Architect directly.

I examined Lord DeVonay as he stood at the door of the tent. He was not a tall man, and had mostly muted features except for an eyepatch over one eye. He was dressed as a common soldier except for the enormous cross around his neck. The light from the tent flap silhouetted him in contrast with the tent's dim interior, and he stood with his arms outstretched in front of him with his palms turned up as a sign of peace.

"You've taken a great risk to be here," August said. "I may not be able to let you leave here alive."

"I don't care for my own life anymore," Lord DeVonay said. "This battle is too important for any one man to hold his own life dear. I've come to bring you something so important I had to deliver it myself." He reached into a satchel and pulled out a yellow box covered with seals. "General August, I'm not sure if you are aware, but the Torch System is complete enough to be fired today."

"What is the Torch System?" August asked.

"My apologies, General," Lord DeVonay said. "It's a kinetic weapons system: A series of seven satellites, each with a rotary magazine of ten high-velocity warheads. My operators have been trying to position them for several days, and in a few minutes they will all be in orbit over the Holy City. This box is the firing module."

"Why have you brought it to me?" August asked.

"Because this is a historic moment. You have done more for our righteous cause than any other person, and I wanted to give you the honor of launching the weapon and dealing the final blow."

"Let's step back for a moment. How do you know who I am?"

"I was given a sign," Lord DeVonay said. "The prisoners you transported here escaped to my lines, and though they were your prisoners, they spoke highly of you. As they came to me, I had them counted. When they had all arrived, there

270

were one hundred and forty four thousand which you had marked. After I was given the sign, I reached out to the other intelligence groups surrounding the city and they told me that you are most likely the Arcani called Ovis. Simon heard that I was making inquiries and he came to find me."

"I don't understand," August said. "Since we are alone, I will tell you that what you say about me is true, but I still don't understand what this 'sign' is."

"You may in time," Lord DeVonay said. "But for now, let us focus on the task at hand."

"There is still a possibility that we can avoid more bloodshed. I'm trying to get both sides to stand down. We may not need to fire the weapon."

"General, The Prophet has withdrawn the Praetorians from the city center. They have met with several regiments of dragoons who just arrived from the north. The Architect is working his way north to Megiddo with as many loyalists as he can muster to form a defensive position. That bastard Kratian Kray has negotiated a fee for his services as well. There's no way this day will end peaceably. The best we can do is try to ensure the outcome. If we fire the full array, we can wipe out tens of millions of The Architect's forces. I will then order a full assault with my forces. It could all be over in a few hours."

"Tens of millions of lives could be saved if we had more time," August said.

"I'm sorry, August," Lord DeVonay said as he opened the latches on the case. "When Ovis asked me to fall back yesterday I did as requested, but I can wait no more. I have to do this. The Architect has taken too much from me. It is time to end him."

As the last seal popped open, Lord DeVonay reached inside and pressed a series of buttons. Lights inside the box began to strobe and a mechanical voice began to count down.

"Undo it!" August yelled as he lunged towards DeVonay, who raised the console high over his head before throwing it violently on the ground. The case and its contents smashed into hundreds of pieces as both men fell to the floor.

"It is done," DeVonay said. "The final battle has begun."

Old Johnny, who had been sitting silently in the corner of August's tent, stood up and raised his hands to the sky. "When the first one blew his trumpet, there came hail and fire mixed with blood, which was hurled down to the earth."

August raced outside. I got up off my stretcher and hobbled out behind him. A low rumble filled the sky. As the kinetic weapons breached the atmosphere, they burned brightly and threw off great plumes of red smoke. The first bolts struck The Architect's forces to the east. The ground trembled as the earth heaved and a massive cloud of debris was thrown into the air. Buildings, vehicles, and soldiers vanished in the cataclysmic blast. As the bombardment continued, the projectiles fell in a precise arc along the northern outskirts of the city.

"Find cover!" August yelled as bits of earth, buildings, machines, and dismembered bodies fell around us. A steady rain of detritus inundated the camp. August and I watched from under a nearby vehicle as the command tent was smashed by a mass of burnt, twisted steel. I tried to spot Lord DeVonay, but he was nowhere to be found. Old Johnny sat praying on the ground just outside the tent.

From our position on the hill, I could just make out the shape of the *Poseidon* still laying beached on the coast. Even though it was twenty some miles away, it could easily target the coalition positions with its twenty-inch guns. It had been steadily firing on the Army of the Americas to our south. Out at sea, the *Poseidon* was a formidable battle station, but lying beached and motionless, it was a mountain of a target.

A single bolt from the Torch System flared through the sky as it descended over the *Poseidon*. It penetrated the ship directly in the middle. A great spout of fire shot out from the entrance hole and the battle station began to roll over into the sea. Moments later, the *Poseidon'* exploded and blinding white light blossomed over the horizon.

I looked away to save my eyes from burning. When I looked back, the sea was a graveyard of broken transports and warships, which had been caught in the blast.

The air was becoming thick with dust. August's communications equipment was destroyed and visibility to all other units was impossible. The Torch's terrible destruction was only the beginning. Now, The Architect played *his* hand. We did not know until later, but despite massive losses, The Architect and The Prophet both survived the bombardment. They unleashed the city's defenses on the coalition forces.

On the cool desert morning after the bombardment, droplets of liquid fell from the sky, soaking the rubble of the city and the parched earth. As the sun rose and the liquid evaporated, it released a gas that seared our lungs. Those already weakened by other circumstances soon suffocated. Soldiers fought in the street for whatever gas masks could be found, exacerbating their inhalation and escalating their demise. The coalition was not the only ones to have developed orbital weapons. And the Architect's penchant for the grandiose was not limited to buildings—it extended to engines of war. Raining a liquid chemical weapon, the satellite named *Apsinthos* killed a great number of coalition and loyalist troops alike.

The next day was almost as dark as the night before. Dust still suspended in the air, along with smoke from burning buildings and funeral pyres, cast the entire city into darkness. I sat with August and what generals he was able to find. His secret had still not been found out by his commanders.

"We need to get out of this city," General Moulin said. "It's nothing but a burning wasteland and smells like rotting corpses. In some areas of the city the gas is still killing people."

"How do we know if we've won or lost?" General Soho asked. "That bombardment was surely the end of the Praetorian, and our scouts are reporting major concentrations of rebels coming up from the south."

"I haven't been in contact with the Praetorian or any Loyalist's for twenty-four hours," General Moulin said. "We don't even know who's left out there."

"We should order a full retreat," General St Clair chimed in. "With no intelligence, we're just sitting here blind, waiting to be annihilated. Other loyalist units have already withdrawn north. Why are we still here?"

"Clear the areas of the city where the gas is still dangerous. It has mostly dissipated on the high ground. Then gather your men and meet me here in an hour," August said. "I want to address everyone."

His generals filed out of the tent and were gone, leaving August and me alone.

275

CHAPTER 30

TURNCOAT

August stood on the roof of a house with a loudspeaker as his forces gathered. He looked out over them for several minutes before raising the loudspeaker to his mouth. The mass of troops was expansive, and they piled onto every scrap of structure and burned-out car or tank trying to get close enough to hear.

"Ladies and gentlemen," he bellowed, "within the hour, Lord DeVonay and his forces will surround our position and demand our surrender." The loudspeaker echoed off the ruined neighborhood. A murmur spread through the crowd. Some soldiers shrieked and yelled curses. "I have been in contact with him, and I have suggested an alternative. I have offered to join him, to hunt down The Architect and The Prophet, and to end this war once and for all." The murmurs and cursing rose to a fevered pitch. Cries of 'traitor' and 'treason' rang out among the crowd. "The Temple is destroyed and the empire has crumbled. There's nothing left to fight for. Nothing left to defend. All of this destruction has been for what? We've suffered for decades trying to bend all the people of the Earth to The Architect's will, and what is our reward? Endless war, disease, famine, and pointless deaths. You can see how little he regards your life and mine. He gassed you, his loyal soldiers, right alongside his enemies. There's only one way for this war to end. The Architect must be defeated."

I tried to gauge the reactions of the soldiers, but they were mixed. Though some still cried out that August was a traitor, the cacophony had settled to a muted rumble as they discussed his words amongst themselves.

At the far reaches of the assembly, the Army of the Americas advanced on our position. Some soldiers at the edge began to press inward, while others turned to face the new threat.

"Hold your fire!" August yelled into the loudspeaker. "For God's sake, hold your fire." I wasn't sure to whom exactly he was speaking, but I assumed it was to both his own troops and to Lord DeVonay's. Several tense minutes passed as August descended to where his other officers and I were standing. The assembled troops opened a path as Lord DeVonay approached us with his bodyguard and some of his own officers.

"I'd like to address your men myself, if I may," Lord DeVonay said as he came into the circle.

"It's unlikely there's anything you can say that will make this easier for them," August said. "They are still digesting what I just said."

"Your kindness and humanity are well known among your men and your enemies, August," DeVonay said. "These men are not here with you because they are loyal to The Architect. They are here because you have drawn them with your actions and compassion. I will appeal to their hearts, as you have."

"If you think you can convince them, then do what you must."

Lord DeVonay and August mounted the house and Lord DeVonay picked up the loudspeaker. "Lay down your arms." August's men hesitantly and reluctantly dropped their weapons at their feat. "Now, pick them up again! Pick them up and raise them high and triumphantly. I do not want to take you as defeated prisoners. I am here today to welcome you as trusted allies. As a sign of faith, you may keep your weapons, your pride, and your dignity. The Architect has been dealt a mighty blow, but the forces of evil will not die or melt away without good men to defeat them.

"I believe that even though you and I have most recently fought against one another, the time of our enmity has passed. You have a chance today to turn your hearts and your weapons over to be instruments of victory, rather than squandering your lives in defeat. The Architect has forsaken everything that is beautiful; he has made the world ugly and cruel for decades. But he and his minions are on their heels.

"Now is the chance for you to join me and say, 'No more blood for his vanity!' If you will join me, turn to my soldiers—who are standing side by side with you—and take their hand in a sign of brotherhood. Together, we will build a new kingdom from today's ashes and end this war forever!"

August's forces looked around at Lord DeVonay's standing silently around them. Somewhat hesitantly, the two groups came together and wove among each other. At first a few, and then many soldiers joined hands and even embraced. August and Lord DeVonay looked at each other and smiled as the alliance solidified. The more enthusiastic of August's men tore off their eagle bands to solidify that they were soldiers of the empire no more.

That night, Lord DeVonay threw a feast. It was a welcome change from the meager rations the Architect offered and helped to convince August's troops they had made the right decision. Many bonfires burned around the city as the coalition took advantage of the lull in the fighting to celebrate. But the joy was short lived. After midnight, several planes flew over the city and leaflets fell from the sky. They were a warning from The Architect, all bearing the same message in many languages:

Woe to those that continue to deny my power over you. I have suffered your attacks, but I live still, and I

shall not be defeated. My legacy is eternal. For those that
wish to live, meet me at Megiddo unarmed, and on your
knees, and I will spare your life. If you do not, I will
unleash the final measures. Submit or be destroyed.

The effect of this message on the soldiery was minimal as
most dismissed it as propaganda. The effect on August and
Lord DeVonay was more aligned with The Architect's
intent. Simon, August and Lord DeVonay discussed how they
should respond.

"What could he possibly have left to throw at us?"
August asked DeVonay.

"Our allies have secured most of the nuclear weapon sites
we know about and have destroyed the delivery vehicles.
However, there are still two units we cannot account for. I'm
not convinced The Architect is bluffing, but surely he would
not destroy the city." DeVonay said.

"Looks pretty destroyed already to me," Simon quipped.

August rolled his eyes but didn't disagree. "Do you have
any idea where the missing missiles might be? Could they be
in range?"

"The missing units are mobile launchers," DeVonay said.
"They could be anywhere. I've ordered potassium iodide pills
to be distributed as quickly as possible, but the doses that
we've brought were hastily made and taste terrible. They seem

to give people stomach aches. Not to mention, that won't help when it comes to the actual blast."

"It will have to do," August said. "Give them something to take it with. Something sweet, if you can."

DeVonay nodded. "I've sent out messengers to the other coalition commanders. They're willing to follow our lead, but they're also concerned about the leaflets. Many of them are wanting to withdraw from the city in case there is a nuclear attack."

"If we withdraw, The Architect will retake the city. This place is a maze of tunnels and bunkers. It could take years to root them out again. It's a miracle they have not already gone underground," August said.

"Then let us go underground ourselves," DeVonay said. "We cannot risk being wiped out. We will continue to send teams to search for the missing warheads, but until then, most of our forces can remain underground. Once the warheads are found, we can deploy to attack Megiddo."

"I don't like losing the momentum we've established, but I don't think we have a choice," August said.

"We also believe the Eastern Army is preparing to attack," DeVonay said. "They've established a staging ground and split their force into four parts. They are so numerous, our scouts on the Euphrates cannot accurately estimate their strength. They are currently spread out over hundreds of square miles. Once they land in the city, their numbers will be overwhelming."

"Do you think we should be preparing for a nuclear attack or for the Eastern Army's assault?" August asked.

DeVonay chuckled nervously. "Why not both? Those tunnels and bunkers can protect us as well as they would The Architect. If he bombs the city, we'll be sheltered. If the Eastern Army attacks, we'll be entrenched. One solution to both problems."

"I'm afraid if we retreat underground," August said, "we will be trapped by the Eastern Army. That's probably why the Architect abandoned them. But if we don't we will be bombed," August said.

"It's a hard decision to make," DeVonay said.

Simon picked up his pack, slung it over his shoulder, and grabbed his rifle. "Let's go. Trapped is better than dead."

August grimaced, but couldn't hide a smile. "I could not agree more."

CHAPTER 31

A ROCK AND A HARD PLACE

DeVonay sent out the message to the other commanders to search for entrances into the city's underground defenses, but The Architect had not left his city totally in the hands of his enemy. There were many traps implanted in the underground lairs. Reports came back from the abyss of ingenious devices intended to maim any intruders. The most common of these was a wall of tiny tubes, each loaded with a small splinter of metal, which when activated launched in quick succession. This soon earned the name "Hornet" or "Locust", for the multiple stinging wounds it inflicted. Some of the traps malfunctioned and fired all at once, filling the tunnels with a thunderous, trumpeting roar. For five days, our engineers worked tirelessly to clear the traps, and we took many casualties from our mechanical enemy. Eventually, our forces made their way underground. Although the tunnel system became crowded, we still had about a third of our forces above ground.

On the sixth day, early in the morning as the sun was coming up, the deafening sound of rotors chopped the air as the Eastern Army's transports blackened the eastern horizon.

The tens of thousands of aircraft made the sky look like a woven cloth with specks of light shining through. The dust kicked up by the low flying-squadrons cast a red haze over the rising sun and setting moon.

The gunships were the first to make contact. They came in low over our lines and let go a salvo of rockets that filled the sky with fire and sucked the air from our lungs. The transports maneuvered behind them to set down and discharge their troops. Wave after wave of them landed for only seconds before rising to make way for more to come in behind them. The eastern army deployed in thick lines stretching for miles along the outskirts of the city.

It was the opportune moment for The Architect to launch his attack. The coalition forces were split above ground and below, and those remaining above ground were outnumbered. The Eastern Army attacked in dense waves against our hastily-made defensive positions. With many of the powerful weapons that had been procured by our forces from the *Poseidon,* as well as artillery from the retreating imperial forces, our troops put up a furious defense and mowed down great swaths of the oncoming horde. What the enemy had intended to be a quick battle achieved by mass charges turned into a hotly contested bloodbath as their attack bogged down in maze of the destroyed city.

Not deterred by their initial losses, and newly informed of the weak points in our defenses, they applied a new strategy. First, they sought out and destroyed our heavy weapons. Although our heavy guns were behind our defensive lines, the enemy pushed hard to penetrate the fortifications. Once they reached our batteries, they spiked the barrels and detonated charges in the chambers, rendering them inoperable. The diminishing firepower neutered our ability to combat their overwhelming strength. Satisfied that our guns were sufficiently silenced, they then began a series of maneuvers intended to make us redeploy our remaining defenses.

At twilight, the sound of rotors again filled the air as transports set down again to the west of the city. Lord DeVonay could not ascertain what portion of the Eastern Army had been redeployed, but guessing by the volume of transports, it was more than half. To protect our flank, some of our troops were redeployed to the west. But as the sun rose, our scouts reported that tens of thousands of empty air transports were sitting there idly with no infantry in sight. A detachment was sent out to destroy the aircraft and prevent another ruse, but having successfully achieved their goal, the Eastern Army renewed their attack on our northern and eastern front. We had little advantage other than the cover provided by the broken, burning city itself. Our hidden soldiers exacted a devastating toll on the attacking enemy, and although they made small gains in ground, they lost a disproportionate number of soldiers.

On the tenth day of the assault, The Architect's forces had nearly decimated a third of our army—and almost the totality of our men who remained above ground. Then, The Eastern Army began a general retreat. They abandoned the positions they had paid dearly for and left behind their wounded and dying. They made all haste to remove themselves entirely from the city. Having wasted many of their transports on their ruse, the fleeing soldiers flowed like a river as they retreated on foot. As news of this spread down into the bunkers, the cheers were deafening in the confined spaces. August, however, was silent as he speculated The Architect's next move—which turned out to be the most sinister yet.

Lord DeVonay was working to get into a bunker several miles away as he sent a message to August. The missing warheads had been located. They were hidden and ready for launch in a grove within range of the city. I stood with August as he read the message to his officers.

Ovis,

A raid has been launched against the missile battery we have discovered, but our forces have been repelled. The missiles are in firing position, and we are expecting that an attack is imminent. Please make haste get your remaining forces secured underground.

Peace to you,

LD

"Get back to your units," August said. "Get them into the tunnels we've cleared no matter what. We must push to take shelter."

We worked feverishly through the night to clear more space below ground, but at eight in the morning our radar operators informed August that missiles were incoming. August was standing just inside the doors of a bunker we were sheltering in as troops shuffled down the tunnel.

"We need to close the doors," a lieutenant said as he helped usher people in.

"I'll do it," August said. He walked over to the door controls and pushed the emergency cycle button. The hydraulics hummed as the heavy steel doors began to close. The panicked soldiers who were in the way started to run towards the shrinking gap, tripping over each other, falling, and some being trampled to death. As the gap closed to less than two feet wide, a few desperate souls leapt into the breach. Those who did not clear the gap were crushed between the doors as they cut off the last rays of sunlight. From outside, we could barely hear the wails of thousands of our men as they pounded on the doors and begged for them to be opened again.

Then we heard the warheads explode.

The high-altitude detonations shook the earth. Debris from the bunker walls and ceiling fell around us. The men who were just inside the door pulled out their radiation pills and took them, and like a wave we saw the rest of the men in the tunnel follow suit. There was a moment of silence as the soldiers lamented their fallen brethren. August stepped off the door control platform and made his way silently through the downtrodden crowd.

CHAPTER 32

THE ROOT OF ALL EVIL

The bunker that August had chosen to shelter in was one of the largest in the city. Though the entrance narrowed as it descended, it eventually opened up into a series of cavernous vaults. It was connected to many of the surrounding tunnels through a network of pipes and railways, all of which were stuffed full of men and supplies. Egregiously well over capacity, the biological needs of the human body soon overtook the bunkers systems. Urine and feces flowed freely across the floor, mixed with blood from the wounded and water from the damaged life support systems. The lower levels were soon ankle-high in revolting sewage.

August inquired among the engineers he could locate if anyone knew of exits outside of the city, but there had not been enough time to map out the tunnels. On the other side of the door through which we entered the bunker was an irradiated wasteland of ash and bone. The filtration systems were not meant for the volume of air needed to sustain millions, and soon the air became dangerous to breath. The need to find an exit became even greater.

On the seventh day, a tunnel-boring machine was found and work began to tunnel north, outside of the anticipated moderate damage zone. Since multiple bombs had been detonated, it was not known where exactly we should try to emerge. The seven days had not been spent idly, and even though conditions were deteriorating, much work was done to link up some of the disconnected tunnels. A network was established which connected most of the remaining coalition units. If the tunnel-boring machine was successful, we would be able to escape our subterranean hell and challenge what remained of The Architect's forces at Megiddo. As the borers worked, scouts continued to search for other openings. On the tenth day after the blast, Simon returned to August with news.

"General," Simon said. "I've found something you must see. No one else knows what we've found. I've not told anyone else. I'm afraid of what it might do."

"What is it?" August said concernedly.

"I can't even say it out loud. I'm afraid it could be the downfall of this army," the Simon replied.

"Very well," August said. "Take me to see."

Old Johnny, who had been sitting nearby, suddenly perked up. "The merchants of the Earth will weep and mourn for her, because there will be no more markets for their cargo: their cargo of gold, silver, precious stones, and pearls; fine linen, purple silk, and scarlet cloth; fragrant wood of every kind, all articles of ivory and all articles of the most expensive wood, bronze, iron, and marble."

August looked at him, then turned and walked away with the Simon. We wound down through the tunnel system to almost the lowest level. The stench of the sewage filtrating down through the passages was overpowering, and we wretched. We had several gas masks among us, which we passed around and shared so that we could catch our breath. The scouts took us to the end of a long tunnel, which had a trolley track running through it. An attempt had been made by the retreating Praetorians to collapse the tunnel, but the scouts had removed enough rubble that a crouched man could fit through.

On the other side was a few more feet of track, then a freight elevator that went straight down. The elevator only held four men, so Simon, myself, General Raptor, and August entered the cab. We rode down the slow elevator for about five minutes. The elevator came to a halt at the bottom and we stepped out into a cavern below. Ankle high water splashed as we slowly shuffled in the darkness. I couldn't even see my hand in front of my face, but I could feel the volume of the room. There was a metallic smell filling the darkness. Simon drew a flare from his bandolier and placed it in his grenade launcher. He fired it, and it lit up a cavern filled with rows and rows of neatly stacked gold, silver, and platinum bars which rose forty feet high for as far as the eye could see. The roughly sawn and bent golden panels from The Temple were carelessly piled in mounds in between the rows and in the isles. We stared in amazement as the flare arced to the other end of the room and fell still burning at the end. The gold shimmered in the light until the flare sputtered out. We turned on our weapons lights to look at the stacks nearest to us.

"It's The Architect's treasure," Simon said. "Presumably, ninety nine percent of all the world's precious metals."

"You were right to bring this information to me," August said. "This information cannot get to the rest of the army."

"There's another problem," the Simon said. "We found a leak. I think one of the city's reservoirs is leaking down through a fissure, and this room will be filled with radiation soon."

"Well, that sounds like one problem solving the other," said August.

"What do you mean?" General Raptor asked. "We'll need this money to rebuild after the war."

"This is too much wealth for mortals to handle," August said. "It will just give us greed for luxury and splendor, and that's not what's going to be needed after the war. Those fruits are gone. I want this filth to be irradiated and lost to us forever."

"It's time to think about how we rebuild," Captain Raptor said. "Who will run the world after The Architect is gone?"

"Those willing to put in the work," August said. "There will be no elites, no castes, and no one will assume their position or have anything without earning it."

"This treasure belongs to everyone," General Raptor said. "It's not your decision to ruin all of this."

"This treasure belongs to no one," August said. "And I will ensure that it never belongs to anyone." He looked at the Simon. "Gather whatever explosives you can and pack the fissure. Once we get the army out of this bunker, we will flood the cavern. I'm trusting you with this task."

"Yes, sir." Simon saluted.

August turned to General Raptor. "The tunnelers tell me that by this time tomorrow, we should breach the surface somewhere around Ramallah. Once we get all of the men out of the tunnel, I will order the charges to be blown and this area will be flooded. If you want to save this gold for yourself, or for posterity, or whatever your plan is, then go and tell the men. But be warned: There is no way to distribute this wealth where anyone will think they were treated fairly. Even if there were, flooding the world with freely obtained gold and silver will unleash something in people that is best not awoken."

We walked to the freight elevator and were silent as it slowly ascended. As we stepped off, General Raptor looked at

293

Simon, "Please fill this tunnel with whatever trash you can find. Make it look like a garbage dump and disable the lift. I'll send some of my men to help you rig the explosives."

We worked our way up to the main chamber and left the saboteurs to do their work. I had been without a penny to my name for several decades, so seeing that overwhelming amount of treasure left me conflicted about what August planned. My mind raced as I lay awake that night, struggling to breath in the putrid air and pondering how the gold could be divided after the war. The coalition was sure to win, assuming they could deploy from a single tunnel without being found out. Perhaps we could delay detonating the tunnel until after we knew the battle was won. Then there would be more time to consider what to do with it.

We could divide it evenly among the survivors of the battle, victor and defeated. However, a gold or silver bar is hard to spend, and the savvier recipients were sure to cheat their way to a greater share. We could gather it all and dispense it to newly formed governments sure to form following the war. But the coalition was not exactly a cohesive force. Often misaligned and with open distrust between zealots and nationalists, there was destined to be further conflict— even without vast amounts of wealth to divide up.

If The Architect and his government did perish, there would be a tremendous power vacuum. Although August and

Lord DeVonay were both prominent within the coalition, they were not the only leaders present in the Holy City. Not to mention the dispersed warlords and strong men who would likely want to claim a portion for themselves. Most notably, Kratian Kray had a sizable force. His whereabouts were unknown to us. He had only agreed to come to the city to secure his own income in the first place. On top of that, he was still aligned with The Architect and likely not privy to August's duality. Perhaps the treasure could be used to entice Kratians's loyalty to turn? What would then stop him from taking the entire haul for himself? There was no doubt that at least a small number of our enemy waiting at Megiddo were aware of the treasure. Should they survive, would they seek to reclaim it either by force or by guile? Even if we did irradiate the cache lying below the city, how do we know that a portion was not removed or lay still unfound in other tunnels and caverns? Would an even smaller hoard be even more precious, and how dearly would fortune seekers sell their lives to get it?

At some point among my musings, I drifted off to sleep and began to dream. Molten gold flowed like rivers through the land and pooled in the bomb craters. Soldiers ran to drink from the glowing pools and were burned alive from the inside out. The air was a hazy red that obscured visibility. Silver bars rained from the sky like hail and struck men down with sickening thuds as their skulls and bodies were crushed. Their broken bodies littered the burned landscape, and from them grew terrible plants and trees with thorns and grotesque flowers that smelled fowl and poisoned the air. I stumbled up a narrow path of a steep hill. I climbed the hill as silver bars crashed around me, and at the top I saw August's mother. Not Diana, but his *real* mother who perished years ago. Her face was as plain to me as the day I saw it. She was lying as I had found her in the street, straining to give birth. I walked towards her, but even though I walked and walked, I drew no closer. From all around her, the red smoke that engulfed us thickened and swirled into a long, red, twisted rope that looked like a tornado, but which writhed like a serpent as it coiled and enveloped the woman. As the tail of the tornado touched the ground, it became the form of a man with burning eyes and robes of ashes. He reached for the woman as August emerged from her womb—.

I was jolted awake as one of August's soldiers shook me violently. "They're through," he exclaimed. "They've broken through and we're trying to get out. Let's go!"

"Where's August?" I asked.

"He's already outside directing the evacuation. We have to clear the area before The Architect figures out what's happening."

I gathered my kit and joined the teaming mass of soldiers hustling through the tunnel system. At the end of the established network the floor was littered with debris from the newly-dug tunnel. It was thirty feet wide and gently sloped up for several mile. Some of the spoils from the excavation had been packed in the bottom half the round hole to make a wider flatter path. A pinhole of light sparkled through the dust stirred up as hundreds of thousands of emaciated and sickened men shuffled up the long tunnel.

As we got closer to the exit, the pace picked up. By the time we were less than a mile from the surface, most soldiers were at a run. Some of them tried to run on the sloping sides of the tunnel to get ahead. Some were successful, but some fell only to be trampled before being dragged to their feet again. At some points, the tunnel was obstructed by debris from minor cave-ins. There had been no time or material to reinforce the sides. It made the going rough, but it could not stop the desperate troops from surging on. Soon, I felt a gentle breeze from the entrance and the electrical odor from the ionization of ozone resulting from the nuclear blast.

I exited the tunnel only to be pushed forward by a team who were urging the men not to stop until they were far away from the tunnel. To prevent a build-up August had deployed hundreds of ushers to fan out from the tunnel and push people onward. The tunnel exited from the side of a low hill into a wide valley. Rather than continue with the other soldiers, I looped around to stand on the hill above the exit. From where

I stood, millions of soldiers flowed out for miles like a wide river delta. I didn't notice him at first, but August was also watching from above and walked over to greet me.

"Sorry," he said. "I couldn't find you when we started the evacuation. I'm glad you made it out."

"This is a miracle," I said.

"It will be a miracle if we can get organized. Lord DeVonay has also found an exit several miles from here. There's no sign of any of The Architect's forces, but it's only a matter of time."

General Soho joined us on the hill. "General," he panted. "This is a mess. There's no food. There's no water. Many of the units are spread apart, and there's no command structure or communications. It's like we're starting from scratch here."

"Tell them to find water first and to form new units," August said. "We don't have time to try and reform the old ones. Appoint as many new officers as you need to create new brigades. Once they've amassed three- to five-thousand troops, have them deploy from west to east, starting at Netanya. Find General Moulin and ask him to try and set up communications as best he can. Find General St Clair and have him send out scouts to locate Kratian Kray, The Architect, The Prophet, and Admiral Hess with what's left of the Eastern Army. We need to strike at the heads to kill the body."

He turned to a lieutenant who was standing nearby. "Go find Lord DeVonay and relay our message to him. He needs to know our plan."

The lieutenant saluted and ran off.

The evacuation continued for three days. General Raptor was given charge of ensuring all the troops, including wounded and prisoners, made it out of the tunnel. August and I waited for Raptor to report back at the mouth of the tunnel as he and a few scouts trudged out.

"It's all prepared," Raptor said. "Here's the detonator. There's thirty-eight hundred pounds of TNT and artillery shells sitting in the tunnel by the fissure. I'm not an engineer, but I do know it's not going to make the hole any smaller."

Raptor handed the detonator to August. August held it for a minute as he stared into the tunnel. After what was now an uncomfortably long time, I reached out my hand. August looked over and handed me the detonator. I gave the dial one long crank, and a second later a low rumble echoed up the tunnel. That was the end of The Architect's treasure, at least for the next thousand years or so.

CHAPTER 33

THE MESSAGE

Presumably surprised at the coalitions escape from underground, The Architect's forces continued to expand his fortification to our north. It was a blessing since August's forces took over a week to get into position. Starting at Netanya by the sea and stretching all the way to Ramallah, the newly formed brigades arrayed for battle. Lord DeVonay did the same with his forces, starting at Ramallah and reaching east to the Jordan river. The remaining coalition forces were put in reserve behind the battle line in anticipation of plugging gaps once the battle started.

Scouts reported a large number of Central Command regulars and loyalists at Megiddo, and from this information August anticipated The Architect was entrenched there. Kratian Kray was encamped to the west but was not dug in or arrayed for battle. He deployed large patrols daily that rode across his sector. To the east, Praetorian, presumably under the command of The Prophet, were spread out in fortified positions with interlocking fields of fire from Megiddo to the Sea of Galilee. Other loyalist units were stationed at positions of importance such as hills, towns, or villages to act as sticking points against the coalition's advance. Although our miraculous emergence from the city's tunnels had surprised The Architect's forces, they made good use of our disarray to organize themselves.

Every night, August ordered an advance towards The Architect's main line. We were, at this point, close enough to the enemy positions that a nuclear strike would enact mutual destruction. Lord DeVonay urged a withdrawal so the bombs he had secured from The Architect's stockpile could be used, but to our back was a nuclear wasteland and before us was the entire Imperial army. Unfortunately for everyone, this battle was going to be fought between soldiers face to faces. When the coalition retreated underground, they were forced to abandon all mechanized advantages. Except for an extremely small number of light small field guns, the coalition forces were completely composed of light infantry armed with rifles and a few magazines of precious ammunition.

Thankfully, the kinetic barrage took out most of the Praetorian's tanks and other armor. Our scouts reported that The Architect was joined from the north by late-arriving reinforcements from Siberia and several regiments of Dragoons, who he deployed in front of his main lines to skirmish. The main body of the Eastern Army was nowhere to be found. However, we could see, behind the Architect's lines, rows and rows of gunships waiting to be scrambled to repel our advance. The Siberian troops brought with them artillery and additional mounted troops to reinforce Kratian's cavalry. The addition of fresh soldiers to The Architect's army more than evened the odds, and the coalition commanders were expressing concern that victory was likely to be hotly contested.

Elements of August's forces closed to within three miles of The Architect's lines. Although there was a limited exchange of artillery fire and minor skirmishes, no major action had taken place. August called a council of war to discuss how best to approach a more conclusive battle. Although many of the coalition commanders were still wary of August's sudden change in loyalties, Lord DeVonay assured them of his genuine intent to defeat The Architect. The coalition commanders reluctantly agreed to meet. From August's camp came General Soho, General Moulin, General St Clair, and General Raptor. Lord DeVonay brought himself and his two most loyal officers: General Nusair and General Perez. There was also General Rawat, who August and DeVonay had appointed to organize the reserve forces and to try and find food, water, and supplies. In addition, there were dozens of regional commanders representing the hundreds of units from all over the world who had come to the siege, as well as runners to relay plans to the dispersed coalition forces.

August was aware the various leaders were wary of his sudden emergence to the forefront of coalition leadership, not to mention many of them were already thinking ahead to their own post war ambitions.

He began with a plea for unity.

"Gentlemen, I have not had the honor of meeting some of you personally, so I will briefly introduce myself. My friends and soldiers call me August, but to you I have been known for some time as Ovis." There were looks of surprise from some of the less well-informed commanders. "The coming battle will test us harshly, and we can only be victorious if we work together. I know some of you are very seasoned and accomplished leaders, but I entreat you to pledge your cooperation with each other and with me to accomplish what must be done. Will you make that pledge?" August's own generals agreed mostly in unison. There was a consensus of nods by most present.

However, not all were convinced. "You must answer for what you did at Bellinzona!" someone yelled from the back of the crowd. A murmur arose as the commanders considered the accusation.

Lord DeVonay was unmoved by the tentative display of loyalty and mistrust from some of the other generals. "I am ashamed of some of you," Lord DeVonay said. "General August has provided us with invaluable information time and time again. How can you believe that he was in any way responsible for what happened there? No one has done more damage to the Empire than he, no one has undermined The Architect more than he, and no one has let us glimpse at any hope of victory more than he.

"It is true. Some of you have faced August on the battlefield before. But reflect on what why that might have happened. I have heard of some detestable things you have done to each other." He paused for moment. "When I first received a message from Ovis I was mistrusting. But when I have followed his advice, I have been met with success, and when I have not, I nearly met disaster. I do not know all your stories, but I assume if you look back on your campaigns you may say the same. I stand with General August because I know he is genuine. He has secretly guided us to countless successes with no thought to glorify himself. Not one of us knew until recently the man who was the legend. If you were the most powerful man in the world could you keep it a secret?" Many around us were looking crestfallen as the scolding soaked in. "Stand up and make your pledge! If we do not show solidarity now, we are already defeated."

Confronted with the fact that their display of cooperation was lacking some of the commanders now stood and faced August. "We pledge our support," they said one by one.

Satisfied there was agreement, August continued, "I've called you all here tonight to learn what you have seen from your positions, and to discuss your preparedness for battle. I know that we are lacking many things, but there is one thing that is not missing: The resolve and the bravery to fight this final battle is in great supply. I see it as I watch our forces every night inch closer and closer towards our enemy. Even so, the effort to win will be the greatest test of our resolve.

"The Architect's forces and ours are arrayed in parallel lines from the sea to the river Jordan. There's little room for complex maneuvers and absolutely no element of surprise. I believe that they are awaiting our attack, and since they know which direction it will come from—and most likely how many men we will be throwing at them—I'm sure they feel well prepared to meet our advance.

"What I am asking you tonight is if there is anything that we can use to tip the scale. I am told that we have only a few days supplies left and almost no water. If we don't engage soon, we'll be forced to withdraw. Since we can't go south or west, our only choice would be to go east across the desert, where it will be no better. If we turn our back on The Architect we may never have the chance to face him again."

"The Praetorians are well prepared," General Nusair said. "They have prepared heavily fortified strong points. If we try to attack their positions, we will suffer heavily. The Architect is still constructing positions, and the Severots are sitting round their camps and feasting. We should mass our forces in the west and try to drive off the Severots. If Kratian Kray retreats, we may have a direct shot at The Architect's flank, and then we can attack the Praetorians from behind."

"It's a good plan," General St Clair said, "but we will be woefully exposed as we move our forces across the entire imperial line. If they wheel around behind us, or if we fail to drive off the Severots, we may be pinned against the sea. I suggest we execute a full-frontal attack all the way across the line. They will be unable to coordinate their reserves if we all attack at once. We will send our reserves into the center and split their forces in two then fight our way from the middle towards their flanks."

"I will not attack the Praetorians in a frontal assault," General Perez said. "Assuming we can even reach their lines, we will be so decimated there will be no hope of victory."

"We should make small, probing attacks," General Moulin said. "Send in the light infantry to find poorly defended areas or areas concealed from direct fire. Once a weak point is found, we will follow up with the rest of the infantry to break through."

General Soho argued, "The Severots may seem like the weak point because they have constructed no fortifications, but their strength lies in mobility. They can travel faster than our foot soldiers. They don't need a front line. They will move their line to meet our advance."

Lord DeVonay and August looked at each other with forlorn gazes. The generals continued to bicker among themselves, trying to agree on a plan.

General Rawat worked his way to where August and Lord DeVonay were seated. "Sirs," he said. "We have scoured the land from our line for as far south as we dare, and all the wells have been poisoned. We have attempted to harvest what food we can, but it is poor quality and possibly contaminated. Unfortunately, I can say with confidence there will be little breakfast tomorrow—and nothing after that."

"Thank you for your honest assessment," August said. "Have you found anything else useful?"

"Just some fuels, but we do not have anything which might use them."

"How archaic," Lord DeVonay said.

"There is one more thing," Rawat said. "My scouts intercepted a Severot patrol, and although the outcome of their skirmish was inconclusive, we did capture one of their officers. Would you like to talk to him, or should we dispose of him?"

"Get rid of him," Lord DeVonay said.

"Wait," August said., "Bring him to me. I would like to talk to him."

The meeting of the generals concluded with no definitive plan of action. August told them that there was no food or water coming, so tomorrow the attack must commence or we must retreat. They agreed on a time and place for a final council and everyone departed. I followed August to a dug-out bunker. Simon was there already, and Rawat brought the Severot officer with him.

"Thank you, General Rawat," August said. "I will take care of him from here."

Rawat saluted and left with his officers and men.

"Untie him," August said to Simon.

August pulled over a small piece of paper from the table beside him and drew a small sketch. "Take this to Kratian Kray," he said to the Severot officer. "Tell no one but him from whom the message comes, and tell no one what it says. If you agree to do this, I will spare your life."

The Severot took the paper and studied it. He nodded in agreement.

"Simon," August said. "Put a bag over his head and retie him. Once you get to the edge of camp, release him. From there, it will be up to him to get the message through. Return to me for further instructions."

"It will be done, sir," Simon said as he retied the prisoner and led him out of the tent.

CHAPTER 34

OCCUPATIONAL HAZARD

We waited for several hours and tried to sleep. Simon came in around midnight and spoke with August, who sent him away again. In the early morning, August shook me awake and we climbed into a small vehicle along with Simon and a few bodyguards. We drove for about half an hour, passing the front line into no man's land. A stiff breeze had cleared most of the dust plaguing the battlefield and a bright moon lit our way. The vehicle's lights were turned off to avoid detection, so the moonlight made the going a little easier. The shadows played tricks on my eyes and made my heart race as every tree and bush seemed to play the part of an enemy soldier. We stopped at the edge of an expansive field filled with tall sugar cane.

We crept through the field until we reached a small clearing. Simon whistled, like a bird. We waited as the stalks on the other side of the clearing swayed in the moonlight. Kratian Kray, mounted on his horse along with his bodyguards, broke through the leaves and into the clearing. In his palace he had been dressed in all manner of finery. Now he was armored from head to toe and bandoliers stuff with knives and pistols hung all over his chest. He wore a great helmet with a large crest in the front. The Severots came to a stop within speaking distance of where we stood.

"Thank you for coming," August said. "I'm sure you're curious about why I would want to meet with you."

"It's you who should be curious," Kratian said, "about why would I meet with any traitorous bastard on the eve of battle. Tomorrow, you and your army will be ashes and dust. I will ride over your bones and laugh."

"I *am* curious," August said. "Why have you come?"

"The Architect has offered a reward for your capture alive. On top of the fee I expect for my part in the battle, there will never be one richer than I." Kratian drew his pistol and his bodyguards sighted their carbines on our party. They encircled us with their mounts. As they drew closer, August, Simon, and the bodyguards threw open their coats to expose rows and rows of explosives wired to their chests.

Kratian's horse bucked as he urged it backward.

"You may take August to The Architect if you want, but it will be in a bucket," Simon yelled.

"I expected treachery from you!" August bellowed. "The gold, the silver, platinum, and gems—everything that you came for—is gone!"

"What are you talking about?" Kratian asked. "The Architect and I have already negotiated my fee. I may be little

310

more than a mercenary, but my services do not come cheaply."

"Your fee will be nothing except death," August said.

"That's a bold threat, considering you and your friends seem to be a little shy about opening this battle," Kratian said.

"I found The Architect's treasure deep in the city," August said. "It's ruined for us, for all men, forever."

"No amount of earth and rock will keep me from my fee. I will dig for the rest of my life to get to it, and I'll use the rubble to bury you and your traitorous friends," Kratian snarled.

"The treasury has been irradiated. It's all been thoroughly poisoned. You can try and dig it out, but you'll never be able to use it."

"I accept many forms of payment," Kratian said. "I had hoped for gold and silver, but I will take grain or wine, steel or lead, slaves, titles, lands. We have not known each other for long, but surely you have heard that I don't care who pays me or by what means. However, I care that the agreements made to me are honored.

"Since it seems that The Architect will come up short when all of this is over regardless of who is victorious, I will give you a one-time chance to make me an offer I can't refuse. What will the rebellion give me that The Architect cannot?"

"I will offer you amnesty," August said. "And I will assure your place in the new order of things after the war. If The Architect wins, you won't need it because the remaining coalition will be hunted down and eradicated. If the coalition is successful, you will need protection from their retribution. I will personally guarantee you will be allowed to return to your lands and keep them to govern."

"What will my role in the battle be for such a paltry price?" Kratian asked.

"All you must do is nothing," August said. "Do not engage my forces, and they will pass you by. If you fail to protect The Architect's flank, his line will likely crumble; and we will defeat him."

"I think I can do better than that," Kratian said as he turned his horse to ride away.

"Does that mean you accept?" August called after him.

Kratian did not reply as he rode away. The stalks of the cane waved in the breeze as his men disappeared into them.

"What do you make of that?" I asked.

"It could mean he has a better offer from The Architect, or it could mean he sees something I do not," August said.

"Shall I take him now?" Simon asked as he raised his grenade launcher.

"No," August said. "It's in his hands now."

We worked our way out of the cane field, checking for ambushes as we withdrew. As we approached the vehicle, Simon suddenly knelt and signaled for the rest of us to do the same. Ahead in the moonlight, our vehicle was surrounded by several dismounted Imperial Dragoons. After a few minutes, a small four-wheeler joined the other Dragoons. As they dismounted, I could see by the gait of his walk and the shape of his body that Ajax had come to inspect their find.

"Take off your vests," Simon whispered.

Everyone threw off their explosive vests. Simon gathered them up and disappeared behind us. A few minutes later, he fired a flare from a hundred yards to our rear. The dragoons jumped into their vehicles and raced into the cane field. As soon as they passed us, we ran to our vehicle. We climbed in and waited anxiously for Simon to return.

The clicks of two pistols safeties made me jump in my seat.

"What do we have here?" I heard a familiar voice say. I turned my head slowly and out of the corner of my eye I saw Ajax standing behind us pistols drawn. "Why don't you all step out so I can get a better look at you?"

We stepped out slowly and faced Ajax. I glanced at my rifle sitting buttstock towards me on the seat next to me.

"Well, I'll be damned," He said as he recognized me. "Looks like another family reunion."

"We're trying to get some information on the rebel positions," August said.

"Well, I find that interesting since you probably know more about the rebels than anyone in The Architect's ranks," Ajax said. "Nice try though. If there wasn't a massive bounty on your head, I might just let you go out of sentimentality."

"I guess it's not a secret anymore?" August asked.

"Oh no. You're a very notorious traitor now. I'm going to be rich as a lord when I turn you in."

Behind Ajax a shadow caught my eye in the moonlight. I tried not to fixate on it or make Ajax suspicious.

"Introduce me to your team here Daniel," Ajax requested politely.

"I looked to my left. "This is Abay Dhar."

Ajax fired a round directly into Abay's head. "Don't need you Abay"

"Stop this!" August shouted.

"Who's this?" Ajax said as he pointed his guns at the man to my right. I said nothing and looked at the ground.

"Don't need you no name," Ajax said as he fired both pistols into the man next to me.

Ajax was standing directly in front of me. "I expected better from you Daniel. We've been fighting rebels for decades. How could you roll over and betray your own kind?"

I glanced over Ajax's shoulder and in the moonlight a shoeless Simon was creeping up the path, knife in hand. I stared in Ajax's eyes. "We're all the same. Just desperate men waiting for our turn to die."

Simon was almost to Ajax and he lunged making a scuffing sound in the gravel path. Ajax ducked down to one knee and as Simon's body flew over him he fired both pistols into Simon's chest. Simon fell face first at my feet. I knelt down and rolled him over. Blood poured from his mouth and nose.

"So close knife boy," Ajax said.

"Hey ass-hole," Simon gurgled, "Enjoy the fireworks." Simon clutched his breast pocket and pressed the button of the remote detonator inside. Seconds later the explosive vests hidden in the cane field erupted in fire and the sound of ball bearings ripping through the cane was followed by the cries of Ajax's wounded troopers. In the confusion Ajax had glanced away for only a second, but it was enough time for me to grab my rifle. As his head turned to look at me again I shot a round straight through his chin which sent a shower of brain and skull flying out behind him in the moonlight. He fell like a log flat on his back without even a twitch. August rushed to Simon who was gasping for air as the blood soaked the ground around him.

"Hold on," August pleaded. "I still need you."

"No. I quit," Simon said. "You're dangerous to work for." Simon went limp and his breathing stopped completely.

August started at his lifeless companion in silence.

"I'm sorry, but we have to get out of here," I said. "That explosion was bound to draw some attention,"

"Let's take his body," August croaked. "I want to bury him."

"Let's leave it," I whispered, "Simon's not in it anymore. He's in here now." I poked August in the heart.

We jumped in the vehicle and headed back towards our lines as fast as the moonlit roads would allow.

August made sure to warn the front line that we would be returning, but we had some difficulty finding the same place where we had crossed when we left. Combined with the changing of the watch, there was some difficulty in crossing back over. Finally, August found men under General Soho's command, and we waited under guard as General Soho made his way to us to authenticate that August was who he said he was. The sun was just beginning to rise as General Soho came racing down the road on a motorbike. He came to a sudden stop just feet from August in a cloud of dust.

"General August," he panted. "You must return to your men. The Severots have abandoned their posts and are attacking The Architect's reserves. We must strike now!"

"This is it," August whispered.

CHAPTER 35

THE ASSEMBLED

August wasted no time getting to his troops. General Moulin had scrounged together enough communications equipment that the Generals could stay in contact with each other. With the help of signal flags and flares, the newly formed network of brigades could be loosely controlled. Moulin procured for August a small tablet which was linked to a satellite network, giving August a bird's-eye view of the entire battlefield from the Holy City to Megiddo and slightly beyond. August asked me to hold the tablet and to give him updates as I saw events unfold. It was a chilling way to see the battle.

Having never seen such a multitude of soldiers, it was hard to comprehend. There were over fourteen-thousand brigades spread out over nearly forty miles. Once the soldiers were amassed, they formed a dark, undulating ribbon a mile deep as they advanced towards The Architect's lines. From all over the world, the coalition had gathered a great concentration of soldiers and mercenaries. Zealots and Nationalists stood side by side in opposition to decades of The Architect's oppressive rein. The soldiers flowed like a tide around buildings and walls, over hills, and through valleys. Where rivers and canals ran, the black ribbon was cut and pinched as they crossed bridges and causeways. From the tablet, I saw the Imperial positions. They were arrayed in a dense patchwork of fortifications and trenches. Behind The Architect's lines, fires burned, and explosions flared as Severots cut wide swaths through his reserves. The gunships which the Eastern Army had brought with them lay smoking by the thousands as Kratian destroyed them on the ground.

General Moulin was commanding his own troops, but he radioed to August to give him updated reports.

"The latest intel indicates The Architect's force consists of at least ten distinct commands, divided among seven different commanders," Moulin said. "In the center are the European Central Command regulars and Loyalist auxiliaries. Next to the European command, the African Central Command has prepared fortified positions. They are supported by additional auxiliaries. Together, these four units are commanded by one general who we have not identified. Directly behind the center, intending to serve as reserves is the Siberian Central Command under a separate general. On the flanks of the Central Command units at the center are the Confederated Loyalists, split between Lord Halifax in the east and General Crease in the west."

"Where are the Praetorians? Have they responded to the Severots attack?" August asked. "We need to capture The Prophet as well to end this once and for all."

"The Praetorians are still on the east of The Architect's position."

Although Moulin did not mention them, between the Imperial forces and ours, darting around and firing wildly into our ranks, were the unpredictable Dragoons. The remainder of the Eastern Army presumably still under the command of Admiral Hess had not yet been located.

With Kratian and the Severots in the west gone there was an opportunity to flank The Architect.

"Signal General Soho and General St Clair to wheel to the northeast," August said to his radio operator. After an hour or so I could see on the console as they pivoted off August's location at the center where he and General Moulin commanded. As they pivoted, General Soho was able to stretch his line far to the north and intersect The Architect's right flank. In the east, Lord DeVonay hesitated to advance on the Praetorians. With The Architect being flanked, and with the Severots behind their lines harassing the reserves, the Praetorians divided their force. Those Praetorian units closest to the center moved to reinforce The Architect. The fortified positions were left with a skeleton crew to man the heavy weapons. Those Praetorians who were farthest east withdrew to the north. As they retreated, they deployed a thick smoke screen and millions of The Architect's best forces seemingly disappeared from the battlefield.

Around noon General Soho reached August on the radio, "We have overrun the Central Command's western flank, but they are redeploying to repel us. You must engage!"

"We have no way to soften The Architect's frontal defenses. We will be crossing open ground straight into their fire. August replied."

"I'm looking straight down their trenches. We have been firing enfilade on General Crease's Loyalists all morning. You must attack now before we are repelled.". At General Soho's urging August and Moulin advanced making a frontal assault against The Architect's defenses. As the remaining Praetorians attempted to move against August and Moulin, Lord DeVonay slammed into their advancing troops and a furious battle ensued. The Praetorians marksmanship was negated as hand-to-hand fighting broke out and stalled the advance of both forces.

General Perez, who had been the most hesitant, now saw a gap between the river Jordan and the Praetorians' eastern flank. He had with him a small contingent of mechanized infantry cobbled together from the armor abandoned by the Praetorians after the kinetic barrage. With these forces, General Perez forced his way through the gap. Now behind them, he harassed the fortified positions the Praetorians had left behind weakly defended.

August and Moulin's troops faltered as the front line became a low mound of bloody bodies. The trauma caused many soldiers to turn and run. Others took their own lives rather than await their fate. Just as Moulin's line was about to thin to the point of breaking, General Rawat applied his reserves, and the momentum pushed the center over The Architect's defenses.

The Severots had mopped up The Architect's reserves and looped around to the east, attacking the Praetorians from behind. General Perez had apparently not been informed of the Severots change of heart, and even though he had a clear shot at the Praetorians' rear, withdrew; thinking that the Severots were reinforcing them. Dust and smoke from the battlefield obscured observation and visual communications. General Perez and General Nusair reformed and slowly advanced. As they pushed north, they observed the Severots, who had now turned their attention to the Praetorians locked in mortal contest with Lord DeVonay. The Severot cavalry reformed a solid line parallel to the rear of the Praetorians, and in one coordinated charge they slammed into their lines from behind. The Praetorians broke and made a desperate dash to rally with the Central Command to defend Megiddo.

Encouraged by the realization the Severots were now allies, General Perez again used his mechanized infantry and he sent them racing northward. They met with the left flank of General Soho. This left The Architect's remaining forces cut in two. The Central Command and Loyalists concentrated around Megiddo were encircled in the west, and the remaining Praetorians—along with a good number of Lord Halifax's surviving Loyalists—withdrew to the northeast.

"I'm looking at the situation," I said to August as the tablet revealed the envelopment, "They cannot escape."

"Ceasefire!" August yelled at his radio operator. "Order all units to cease fire." But the momentum could not be stopped.

August gathered several radio operators and I followed him as we raced to a waiting vehicle. We raced across the killing fields. The coalition forces constricted until only Tel Megiddo stood above the writhing throng. An ancient hill of ruins which overlooked the plains beyond, it was the tallest landmark in that area of the battlefield. As we approached the hill August dismounted and joined the mass of soldiers assaulting the last remaining fortifications. The coalition soldiers forced their way up the hill, as the loyalists threw down their weapons and begged for mercy.

As August approached the center of the hill, the fighting died down. A ring of Praetorians, fully armored and holding ballistic shields, formed a testudo around a cloaked and hooded figure. The soldiers surrounding the testudo backed away to let August walk around the formation.

"It's over!" he yelled at the figure. "Give yourself up so you may be judged." The Praetorians did not flinch as the coalition soldiers began to close in around them again.

"It's never over," said the muffled voice of the figure buried deep within the Praetorian ranks. "The ending of each battle is the beginning of the next. So it has been, and so it will be forever."

"That may be true," August said, "but this day is done. *Your* battle is over. Your temple is destroyed and your empire has gathered here to fight against you."

"*Your* battle is just beginning," the hooded figure growled. "You have not won half of what you think you have."

A look of concern grew on August's face.

"Reveal yourself!" August yelled.

The testudo opened like a flower and the hooded figure removed his disguise to reveal himself as The Prophet. August was obviously shocked. Without The Architect's death or capture, the war would continue.

"As I said, young August," The Prophet laughed. "It's never over."

Though it took great force of arms and battering, the coalition on Tel Megiddo finally beat their way through the Praetorians to kill or capture them, and eventually to take in hand The Prophet, who laughed hysterically even as his captors beat him. August was standing with his radio operators, trying to understand the status of the rest of the coalition units, when General Moulin came bursting through the crowd. He frantically shoved people away and tripped as he made his way to August.

"August! We were wrong," General Moulin yelled. "Lord DeVonay has learned The Architect isn't at Megiddo, he's at the mountain seen from Megiddo. He must be at Mount Tabor."

Far away across the burning plain piled with the dead and dying, Mount Tabor blackened as the remaining Praetorians ascended the slopes. They took up the positions which had been prepared for them by the Eastern Army. While the coalition had been focused on Megiddo, The Architect had been busy fortifying the mountain with the remainder of the Eastern Army. August grabbed the tablet from me and zoomed in on the hill. I looked over his shoulder as he examined the images. It had become a terraced mound of trenches, fox holes, low stone walls, barbed wire, and landmines.

"Do we know how Lord DeVonay's forces are holding up?" August asked Moulin. "I can't contact any of his units.

"I've just been in contact with his headquarters," Moulin said. "He has peeled off and is making a drive for Mount Tabor with all of his forces."

"He must wait for reinforcements!" August exclaimed.

"We have another problem," August's radio operator said. "There's a whole division of the Eastern Army that was late in arriving. It's mostly armor, so they are still days out, but they are sending air transports to extract The Architect. If we don't get to him before they do, he may yet escape."

"General Moulin," August said, "order all units to redeploy to Mount Tabor."

"It's fourteen miles away and the bulk of all our forces are concentrated here," Moulin said.

"I might have a solution for that," a voice from the crowd said. Kratian Kray approached August through the throng of soldiers. "I will send my horsemen across the plain and reinforce Lord DeVonay until you can form up your men."

"You have saved us all already once today," August said.

"I told you I could do better than your offer," Kratian said.

"How could you turn so easily on The Architect?" August asked.

"If there's one thing I hate, it's a man who owes me money," Kratian smiled.

CHAPTER 36

REQUIEM

The Severots rode at a gallop to the base of Mount Tabor. Their horses foamed at the mouth and sweated profusely, spent and nearly dead. Lord DeVonay nearly, mistakenly engaged them as they approached his exhausted troops. But after the change of loyalty had been discovered, together they circled the mountain as the Praetorian attempted to repel them. The thundering hooves drove up a cloud of dust that nearly obscured the mountain.

General Perez's remaining mechanized infantry arrived next. He ordered them to charge up the hill, but as they began to ascend, a ring of landmines destroyed them one after another. The burning hulks blocked the path of those behind them, and the assault was stopped in its tracks. Although the result of the charge was not as intended, the mangled personnel carriers now provided cover for the infantry and the survivors as they dismounted and returned fire.

The bulk of August troops, already exhausted, traveled slowly and were stretched out between Megiddo and Mount Tabor. They trudged along through the searing heat. Some of the more cohesive units formed columns and marched with purpose, while the other disjointed and unaffiliated soldiers took their time and looted the dead along the way. August had been able to secure vehicles for himself and some of his officers, and they arrived ahead of the men to establish some form of a line of battle. Lord DeVonay had suddenly become blind with rage and overcome with blood lust. August tried desperately to temper his desire for a hastily prepared charge. With August's forces now beginning to form up in some density on the west side of the mountain, Kratian Kray took up position on the east side; effectively surrounding The Architect's forces and trapping them. This was no surprise. The Architect and his followers had already sealed their fate intending to either die on the mountain or make the coalition break themselves upon the defenses.

No headway was made on either the east or west side of Mount Tabor, although there was a furious and continuous exchange of fire throughout the night. By morning, August and Lord DeVonay accumulated enough of a force they felt ready for a final push. The order was given to advance across the line. As the troops moved forward, several dozen Imperial aircraft emerged from the clouds and descended towards the mountain top.

"We're too late!" I said to August.

"The Architect may escape this battle, but he will not escape his fate. I will hunt him to the ends of the Earth," August said.

Again, it was Kratian Kray who would prove to be the key to victory. He had reserved a variety of man-portable surface to air missiles. His forces on the eastern side of the mountain unleashed a barrage of missiles at the hapless transports. Some of the aircraft took evasive maneuvers while others released their countermeasures, but the mixture of guided and unguided weapons, combined with the sheer volume of fire, brought down the entire squadron. They crashed onto the mountain, raining down fire and shrapnel over the entrenched Praetorians. A momentous roar of applause and celebration erupted among August's army and they surged forward with renewed zeal. The Severots, now rested after the previous day's hard ride, charged up the mountain as well.

Layer after layer of The Architect's defenses were overcome as the Praetorians ran out of ammunition and were reduced to fighting hand-to-hand in narrow, rocky trenches. Some loyalists and remnants of the Eastern Army did not even put up a fight. They laid down their arms and were passed by as the coalition strained to keep up the momentum.

Throughout the day, the coalition made steady progress, although the fanatic Praetorians made them pay dearly. By evening, August's forces and Kratian's horsemen, who by now had dismounted, met on both the north and south end of the mountain, leaving an eye-shaped pocket of resistance at the mountain's top. In the center, The Architect's hand-picked bodyguards and the most elite unit in the empire—the 1st Praetorian Grenadiers—maintained a strong resistance. With thick armor our rifles could not penetrate, and draped with many bandoliers of grenades, the 1st Praetorians rained down explosives on our advancing troops, blowing great holes in the ranks. The high crests on their helmets flashed in the setting sun as they lobbed volley after volley down the mountain. Throughout the night, as the bodies piled up, the assault bogged down. Although General Rawat had found little food and water he had been busy thinking of a use for the fuel he had found. By morning, his troops were prepared to join the assault. In the twilight they rushed up the mountain. Just before they reached the Praetorian lines, they hurled flaming bottles and canisters into the enemy ranks which broke and showered the enemy in fire. The remaining lines of defense unraveled as burning Praetorian elites rolled on the ground or were overcome by the smoke from their own burning kit. Those still bedecked with grenades exploded in a gruesome fountain of flesh and bone. Geysers of blood filled the air with pink mist. Those Praetorians who had not been immolated fled to the ruined grounds of the monastery which once adorned the top of Mount Tabor. The coalition forces closed in around them until only one small band remained.

At the top of the mountain, standing among the broken columns of the basilica and surrounded by a ring of the last Praetorians, was The Architect. He was tall, thin man with short, greying hair. He stood motionless as his ministers were tending an enormous pit filled with burning books and paper. Records of his misdeeds and conquests, as well as ancient religious texts he had taken from his destroyed temple. The fighting stopped as August approached the pit. Behind him, Kratian Kray led a bloody and beaten Prophet. Lord DeVonay marched purposefully through the mass of soldiers as they parted. All but a few of the soldiers protecting The Architect laid down their weapons and melted into the crowd. August was weak from lack of sleep for several days. As he crossed the marble floor of the destroyed basilica, now slippery with blood, he lost his footing and fell to the sodden floor. I rushed to help him stand along with the aid of several other soldiers. His coat was soaked in blood. I tried to help him take it off. but he waved me away. He walked forward and stood before The Architect as he turned to face August. The burning parchment enveloped The Architect in a smoky, dusty breeze. He looked at a book he was holding as he spoke to August.

"Welcome, young August, to the end of the world."

"This isn't the end. This is a new beginning." August said.

"You betrayed me August. You betrayed the trust of your men. You betrayed the empire."

"I was never with you. My actions were just a means to an end."

"To what end? You could not possibly have envisioned yourself here before me victorious."

"I do not preoccupy myself with you as a person. Only you as an idea. I have dreamed of destroying the idea of you since I was very young. Since I became a slave. Then again when I became your prisoner at school. When I was finally free, when I finally had some control over my own destiny, I vowed that I would be the change I wished to see in the world."

"It's a noble goal," The Architect said. "When I was young, I thought ruling the world was the greatest achievement a man could accomplish. And it was my nature to create. And so, I built a world where I thought all men could live in peace. I forgot only one thing: God. I never needed God when I was young. *My* gods were stone and steel. I could find in them all the truth I needed to understand my purpose."

"Where is your god now?" August said.

The Architect turned away from us and spread his arms towards the smoking landscape full of death and destruction.

The gory piles of bullet-riddled bodies lay in long lines across where the two armies had clashed. Blood ran down the slopes of the mountain in long, sticky rivulets as the hot sun baked the battlefield. As far as the eye could see in all directions, the land was littered with the smoking waste of battle. The air hummed with the sounds of the wounded men and was pierced occasionally by the screams of dying horses. A more gruesome hellish sight there has never been in the sight of mortal man.

"Where are all of our gods now?" The Architect said. He turned to look at August again, "Do you fear death? You should not. It is inevitable; everyone dies. What you should fear is being forgotten. To slip into oblivion. To have nothing left of you. Your entire being erased with no thought ever given to you again. That is what you should fear. It's the only thing that troubles *my* mind." He held up the book he was looking at. It was an ancient Bible. He tossed it into the fire behind him.

"You should have kept that. Religion is how most people comfort themselves against that thought," August said.

"That, too, will be forgotten," he said. "But look at the Pyramids, the Greek temples, the Mayan ruins. They have lasted. They have endured. I made my own temple for the world to remember me by, and you destroyed it. You have stolen from me my legacy. Now, I will slip into oblivion, just like you and the billions of others who have passed through this world—small and unremarkable while they were alive and forgotten soon after they were dead."

"It will be a long time before anyone forgets you. Your name will be cursed forever," August replied. "You will be held accountable for your crimes."

"What crimes?" The Architect laughed. "I am the law. I decide what is a crime and what is not."

"Starting today, that will change," August said.

"And who will rule after me?" The Architect asked. "You? A poor boy from a backwoods upbringing. A slave. A traitor. You cannot rule an empire. You can't rebuild it."

"I don't know who will inherit this mess," August said. "I can say only this: We will not rebuild a single thing you created. We will raze every edifice of your existence to the ground. Every building, every office, every symbol of you will be erased. What we build will be new and thoughtfully crafted. Mankind's very existence depends on it."

"And in this new creation, how do you intend to make me pay for my crimes?" The Architect asked.

"You will watch as we dismantle your legacy, and anguish as we build a new world without you," August said.

"You will fall victim to the same disease that has ailed my rein. The oldest and most powerful sickness, called human nature," The Architect said.

"There is good in human nature as well," August said. "You've hidden it from us, but it is still there. I intend to make it shine again."

The Architect had not noticed Lord DeVonay before but now turned to him. "Do you hear this dribble, DeVonay?" The Architect asked him. "I almost didn't recognize you with one eye."

"I've heard quite enough indeed," Lord DeVonay said. With that, he grabbed the Prophet from Kratian Kray and shoved him into The Architect. The Architect tumbled backwards and both he and The Prophet fell into the burning pit. They were instantly consumed by the loose paper ash which plumed as they fell. There were no screams or struggles as the ash filled their lungs and the collapsing sides of the pit folded in around them. The Prophet and The Architect were no more.

All but August cheered. Soldiers fired their rifles in the air, clasped hands, or embraced.

"You've done it!" I said to August as he stared into the pit. "It's over!"

"It's never over," he said echoing the words of The Prophet. "The ending of each battle is the beginning of the next."

August was reserved despite the momentous occasion. I watched him closely as the Generals made their way to him to congratulate each other. I reflected on all that he had achieved. So humble and unassuming, from the day he was born to this day. Yet controlling and forming the destiny of millions and the future of the world altogether. I wondered if I had left August in the street the day he was born, would he have survived? If I had abandoned him to the elements, or to the violence of the day, would another soul have taken him in and kept alive the potential he held? Whether I came into August's life or he came into mine is unclear, but the truth is together we did our part as fate intended. In that way the world was remade by one simple act in a place far away, on a day not so long ago.

www.ingramcontent.com/pod-product-compliance
Lightning Source LLC
Chambersburg PA
CBHW070735180626
46818CB00007B/2850